EVERYONE DESERVES A HOME

BAER CHARLTON

CONTENTS

Dedication   vii

Prologue   1
1. Walter Nathan Humphrey III   5
2. A Change in the Household   17
3. Betsy Turner   25
4. Leatha   29
5. Hannah Mariah Rose Humphrey   38
6. New Orleans   50
7. Welcome to England   67
8. Welcome to London   74
9. Welcome to King's College Hospital   81
10. The Pig and Duck   91
11. Surgeries and Percy   100
12. SoHo   108
13. God's Work   119
14. 1938   128
15. St. Crispin's Day   140
16. 'Twas the Night Before Thanksgiving   147
17. 'Twas the Knight Before Christmas   155
18. Christmas Gift   159
19. War   171
20. Death, Buried, and Life   180
21. Life Above and Below   189
22. New Life, Same Old Eagle   198
23. Finding Spine Under Ground   207
24. Over Here   216
25. Sanctuary   225
26. End of Summer Is No Relief   232

27. Bristol 240

28. Come to Visit 248

29. A New World 256

30. Welcome Home 264

31. Midsummer Dream 274

32. Going Home 284

33. Seattle Morning 289

About the Author 305

Cover design by Roslyn McFarland, Far Lands Publishing

Rogena Mitchell-Jones, Literary Editor
RMJ Manuscript Service, www.rogenamitchell.com

Published by Mordant Media, Portland, Oregon

ISBN: 978-1-949316-51-3 (Print)
ISBN: 978-1-949316-50-6 (eBook)

10 9 8 7 6 5 4 3 2 1

To Marie "Daisy" Charlton Portberry — His Majesty's Motor Messenger Service for whole blood 1914-1920

Born 1899 - 1978 — Photo by London Times 1916

PROLOGUE

"Our mother was never married. And we weren't born her children."

I looked over the reporter's left shoulder at my sister Betsy as she talked to me. It had been a lengthy interview, and she had sat patiently, waiting for her turn. Her long, blonde curls were turning gray, a testament to her disregard for vanity as she followed our sister and me into the life of the retired or tired. Her speech was as beautiful to watch, fluid and graceful, as the day she graduated from the Norman Tyson Preparatory Academy for the Deaf. The reporter was unaware that my sister was speaking. She spoke to me in sign language, as the three of us were deaf.

Her cornflower-blue eyes sparkled as the reporter sensed something behind him. Looking up, he turned in the Edwardian leather club chair we always, with a wink, had called Papa's Chair. He stared, fascinated by her sign language, as were most who watched her speak, or took her English writing class at the academy. As I watched the back of his head, it was clear his eyes were dancing with her fingers in a silent waltz, a haunting image that would stay with him in his dreams for nights to follow. She had a kind of captivating effect on people.

His head turned and cocked toward me. I studied the side of his jaw moving as he went to ask a question.

I reminded him. "You must look at me so I can see your lips when you talk."

His face flushed at his lapse of memory as he turned around. "I'm sorry. I forgot."

"It's okay. Most people do." My speech is often mistaken for being somewhere between a Boston accent and a London accent. So I would guess it means a wet mid-Atlantic. Extensive speech therapy and tutoring have made my speech almost indistinguishable from that of a hearing person.

"I was curious about what she was saying."

Ignoring her pleas for us to end the interview and go to our sister's for dinner, I pressed another crucial point. "She wanted to remind me about our mother not being born white."

The reporter looked down at his notes. His confusion with his notes made it obvious that what I had just said was news to him. His head jerked up, and his eyes scrunched. He assumed he had heard me wrong.

Looking at him, I realized he had not known our mother was part black. I set him straight. "Our mother was born of mixed black—not white. She didn't become white until she started school when she was five, in 1910."

My sister realized what had just occurred, and I saw her shoulders slump as she fell into defeat. Her freckles lost their luster as she pulled out her cell phone and typed in a text. I assumed it was our sister, who was hosting Sunday dinner.

She read the return text and put the phone away in her pocket. I translated her message to the reporter. "My sister says you are joining us for dinner." As I got up, I noticed he was making noises of protest about the intrusion. I cut him off.

"If you want to understand about the hospital and school, you need to understand our mother. But to understand our mother, you'll need to come to dinner at my sister's house." I reached the coat stand in the corner and grabbed my raincoat. Putting it on and turning, I saw the young reporter talking. I cut him off again. "If you don't know or understand about my mother, then you can't write about the hospital and school." Turning, I opened the door. Turning back, I continued. "And you can't understand about my mother, unless you know about her parents—Walter, Leatha, and Betsy."

As we followed my sister out the door, I continued. "You are too young to understand the weight of the black-white problem. By the end of tonight, you might grasp what it meant for my mother and her parents to navigate a world where they were black but lived like whites."

I closed the front door behind us. As we walked to the car, I started his education. "It was called passing."

1

WALTER NATHAN
HUMPHREY III

THE OCCASION of my birth in 1857 probably came as much of a surprise to my mother as to her husband. A probable reason for my being alive was because of my muddy green eyes and the wisps of russet hair, which were reported to *Himself* by the midwife. My mother always measured the fact that the midwife held a special place in his heart as both his favorite yard slave and his bedding toy.

I took my first breath of life and most heartily lodged an angry protest for being thrust into the frigid January night in Black River, Louisiana. At the time of my birth, my father was the proud owner of over ten thousand acres of prime bottomland, four thousand head of cattle, eight hundred pigs, twenty-seven horses, forty percent share in two riverboats, and exactly nine hundred and forty-seven slaves. Fourteen slaves carried children; two were his. The Master of the land, Walter Nathan Humphrey Jr., was an icon of the Southern landholder, if nothing else.

Early mornings were his habit, regardless of where he slept. With coffee, toast, and a touch of rum, he rode the fields until suppertime. Riding the levies in the afternoon usually followed a rest after supper or a visit to a slave quarter if the spirit moved him. Usually, the spirit was restless and moved him to no end.

His riding the levies was more about showing off his prized Tennessee walker horse. Talking with the other landholders superseded checking the vitals of the retainers, which kept the great river from consuming his plantation. Passing flasks of sipping whiskey or bourbon was a minor detail in the Southern Gentlemen's dance.

I only mention my birth and parentage to illustrate that "passing" for white is not a new contrivance of the modern century. It likely started with the Athenian Amphitheater women players. However, most definitely, since the all-women acting troupes who put on wigs and mustaches to portray the male characters in the plays they perform.

The happenstance of my real father being a mixed-blood house slave with a complexion of high color contributed to the color of my skin. The wavy reddish hair and green eyes were a bonus that didn't surface until months later. But those did nothing for my father's humor at not having sired me, nor having shared my mother's bed for almost the duration of their marriage.

Shortly after my birth, Thomas, my blood sire, was sold on the auction block in the center of Natchez, Mississippi, for the total consideration of $421. The bidding lacked a reserve floor. Cora May, his wife, remained and nursed me for my first year. Not because I needed a wet nurse, but because it resulted in her being in the big house, and easier access to my father's preferences.

What didn't figure into our lives was the war. With secession and conflict looking imminent, my father sent my mother and me packing to shirttail relatives in the Texas Territory. Most of the house slaves, except my wet nurse, as well as some of the preferred yard hands, were sent along to care for us. Many my father kept on after the great emancipation as indentured help. But conditions would never be the way they were in my father's prime.

My father's summons arrived long after the war's end; I was nearly twelve. The Army occupied the big house for much of the war. My father secured funds and gold to cover rent and what passed for medical expenses at the time. Surgeries mainly comprised cutting away rotting limbs and removing offending scraps of lead and shrapnel. Anesthesia of the day involved nothing more than a stick between the teeth.

As I matriculated into my secondary studies, the final plantation sale concluded, we were shunt of acreage and retainers.

We moved into the Townhouse in Black River. The house was a forward-thinking affair. The plumbing was indoors, as was the winter kitchen.

My father pioneered household electric wiring via gas pipes, following Edison's arrival in Louisiana in 1886. Then, workers installed Edison lighting bulbs where gas wicks and flames previously adorned the walls. The light from the electricity was dim, but the electrification allowed us all to sleep at night. No one needed to remain awake guarding against gas leaks from a dimmed lamp or one that had blown out.

"What's this old bicycle for?" Anthony Jamison was the son of the dry goods owner from whom my father had bought the contraption the year before. "You kin have your slave drive you anywhere in your'n wagon."

I never thought of our gardener, Samuel, as a slave. "He is not a slave. He is our gardener and manservant." I was already having a confusing feeling about how nice the man smelled when he manicured the front yard, complete with its showy bushes and tightly mowed grass. "He's my father's retainer."

"Do he sleep in the barn with the horses?"

"Yes. Because it smells good out there."

"Hah! He be a slave. Same as that woman, Leatha."

"She don't sleep in the barn. She sleeps upstairs with me." I pointed to the attic window above the third floor.

The house was a big white affair on the corner of Jefferson and Elm. I could see both ends of town from the two ends of the attic above the third floor, which I shared with my nanny, Leatha. My only play area: the small back-yard, nestled between house and barn. The front was the "show" yard and was constantly being manicured by our gardener, Samuel. Samuel had been one of my father's favorite field slaves. We had taken him to Texas with us, and he now slept with the horses. Leatha was a colored girl my mama found in Texas, to look after me.

Her name was truly Alisha Jones, but since I couldn't pronounce my "S" sounds, my mama simply informed the girl that she was now Leatha. Years later, Leatha confessed to me she loved the sound of her name coming from my mouth, just the way I had done it upon first meeting her. As I matured, there were other aspects of me that she found to her liking. Our bond was why, when I was in my secondary school, I insisted I could not sleep or eat if Mama turned her out. So Leatha Jones became a family retainer.

Upon my matriculation from secondary school, my father had arranged for me to sit my college at Tulane University. It was his alma mater, and with the correct palms greased, it would see me through my medical education as well. Not having been able to control my inception, he would be damned if he would not control my destiny. I was supposed to be the next Doctor Humphrey, practicing in the parlor of the big white house in Black Water, Louisiana.

My first semester away from home was nothing short of turning loose a pent-up stallion in spring. Securing nearby housing—close to classes and the French Quarter— consumed a day. As luck would have it, the artistic humors of mankind lent themselves by many in the quarter to my predilections of bed companion or companions, as the event may be.

Many late nights and excessive drinking resulted in grades unbefitting a prospective doctor. But as luck would have it, my mother prevailed in her explanation. It was simply a case of my being alone and away from the dedicated care of my beloved Leatha. So, I secured a new apartment, distant from the French Quarter, to allow for a caretaker and, as I would soon find out, a disciplinarian.

The morning after returning to the new apartment with a young trumpet player, the shock of icy water jolted us awake. The pan clattered to the floor, and the once-cozy sheets clung to our skin, now a sopping mess. Blinking through the haze of sleep and cold, we lifted our heads to see Leatha standing over us, her expression a storm of anger. She had already put on her crisp uniform, a stark contrast to the disheveled scene she had created. Her eyes were wild, rimmed with red.

"I have worked since dawn preparing your breakfast. The biscuits will be ready in twenty minutes. I expect no less than two fresh-washed and well-dressed gentlemen sitting at the dining table."

The musician wanted nothing to do with the fiery Valkyrie and departed. I never saw him again. But as I quietly slipped into the chair, minutes later, she placed the food on the table, sat, and served us. It would never change.

Her delicate fingers prized open the biscuit. "I have no problem with you having gentlemen callers. Those tendencies in you, you was born with. But this here be a day's ride from your father's hands and penis? I will not let this opportunity slip through your sheets. You will study and act like a gentleman in this house. By midterm, I expect none other than you be the top in your class." She paused with the sharp paring knife filled with butter at the mouth of the biscuit. "And if you ain't..." She jabbed the blade into the biscuit. "You won't like it."

So Leatha and I returned to our old ways. While I studied until the late hours, Leatha also took to improving her language and mathematical skills. By the time I was sitting my medical studies, Leatha had secured a high school diploma and was learning the healing arts as well. While I was at the university learning the art of medicine, she was deep in the city's underbelly, learning the island arts of voodoo. Her newfound knowledge of herbs and spices also had a profound effect on our dinners. Any companions I was allowed on the occasional weekend did not overlook her culinary skills.

Long after I had matriculated from medical school and set up a small practice in a fine Victorian home I had secured in the Garden District, word came of my mother's ill health. The consumption would take her the following year.

My medical practice was a going concern, as I catered to the more delicate illnesses of the ladies and gentlemen of the underside of New Orleans. Well-dressed people in the district concealed their real lifestyles. Social diseases hit those who were extremely sensitive the hardest, such as syphilis. I barely managed to avoid it and made a commitment to always use protection.

Dealing with pregnancy occurred occasionally. A burdensome obstacle hindering lifestyle and career pursuits. These, I referred quietly from the parlor into the kitchen, where Leatha practiced her art. Only in rare instances did they need any assistance of a more surgical nature. If so, then they would become houseguests for a week, on the third floor.

So, with the dawn of the new century, our two businesses nestled comfortably into the lush, green embrace of the refined Garden District. We explored the city's rich culture while maintaining a public image of a gentleman and his servant. Beneath this social facade, however, lay a profound bond of deep love and mutual respect for each other's beings. I could scarcely envision any conventional married couple enjoying a more affectionate and nurturing relationship than the one shared between Leatha and myself. In essence, we were like two little mud bugs content at the bottom of a warm, tranquil bayou, blissfully unaware of anything more fulfilling—until that fateful, balmy late-summer evening when a gentle, almost tentative knock sounded at the kitchen door.

Leatha scooted her chair back as she placed her napkin on the tablecloth. "Excuse me."

I sipped on my white wine with an ear toward the proceedings. The back door opened with its characteristic mouse squeak of a complaint.

"Oh, miss, this is the back door. The doctor is through the front door."

"Are you Mistress Leatha?"

"Yes, miss."

"Then I believe I have the correct door."

I could hear a strange, delicate footstep advance into the kitchen.

"But, miss, white folk—" Leatha tried to continue.

"I'm not white." The soft voice of a child sighed. "But I am pregnant."

I carefully pulled my napkin from my lap, folded the cloth, and patted my lips as I rose. Still holding the white cloth as if it were a handgrip for reality, I stepped into the warm kitchen. Standing before Leatha was what appeared to be a white girl of only sixteen. As we discovered, she wasn't white, and my age estimate was incorrect by two years. Betsy was a child of fourteen and in the initial stages of bearing a child.

I cleared my throat and took charge, a privilege of manhood, which I was about to lose for the rest of my life. "We were just starting our dinner, if you would care to join us. Miss ...?"

"Turner, sir. Betsy Turner."

I extended my arm toward the dining parlor. "Well, Miss Turner, Betsy, Leatha makes some of the best pork loin in all New Orleans, and she does not boil the greens to death. She has even assured me that in the event of my behaving myself, there is a Shoo Fly pie in the offering with the coffee. So please."

"It all sounds good, sir, but I can't." She hesitated as she studied Leatha. "I'm not white."

"Leatha clearly isn't either. And our table awaits three diners." I pointed my hand and napkin at the door to the dining parlor. "Please." I omitted my gentleman friend, having not shown as promised—an occurrence becoming increasingly perplexing as I grew older.

A most pleasant first dinner revealed Betsy Turner's

captivating, albeit brief, life. Being the daughter of a janitor at the Bijou Theater, she grasped the skill of transforming into a different persona early on. For a young girl, it was looking older; but for a young girl of color, it was also to appear white.

She has been dating some of the young swells in the city since she was twelve. She publicly portrayed herself as coming from a wealthy family. The family quietly had taken up residency in New Orleans to avoid scandalous activity where they were from. In street terms, they were lying low.

Possible suitors understood that reaching her required using the theater's back-door staff.

Things had gone along remarkably well until recently. A particular suitor had become more than persistent in their amorous activities. He was unwilling to be guided through volumes of undergarments, and unsuspectingly, into a gaffe. Or if she was feeling up to the party, her buttocks. On the fateful night, he had stripped her naked, found the gaffe, and in retribution, brutally raped her—repeatedly.

The result, to her great discomfort, was that her clothes were rapidly becoming ill-fitting. The thought of dealing with a child in that scenario completely overwhelmed her. Despite having a remedy at both doors of the house she came to, neither option was her preference. She had turned to us not for our medical knowledge, but as disinterested parties for knowledge and ideas, for it was her full intent not to abandon the future soul.

As the first evening drew to a close, we made her as comfortable as possible on the third floor. Leatha and I talked over the young woman's predicament on the second floor. Well, I spoke while Leatha had her way of convincing me of her mind, which was best while her mouth was full of my manhood. By the morning light, we were resolved. Forthwith, Betsy and the future bundle would become one with the household.

Over the morning's repast, we informed the forlorn child that her predicament was fortuitous. Leatha's household duties were becoming more burdensome as her reputation in the darker arts spread across the city.

So Betsy, while she was able, would assume the household duties of cleaning and caring for the two medicine practitioners. The Gordian knot of her upcoming life would have to wait until after the pending arrival was breached.

A sweltering New Orleans summer of 1904 brought hope of new beginnings to the stately mansion on St. Charles Avenue.

The lush green foliage seemed to droop under the weight of the sweltering heat. Our sprawling manor stood as a beacon of elegance and hope amidst the steamy haze. Its majestic columns gleaming in the relentless sun, hinting at the promise of new beginnings and untold stories within its stately walls.

We had to forgive the noise and dust of the constant construction efforts of the electrification of our street's favored trollies. The likes of which allowed for a gentleman and his housekeeper to both ride together regardless of color, by mandate since the 1830s. The trolley's accommodation was essential to the success of our practices and promoted a peaceful household.

Open windows and the constant dust from the construction allowed us to learn the coarsest language any French sailor could teach a young girl. But mostly, Betsy was happy with her new family, and we were with her.

2

A CHANGE IN THE HOUSEHOLD

THE SQUALLING of a newborn child is not a pleasant thing—but it is life-affirming. In my practice, I had not birthed a single child. In fact, much of my practice was the cessation of the progression of nature. Therefore, it was called upon us to engage a midwife as the time drew near, especially as Betsy lay ensconced on the third floor.

Over the summer, I hired skilled workers to modernize our house before the new addition to our family. I considered the modifications to the house to reflect the new electric streetcars that would quietly pass by our fine old Victorian lady.

As the construction progressed, we found ourselves being pushed from one side of the house to the other and from one floor to another. But eventually we ceased our suffrage and were left with many new conveniences. The Otis Lift off the back hall wouldn't experience its actual value for entertainment until a few years later. The rooms, equipped with baths and toilets and featuring hot and cold running water on every floor, were enjoyed by all. Importantly, two toilets were available on the main floor. The status exposed to the public paid well for its dividends.

The telephone was originally to be installed in the front entry. But after a very pleasant dinner, entertaining the new telephone installer, a young, good-looking man with a healthy handful of almost white-blond hair and a slender body. We had several phones placed in strategic locations around the house. Jack was also a wizard at installing a telephone system for communication in any room in the house. This included secret ones hidden in cabinets in the bathing rooms and toilets.

While it was a pleasure for many years to have this efficient means of communication about the house, I was despondent when Jack no longer found reasons to spend long days stripped to the waist and sweating in our home. It prevailed upon me as host to allow him the use of my large stand-up bath, with its fifty-eight nozzles and sprayers, which could drench two male bodies in almost any position.

I never asked if Leatha had forewarned Betsy of my nature. But she seemed unaffected by the extra-curricular male gymnastics and engagement, which most times went on quietly that summer.

It was in the last month of summer heat. As I grieved for my Jack, we were finally getting settled after all the construction. A message arrived from Black Water of my mother's passing. I was to return posthaste, as she wished to lie in state until I arrived—even if it was the height of the summer heat.

Upon my arrival at the white house, I was thankful for my father's medical training in formaldehyde. He had also respectfully moved the body to the icehouse before the ceremony.

Although my father was the only doctor for many miles, his manners prevented him from endearing himself to the populace. The man displayed a disagreeable and tedious nature, lacking any shred of gentility.

The forty people attending her graveside stood as testament to my mother's efforts to connect with the community —despite her husband. Only the banker and my father's lawyer attended the following reception at the house. Which was a blessing, as the housekeeper, Cora May, had only made a single platter of cucumber sandwiches and a single pitcher of lemon water.

Her off-putting attitude and shortness, I chalked it up to the heat. I knew she adored my mother and followed her into the kitchen to the dry board. I wedged what may or may not have felt like my manhood in the fold of her ample behind. Reaching around, I cupped and gently played with her teats as I nuzzled my nose and lips in the softness of her neck.

Shortly, I was rewarded with a disgruntled chuckle, and then the sound of stifled giggling. The tall glass of sweet tea came after I stopped, and she regained her composure enough to turn and greet me with a smile, a proper hug, and a teary kiss. We both missed the great matriarch of Black River.

I reached to steal one of the small cucumber sandwiches she had arranged on a silver tray. She slapped my hand.

"Them cucumbers ain't for you. Thems for *Himself* and his friends." She winked as she left the kitchen. "I be right back."

As I found some biscuits in the bread tin, she returned. "No, sweet child. I have your food over here." She reached deep into the icebox and withdrew a plate with cold meat, fresh slices of tomatoes, and cucumbers. She leaned over my head to whisper. "These cucumbers I haven't pickled with my brine." Her evil smile slightly tempered the fire in her eyes.

The menfolk sat in my father's study, smoking cheroots, sipping whiskey, and ignoring Cora May's sandwiches. The two of us prowled the house, retrieving a large, heavy suitcase and several baskets my mother had secreted over the passing years.

"What is all this?"

She placed her finger over her pursed lips. "Shh. I'll explain later. Bring them. They be your inheritance." And so during the heat of the day, we un-secreted and carried baskets and boxes out the back door. We packed them all into a sturdy wagon, which remained under the cover of a large oilcloth. The wagon, I was sure, did not belong to my father. He was now the proud owner of a horseless carriage, and there was no barn left on the property to house the required foursome needed to pull such a conveyance.

We quietly skulked the entire three floors and finally the almost forgotten dungeon of a basement. Pulling me close.

"There be no last will and testament. This is all from your mother. She knowed what you take away now, is all there is. That's what that banker and lawyer type be sniffing around for."

Cora May explained in her own way. As the years passed, my father grew increasingly bitter about the Confederation's defeat at the hands of the Northern Aggressors. He also placed the blame at the feet of my mother, and more so, the siring of her son.

I asked her what was in the extremely heavy containers, but she said all would be clear once we were done with what we had to do.

As we passed through the foyer, we could hear the menfolk. They had succumbed to the indulgence, usually following heavy drinking on a hot Louisiana afternoon. There were three distinct snores. Devilishly, Cora May sought to assess the fortitude of their slumber and promptly dropped the silver platter full of sandwiches. The same platter she slapped my hand for trying to grab one. As the platter clattered on the marble floor, she pointed to the food and held her nose as she made the most gawd-awful face and stuck out her tongue. The sandwiches were not made for me or any decent folk to eat. She had pickled the cucumbers in her own urine and cane sugar.

The stairs creaked as she led me to the basement. Thinking of Leatha and now Betsy, I hit on a grand idea. I reached for her arm. "Cora May, we have a baby coming. Why don't you return with me? We have plenty of room."

At the bottom of the stairs, she turned to me and pulled

my shirt until our breaths mingled. "Sweet child, I loves you dearly as if you was one of my own. I loves your Leatha. But as much as I loves you two, I will exact my revenge on *Himself* for all the years of his torment."

I had forgotten about her being born on the plantation and her virginity being taken from her by *Himself*, the year before I was born. She was only a mere thirteen years older than me.

She took my hand and guided me back into the darkest back area of the basement. "This is where my father cast all his lead soldiers, cannons, and wagons. What are we doing here? Is that what's in those baskets?"

Casting the lead objects, he later painted and arranged them on a table in the foyer for war commemoration days. They were always the good battles; never the ones where the North carried the day. The smell of the lead, the Japanese paints, and every memory came flooding back. Not pleasant memories, just detritus of the mind.

Cora May nodded, but then held her finger up to her lips. She raised the lid of a box containing the crucible. What crusted the edge was not lead, but glowed a soft yellow. She reached up and, grabbing my ear, brought it to her lips. "He done cast everything in gold, not lead."

It was at that instant that I realized why there were no large deposits at the bank from the only doctor in the area. The banker was snooping around to find out where my father secreted his success. He entrusted the lawyer with his will, but it didn't reflect the true nature of what my father's worth should be. I am sure they both knew that over the years, the six-thousand acres of prime bottomland had been pieced off. And now, there were only three of us who knew where the proceeds hid—all in plain sight.

In the kitchen, she sat me down with some sweet tea. Stepping to the wall, she took the receiver down from the Bell telephone mounted on the kitchen wall.

"It's time. Send him." She hung up the phone and turned to me. "Hurry and eat that. Then, you need to go pack. Quietly. You be leaving now while the men sleep."

As I returned with my grip and coat, I looked out the window where a square brace of horses stood attached to the wagon. Cora May once again embraced me and kissed me on the cheek. "I'll see you when he be dead. Now take this here food and be gone. The boy know the way to New Orleans, but you show him to your house. He won't stop." Shoving a basket of fresh food into my hands, she instructed the young man that we were not to stop until I was home safe and the wagon properly unloaded.

We rode through the entire night and day, arriving shortly before a late supper, as Leatha bribed a couple of neighborhood boys to carry in all the parcels. We secured lodging for the animals, and the young man who had silently transported me for more than a day slept the sleep of the dead on my examining table.

It wasn't until after he was gone that Betsy mentioned he was a nice man and polite too. He had enjoyed my regaling him with stories, as they had helped to keep him awake. She said Cora May had also warned him that if he were to fall asleep, I would most likely try to have my way with him. The latter would probably account for the way he pushed the team of horses, and would only urinate on the other side of the wagon when we stopped.

I told her he had not spoken a single word in my presence, and I stood in marvel at her having gotten him to talk to her. She just laughed as she lowered her head in a sad swing. For all the smart doctor training, I could not detect a mute when he sat inches from my hip for a full day and night.

She showed us the language of signs many of the stage-hands knew, so they could silently communicate from one side of a theater to the other. Her language skills opened her to more than just a subculture of deaf people, but also to watch for many things others did not see. As she sat down in front of me, she informed me of the first moment she had seen me in the light. She knew then that I was not as white as Leatha was or I pretended to be.

From that night forward, the language spoken around the dinner table was of signs.

From the moment she started walking, Hannah could communicate her wants using signs and joyful sounds. If the three of us stayed simply entertained, little Hannah was in heaven.

3
BETSY TURNER

ON THAT SWELTERING SUMMER NIGHT, an unfamiliar cold gripped me. Since I was eleven, I've been on my own after my father disappeared with a dance troupe one night and was never heard from again. While troupes may change with frequency in a large theater, the stagehands remain a close-knit family, always looking out for one another. So I never felt abandoned until I stood with my hand poised aside the glass window of the kitchen door. I had never felt so alone, and thank goodness, never since.

Knocking on the wood with a light rap, I watched through the glass of the door.

A dancer's recommendation brought me to this door. She had missed her monthly after a weekend with one of the swells who knocked on the stage door. The young men typically used their French purses, except for one instance. Her resulting discomfort from Miss Leatha's concoction was only minor. Nowhere as unbearable as never dancing again because of an unwanted child.

I sought a different solution. Vacating my womb was not my wish. Nor did I wish to serve nine months to a growing thing, only to discard it into the arms of someone else. My desires were unclear. However, I sensed solutions existed outside my present scope.

The glass was cool on my white gloved knuckle.

The door swung into a cheerful kitchen. I felt I had found a friend, as I beheld the freckled, warm, high, rounded cheeks of the woman. But I knew I had found a home when I walked into the grand dining room, dwarfing the small table, but paneled with shelves and shelves of books.

There was a certain relationship between the master of the house and his housekeeper. Not a usual one, and I couldn't put my finger on it until later that night. It was not of a white man and his colored housekeeper, but the moving of two equals showing their mutual care and support.

I rested, intrigued by the soft bed and the comfort surrounding me.

I remember the table. In a room large enough to accommodate all four leaves, it stood reduced to its smallest configuration without a single expanding leaf. The simple table hinted at a modesty and closeness seldom seen in grand houses or those of the city's elite, specifically in the Garden District. It was most certainly unexpected in the home of a doctor whose practice was right on the primary thoroughfare of St. Charles Street.

I almost ran at the thought of sitting down in this house. Two people, three settings: the mystery compelled me to sit. If nothing more, but to discern how they had foreknowledge of my arrival. As nothing else now could explain the extra service laid out in this intimate arrangement. I found the seating arrangement most intriguing: I sat at the table's head, flanked by the two others. Three other chairs remained unoccupied at the room's far end, appearing unused.

The meal and conversation were a flurry of activity. Food melted in my mouth like a confection known as sugar cotton. The tastes were beyond any I had ever experienced, yet the food looked not unlike any other I had experienced in fine dining establishments. The doctor bowed to the expertise of Miss Leatha for the culinary experience. He even pointed out where they used to roam the city at will, enjoying the culinary delights. They now found the offerings pale or pedestrian when compared with Miss Leatha's talents. The company was also without impingement.

During our conversation, the good doctor inquired if I was familiar with the upstart English humorist Mr. Shaw, bringing up the topic of the theater. Shaw. I remembered the sad story of our having performed just last year, his *Mrs. Warren's Profession*. I recounted how, at first, I had identified with her daughter, Vivian. But in the end, I found Mrs. Warren's aloneness, after high hopes, most reflected my life and the abandonment by my father.

This somehow led to a discussion of Voltaire. I knew his views on religion and tolerance could turn a cool conversation into a battle of hot tempers. So I tread carefully by quoting his essay from near the end of his life. "Verily, are we not all children of the same father, and beasts from the same god?" I begged to be more familiar with playwrights than philosophers. But I could see by the exchanges of looks between the good doctor and Miss Leatha. The evening had ripened its fruit and was now drawing to a close.

Unexpectedly, they led me to a refined room on the third floor, where a soft, down-filled bed sat between two walls of floor-to-ceiling windows, providing a refreshing breeze for a gentle night's sleep. I almost didn't notice the large fan high above me on the ceiling. When Miss Leatha informed me this was my room, I assumed it would be for the night, and they would deal with me in the morning light.

As she closed the door, she admonished me that she and the good doctor were on the floor below, should I find myself in need of anything. As I heard her step away from the door I was staring at, I could have sworn I heard her softly say, *Welcome home.*

Or maybe it was just a figment of my dream.

4
LEATHA

Our household had become interesting, without drama. The early years of raising Walter, and having to fend off or finally deal with his father's advances, made my life a muddled mess, with too much hell on earth. His mother, being beyond caring, as long as her husband didn't broach her bedroom door, required the household to be an armed camp of every vigilance.

The night he first found out he was going back to New Orleans, I held Walter's manhood in my mouth. I then took it in my left hand and held a meat carving knife against it with my right. No fear emanated from him.

"Leatha? Why have you stopped sucking?" He stared at the carving knife I held to his manhood.

"I'll never threaten you again. But if'n you don't take me with you, and away from your father, I will be sure you never derive pleasure from this here manhood again." I knew he could see in my eyes that it were the muck in the tobacco rows truth.

He, soft as a kitten, rested his hand on mine. His smile be like the cherub I fell in love with years before. "You are my savior. I would straight pass away if I were ever separated from you again. You have been my sole purpose of living in the hell world of my father. But now, with my mother's help, we will return to New Orleans together and never be apart again."

His passions weren't common or even acceptable to society. But then, it met my needs, as I no longer had to be molested in ways I did not wish. Under the cloak of night, we vowed eternal loyalty. Whatever the new century would bring, we would face it together—without sorrow, suffering, or ill humor.

It was into this loving, supportive household that our young Betsy Turner entered.

Betsy be a curious thing. With a bit of makeup, she was the whitest of the young ladies. To hear her speak, one would expect her to have flourishes of an education at some university abroad, or the very least, a few years spent on the popular Grand Tour. While her French was most impressive, it was the sign language she brought to the household that I found most amazing —and yet, so easy to overlook. Once somewhat mastered, we could speak many secret conversations while in public, which offered immense freedom. While we were about the city, she was presented as Walter's young cousin, but I, as always, was the attentive servant.

In the early days, I was taken aback as I felt my relationship with Walter was confounded at the dinner table, where the two discussed books and ideas I had never heard of before. But I told myself it was just my imagination, and the boning knife remained in the kitchen when we retired for the night.

Shakespeare's bedroom was the subject of a heated dinner conversation that third week. During the salad course, the subject of his leaving his second-best bed (the one with the knothole in the headboard) to his wife came up. Walter suspected that Frances Bacon, another playwright, had taken possession of his best bed. At first, I thought Frances to be a woman's name. But the subject did not end there. Their love for each other, despite being men, went unnoticed, but in today's enlightened society, it is now viewed with disapproval, or worse.

Betsy held her butter knife like a sword, with butter on the tip instead of blood. "Yes, but in Midsummer Night's, he refutes it by having her wake up having lain with an ass. And there is only one way an ass has sex."

Walter lay back against his chair, his arms spread like he was about to take flight. "Oh, please. They just slept. But what about Portia? She is the real ploy."

"Because of her love for another woman? Please. Switch a woman with a woman, and you have a man with a man. It's the same. He is talking to Frances and reinforcing his advances with the donkey."

I sat lost and no longer cared.

The silence settled down on the table like a winter blanket. I looked up to find the two looking at me in silence.

"Is something wrong?" My heart sank at the sight of his sad face.

Walter covered my right hand with his left. The contact was comforting and gentle. Though even light, his touch was filled with the heavy weight of his caring. "We were wondering the same about you."

As I dabbed my mouth, I thought. Laying my napkin folded by my plate, I peered into his concerned face. "I don't know..." I shrugged. "I be in fine health. I live in a grand home with a man who cares for me. No matter what trouble, he be there... except..."

"Except...?" His hand stroked mine. "You don't feel included?"

I shrugged. I straightened my napkin. And that was when I looked into the eyes I be needing. She knew.

Betsy reached out both hands and gathered my hand into her strength. "We will teach each other so much. For I have so much to learn from you."

It was in that moment that I knew I was in love with this young woman. I had the sister I had prayed for most of my days.

I don't remember if we finished dinner, but I know it was well past midnight when Betsy and I blew out the lamps in the parlor as we retired for the night. My head was spinning with words and names and scenes from Mr. Shakespeare's plays. But most of all, the chest-fluttering words of love in his sonnets. All of this, from my newfound sister's mouth. She had read or recited from memory her favorite words of the man long dead, and yet so alive.

At the right time, we would allow Walter back into our nest of learning. But for then, we lay about curled on the floor, dipping our eyes into first one play, and then another. We gathered a sense, more about the man than his plays. And who we were. By then, little Betsy could no longer be called little.

It was about this time that Walter's mother passed away. We scarcely noticed his time away, as we were busy with the back-door medications and ministrations and Betsy's education into the arts of my calling. I never had to show her anything twice, not even complicated recipes. She became a second set of hands. After a brief time, she already knew what I needed next. All the while, we communicated through French and sign language. It seemed to add an air of even more powerful mystery to the ministrations.

With Walter gone, we fell into late meals held as a picnic in the parlor, as we studied well past the midnight hour. Occasionally, the morning light would find us still lounging in the pile of pillows with Betsy's head resting in my lap. We had become like two little puppies and fell into slumber wherever the mood took us. Besides Walter, she was the only person I ever trusted to fall asleep near.

Walter's return wasn't a grand entrance, but more of a waking up and finding the master home. But his sensitivity to changes drew him back from his usual boisterous self, and he became a quiet watcher for a few days. I feared a change he couldn't share.

The night he shared was the night Betsy unpacked the wagon load of trunks and baskets. Her discoveries—toy soldiers and knickknacks—made no sense. But in one basket, she found a pair of lovely, simple candlesticks. The tarnish had hold of the brass something fierce. They be the devil for her to clean and polish. But polish she did, until the two lovely candlesticks, shining as if made of gold, stood in the middle of our little table.

She hadn't shown me what she was doing the entire afternoon. She had informed me we would have our dinner only when she told me the table was ready. Not wanting to disquiet her enthusiastic endeavor, I prepared a cold meal we could serve at any time.

As we took our places, Walter eyed the candlesticks glowing in the dancing light. I couldn't fathom the depths of his wry smile, but I knew he was about to have fun, as he could never hide the dancing sparkles in his eyes.

"It would appear that during my separation from the household, someone has made additions to our table."

I looked about the table, feigning innocence. "No, Master Walter, these are the familiar place settings we always use. The linens are the ones you bought just last year. And Miss Betsy was here before you left." I fluttered my eyelashes as I ladled us all some cucumber soup.

"I was referring to the new brass candlesticks."

"Oh, those aren't new. Those are the same ones who sat on the table in your mother's home. Although I must admit, Miss Betsy's afternoon restoring their beauty was well spent. I cannot fathom why I never polished them for their former table setting."

He turned his attention to Miss Betsy. "Did you find a fresh knife cut on the bottom edge of one of them?"

"Yes, sir, I did." She answered.

"Indeed. I put said cut there." He turned to me. "It took less trouble than shaving a little off a double eagle coin. For the coin is only sixty-five percent pure, as the South was not beyond cheating and added brass to the minting, which made it harder." He pointed at the candlesticks. "These are better gold."

We sat stunned at his revelation. He continued by pointing at the candlesticks with his butter knife, between applications of hard preserves to his biscuit. "Those are almost pure. As well as the toy soldiers and knickknacks, you most certainly also found."

Miss Betsy picked up her side plate and fanned herself as she flushed and gasped for air. Sitting opposite Walter, I struggled to breathe. I thought I was used to finery, but solid gold candlesticks are a whole different kettle of bayou stew.

Walter reflected on the meaning of this. And now, with the cat out of the bag, he was ready to share.

"I have observed these last few days that the household has taken a turn. This change appears positive and lasting." He pointed his knife, loaded with strawberry-rhubarb preserve. "The relationship of our guest has become instead one of the family. And it is welcome to remain such, as I believe I have found a certain fondness for your company as well. Vrai, mon Cheri?" True, my sweet?

Muted, Betsy and I nodded, "Oui."

So, with the family settled, Walter told us about his visit to his father's domain, as well as his packing to skulk away in the middle of the night with Cora May. As he spoke, I envisioned a new use for our basement, as well as some new, extensive curios we could gain for the hiding of our newfound wealth, which would also be useful for concealing the wealth yet to come. As it was, there were already a small chest or two brimming with coins and other forms of payment. All which we did not wish to expose in the usual banking. As Walter found out, we were not the first to have this problem.

With the waving of his butter sword tainted with the blood of jam, Walter explained the truth about the gold. "Throughout the war, the pay received by the living soldiers was less than the value of one of those three-inch-tall Confederate soldiers. A cast general on the back of a horse would most likely have bought a few field cannons, as well as paid the squads for the duration of the war." His biscuit lost a bite, but his teaching continued. "Just one of those lead-colored wagons with a cannon caisson drawn by a six-team of horses and drivers would have bought and paid for the entire company."

I felt a chill thinking about what was in the basement full of baskets. They brimmed with more soldiers than mounted the field at Appomattox and Gettysburg combined. For as long as Walter had lived, the old devil had cheated the taxman.

The new century was looking mighty golden. My smile reflected on my newfound sister and our man. The only thing left to determine was what was in Betsy's belly, and it wouldn't take long to find out.

Her midwife arrived the next day, and Hannah Mariah was born three days later.

Her almost pink skin, tiny nose, and wavy milk-chocolate hair sealed her fate. The story of her birth and the death of her mother would come later.

5

HANNAH MARIAH ROSE HUMPHREY

HER FIRST MEMORY of being different was as a new child in a small town, four days after her ninth birthday. Prior to that fateful day, she lived as one of the special princesses on St. Charles Street in the finest neighborhood the South had to offer. Children living in the Garden District received special care and attention. But only Hannah enjoyed the true status granted by being so anointed by her colored housekeeper and closest confidant, Leatha.

To the neighborhood nosy bodies, the good doctor, on undertaking the wardship of the tiny baby, had the presence of mind to engage a cultured French au pair. As the tongues wagged, the small girl would receive a proper upbringing, learning to speak the cultured French. Others could learn lesser-known languages spoken by the local cultures other people engaged for their child.

Little did they know French was only a minor language spoken in the household. Languages of the day included Latin, German, Spanish, English, and Sign Language—the sign language they signed in all three subsets of American, English, and French. The French signs were usually spoken during the circus when all four of them bustled about in the kitchen, preparing a meal.

Sign language became the primary means of communication as time passed. They exchanged requests and answers using English and French sign language. Daily, the first punster, regardless of language, earned a chalkboard tally point. Any pun made in sign language received an added point. The person with the highest points for the week chose the main course for Sunday dinner. The highest for the month decided the next month's special outing. By the age of six, Hannah had become a true competitor in the daily count.

She spent her days in free rein to roam about the house, except during surgery. At those times, Betsy and Leatha kept Hannah occupied in the study, using the books as they all studied. Leatha and Betsy studied for general knowledge and their love of the theater alongside Hannah, who read everything in the library.

As the good doctor's practice branched out to cover other maladies, it was common for her to be sitting on his lap, paying rapt attention to the medical consulting going on. Nobody ever suspected a six-year-old of understanding the word "carbuncle," much less knowing what it meant. When she started making up fresh signs for the maladies, and then diagnosing other passengers on the streetcar. The girl's insightful diagnosis surprised the adults, but then they recalled past similar illnesses of patients who had visited the good doctor.

The end of the halcyon days of New Orleans came not with a bang, but with the wheezing final breaths of the once-great Dr. Walter Nathan Humphreys Sr.—the scion of all he surveyed, at least in his mind. Cora May found his father suffering a massive heart attack as he lay clutching his beloved lead soldiers. Cora stood on her tiptoes and whispered in Walter's ear, "He had figured out they was truly jus' lead—not the gold he hoarded." So it was time, and the large corner house, some distance from St. Charles Street, became Doctor Humphrey's new practice location.

"Is there a theater there?"

"I don't think so, darling. It is a tiny town."

"But father, Nana Betsy loves the theater, and I love going with her."

"Sweet child, endure until we can journey into the big city and partake of such entertainment."

"But that could be months or years before we can go."

"You will surely waste away right in front of us. Eh, petit chue?" He nuzzled her cheek with the side of his finger as he called her a little cabbage; the name of endearment for the center of the three adults' lives.

"Suus non poultry."

"It's not chicken?" Walter laughed. "Didn't you mean Suus non pulchra? It's not fair?"

The girl crossed her eyes, pretended to be a simpleton, and nodded her hand vigorously to sign an agreement.

Although her language faux pas were becoming fewer and fewer, they were still there.

He reached out and gathered the young girl in as he turned a dining chair to sit on. Hannah leaned into his open legs and stood more in his lap than sat. She leaned her slender shoulder and head against his shoulder and smelled the mix of the starch in his paper collar, and the citric tang of his cologne. "Oh, Papa, but I so love living here."

He smoothed the waves of her long, curly, dark hair falling to her shoulders. He leaned his cheek against her head and gave a tiny moan of his own. "There are many fine memories within these old walls, honey." He surveyed books, paintings, and his lifetime of collected items. "Certain memories will accompany us; we can return to the rest."

She lifted her head and looked at him. "You aren't selling the house?"

A slight look of mock horror flittered across his face. "Mercy, child, I'd never do such a thing! Where would we stay when we come to visit during the theater season?"

She giggled with him as she hugged him and snuggled deeper into his chest. "Thank you, Papa."

"Oh, it's not just for the theater, my child. In a few short years, you will need a place for you and Nana to live while you are sitting at your schooling at Tulane, and then medical school. You certainly didn't expect to hole up in some sleazy back alley of Bourbon Street, did you?"

She smiled with devilment, "Why not? You did."

He pushed her away in mock horror. "Who told you such a nasty thing?"

Hannah struck a diva pose and pushed her hair back on one side. "Nana Leatha told on you. She even showed me the alley where the bums and drunkards threw up on the walls and one another. She even showed me the rickety falling-down stairway you made her climb while you rode in the gold-plated Otis inside."

He roared with laughter, "I see now I am rescuing you from the den of iniquity your nanny drags you off to every Saturday when you should be studying your Latin."

The diva snapped back into a child as she remembered the theater. She leaned excitedly back into his lap. "Oh, Papa, I just remembered. This weekend, a troupe is performing Shakespeare's *A Midsummer Night's Dream*, and a friend of Nana's is playing Puck. Leatha needs a box to attend. I'm sure she would enjoy it as well."

Walter drew a long, serious face as he stroked his chin. "A box is a serious commitment. I'll have to think about it."

She squirmed. "Please, Papa, it is an excellent play, and it is Nana's friend."

"Well, maybe there is something in the envelope on my desk. The envelope next to your Latin and German textbooks. The ones you're supposed to be studying right now?"

Her shoulders fell. "Oh, do I have to?"

"Only if you want to join us in the box this Friday night."

She quietly hugged his neck and smiled.

The cleared throat at the kitchen door was a deep rumble.

Walter pushed at the lithe body as he stage-whispered, "Es ist die polizie." It is the police.

Hannah slipped out of his lap as she posed the ancient Greek question, "Quis custodiet ipsos custodes?" Who will guard the guards?

The girl's giggle rewarded Leatha's striving for a stern expression.

Leatha wandered in slowly as she shooed Hannah toward the study. Watching the child gather her books and leave, she sighed as she wiped her hands on her apron.

Turning another chair around, she sat facing her oldest friend. "So, we're keeping the house?" She pushed a waft of wandering hair with the back of her hand. Her deep brown eyes watched every feature of the man's face. Her thin smile was more of a relief than any condemnation. The house represented freedom for her.

He shrugged in on his body, and the eyes cast about the large Persian rug he'd received from a city elder with a wayward daughter, for services rendered. His lips tightened as he observed the four custom-made display cases filled with thousands of cast soldiers, cannons, horses, and a few new painted knickknacks.

His green eyes, filled with water, scanned the room until they landed on the one person who truly understood him. "How could I ever sell this? How could we allow a stranger to wander in the remnants of our memories? Our secrets?"

He reached out and took her hand. "We escaped to here to get away from my father. We created our own family. As strange as we are, we are a family. And this house... Well, it is a member of this family."

"And what if our daughter doesn't aspire to be a doctor?"

He sat, thinking. He looked out the window toward St. Charles Street as the streetcar went rumbling by. Turning back, he shrugged. "Then I guess she will just have to be some mean laborer... Like a surgeon."

Leatha sat mute and calm, but Walter could see the laughter he jokingly insisted on percolating up from her lower bowels because it took so long. "Before you laugh, think about it. On the streetcars, on the street, in stores, she has been diagnosing people's ailments for years. And she has become more accurate over time. She has even invented new signs for the ailments. She has known medicine all her life." The laughter finally worked its way into her chest, as the unrestrained teats bounced about on her jumping rib cage. Her laughter was like that of a little girl again. "You are correct. As painful as a stubbed toe in the night, you are completely correct. And as she has learned, so have I." She wound a finger under her head wrap. "Betsy introduced us to the theater but also took me under her wing and intro-duced me to philosophy, as well as the plays."

Walter rested his hand on her knee. "Don't forget you're teaching her the healing arts of voodoo." He leaned back against the chair and sighed. "Where would we be without each of our contributions to the combined whole?"

And with stumbles and bruised limbs, as well as ego, the lithesome little girl was all too soon a young woman. And, as her father had predicted, she followed in his footsteps, sort of.

❧

HANNAH STROLLED along the main street of Black River. Her white jumper glowed hot in the early spring afternoon sun. The wool plaid skirt was even hotter. Her feet ached to be bare and free from the hot black patent leather shoes. The heat bore down, making the five schoolbooks as heavy as the lead in her heart.

From the corner of her eye, she watched a girl dressed similarly. The girl was about the same age, and yet she wore no shoes. Hannah knew the colored girl across the street was wearing pass-me-downs or clothes from the church box.

It was only about sixty feet; thirty strides for either girl, separating the two physically. The street on Hannah's side was the new macadam called asphalt, smooth and dark gray. At the center of the street, the asphalt abruptly turned into dirt. Deep potholes and ruts ran like snakes winding between large dents in the earth. Nothing but horse carts and ox carts ever fought their way down the colored side of the street. On Hannah's side, the shiny new horseless carriages rolled smoothly. There, white folk went about their daily business or were just out for a Sunday drive, to see and be seen in their choice of automobile.

Hannah ached as she watched the other girl. The only distinction Hannah perceived between herself and the other girl was one of coloring. She even knew the girl's name was Edwina May Holder, and she lived next door to the colored Southern Baptist Church.

Hannah had learned that the other girl was an excellent student and may even be the best in the colored school. However, Hannah also knew that there would never be enough money to send her to college. Without help, the girl could never rise from the other side of the street—the side with dust in the summer, and mud in the winter.

Hannah made a mental note to pack a special bag of clothes. They would drop it off at the colored church when Leatha, Walter, and she made their medical rounds on the colored side of the town the next night. Perhaps one of the new jumpers or dresses would suit her. Her jumper, though nearly a year old, fit perfectly. A couple of months more was acceptable, given summer school.

THE SURGEON, satisfied with her work, raised her gaze to the assisting physician and communicated with him in perfect High German. "You may close. Mind you, she is still growing, so use the cotton thread, not the silk. We want her gut to absorb the internal stitches before she really starts growing. I don't want to find myself in a situation where I must explain to her that in twenty years she is hunched over and experiencing stomach pain because my assistant surgeon used silk and tied her guts to the size of an eight-year-old."

The seventeen-year-old surgeon gave her assistant the

hard, one-eyed stare and asked in French, "Comprendre, Papa?"

Walter laughed. "Oui, mon Cherie. This was a surgery of perfection. If we had a young girl here instead of this suckling pig, she would grow into a young woman with a perfectly missing appendix. Her left kidney lives on the right, her right on the left. We could mend the heart," he suggested, glancing toward the woman wielding a large knife near the kitchen entry. "But I think our patient has a pressing engagement for our Sunday dinner."

Turning, Hannah asked Leatha, "Can we butcher it in any way special for you?"

The colored woman, with her trademark three-colored scarves wound about her hair, pushed off the doorjamb. "If you could remove all your homework from the cavity, then we can stuff him before your esteemed father and house doctor sews him back up. The coals in the pit are almost ready, so no more surgery today."

"Just as well. I was getting hungry just watching Hannah move the kidneys around."

"If we had been wearing masks, I think I would have soaked mine with spit myself."

Leatha stood up straight and gave the young woman a hard look. A young woman in society does not use the word "spit."

Hannah blushed. "Mia culpa. You're entirely correct. It would have been awash with saliva."

As the woman embraced her warmly, the trio shared a laugh while she glanced at her closest friend and the head of the household. "Oh, child, what are we going to do next year when you go off to college? Who will hold us accountable, and yet make us laugh?"

A muffled voice, "Well...," issued from the woman's chest, "as we have discussed, all of us shall decamp Black River for the duration of the theater season." Pulling into clear air to speak, the surgeon continued as she set about clearing the cavity of the pig. "I believe this will give the two of you until after Christmas to prepare yourselves."

As she turned to look at her father, her hands worked in the pig's cavity, more by feel than guided by sight. "Unless, of course, you were to retire to New Orleans," Turning back to Leatha. "Which would mean we never have to separate, nez pas?"

"Sempre unum; but never to be." Walter slowly slumped into a chair, feeling all his years. "One day, there will be a time when we will all go our separate ways. It is the path of life we all walk at different paces. But for a moment, let us walk together on the path and enjoy the sunshine for a day."

"Nathanial Longfellow, that was not." The young woman with the bloody butchering knife rested her fist on her outstretched hip as she closed one eye, trying hard to find the passage in her memory.

"Walter Humphrey, 1922; and I better go write it down before I forget such an exquisite epitaph for my headstone." Rising, he added. "My stone will bear witness to my extensive wisdom."

"Yes, Father, we have all read the tome, and your headstone grows at the pace of your head as you swell to make anew. As it is, we shall go broke just paying for the granite on which to inscribe the wisdoms." She gathered the last of the entrails and waxed poetic. "Ah, but what is life? But with fewer years, one gains less knowledge of the craft needed for life. The Earth's interior pulls us down; we yield, becoming food for Earth's rightful owners."

Leatha rolled her eyes. "I guess I'll have to go out back and kill a rutabaga for my supper because I have watched you two trying to cook this poor pig by telling it to be done. Its only action was to try to stand and walk away from the chatter."

6

NEW ORLEANS

The tiny woman finished the hand, announcing, "Gin."

"Oh, Nana, when will I ever learn how to win against you?" Hannah laughed as she tallied the score. "And that is the game." She settled back into the large leather club chair. "And the travesty wasn't even close."

The older woman pushed at her glasses, which had slid down her small nose. Lowering her head to one side, she looked over the top of her glasses. "Quia ego viceroy decipiat." I win because I cheat.

Hannah chuckled. "Not as much as Papa. Or as bad."

"Oui, Cherie, he is the worst. But he only cheats blatantly when he wants to be caught. It is when he cheats wisely that you do not see. But these days, he only cheats to entertain." She lay back into the comfort of her club chair and drew the ottoman over with her toes. The two shared the rest with all four feet.

"Nana, I have a question. I am fairly sure I know the

answer, but I want to ask it, anyway. It is just for me to know. No other reason."

"Que vous inquiète pas?" What worries you so?

"You are my mother, oui?"

Betsy's head rolled to the side. She thought of nothing as she just watched the late January storm wept slowly against the windows. A streetcar glided through the soft drizzle on St. Charles Street. Over the years, she knew the question would eventually surface. But she had always hoped the older two to be asked to deal with it.

Carefully, she looked back at the face of her young reflection. In a soft voice from afar, she heard herself ask. "Have you pondered this matter for a considerable period?"

"Since I was six. It was when I realized I was not exactly white."

Nanna's brow furrowed as she looked straight at the girl. "How was that?"

"Papa was performing an abortion on the cotton gin owner's daughter. She had hair darker than mine, but her womanly parts were pink as her lips—mine are not. Not as dark as Leatha's, but as dark as yours."

The older pushed her head back into the cushion of the chair. "Oh, my lord. When did you start looking at our womanly parts?"

Hannah giggled. "Well, our household isn't exactly a bastion of modesty."

The other shrugged with her eyelids and brows. "But that isn't my question."

Betsy wrinkled up a few freckles on her nose as she

stared at her daughter. "The revelation of my being your mother wasn't your question?"

"Oh, heavens no; I had laid that corpse to rest before I was ten. I just figured you preferred to be called Nana instead of 'mother' or 'mama.' Any possibility of you thinking I didn't know you were my mother? It never entered my mind."

"Then what earth-shattering question could you not answer?"

"Walter."

"What about Walter?"

"Whether or not he is my father?"

Betsy swallowed hard, but tried not to show it. How can she articulate the peculiar yet affectionate connections which thrive solely in the night's quiet? "What do you think?"

"Well, it's confusing. The world thinks he is white. And yet, he is not. Or at least partly. He does not sleep with you, but Leatha never sleeps in her bed except to nap in the afternoon. Occasionally, you sleep with them in the big bed, but seldom. And then there are the gentlemen. They stay the night, but don't sleep in the guest..."

"Stop right there, young lady!" Betsy glowered at her daughter. "How do you know all of this?"

Hannah rolled her eyes as her fingers signed her answer, "Oh, please, Mother. I'm not blind."

The older woman sighed as she laid the back of her wrist against her forehead in a dramatic swooning motion.

Hannah snickered, and it drew up a resonating chuckle from her mother.

"We thought we were so discreet. But habits are habits."

"Well, Mother?"

"What?"

"Is he?"

"Biologically? No." She sagged into herself. "But he is as much my father as he is yours." She stood. "I need some tea before recounting our arrival."

"Maybe I can help, and we can make an early supper out of it. And then I need to study."

The temperate wind rose ever so slightly outside, just enough to rattle the shutters softly. It echoed the movement of the pot and pan as they made the meal. The candles glowed softly off the dull gold of the candlesticks as the two finished their meager repast.

"Well?" Hannah laid her utensils at the five o'clock position of her empty plate. She wiped her lips and waited. She could tell her mother was gathering her story. Throughout Hannah's life, her mother always prepared herself to tell a story. It mattered not whether it was about seeing someone on the street or recalling the glory days in Troy.

"I was just about fifteen when I knocked on the back door. I was also three months pregnant with you, and out of answers."

The streetcar's last run was ending, leaving the two women isolated as the night's hush deepened. One finally learning of her heritage, the other discovering what a woman her daughter had become. Nineteen twenty-five looked better than expected.

The wheels on the streetcars roll predictably smooth. Enormous wheels on the sterns of the ships plying the Big Muddy are smooth and quiet. As the wheels of time grind ever on, some realize time is slipping away from them, and those they love.

The shade rose quietly, and the drapes drew back in a slow reveal of the morning sprinkled with drops on the windowpanes. Hannah stretched, yawned, and opened her eyes to see the rest of her family standing at the foot of her bed with presents in their hands.

"Morning, youngest woman of my heart." Walter boomed.

"Merry Christmas, Cherie." Hannah squealed with surprise and glee as she sat up to receive her hugs.

"Joyeux Noël mon petit chou." Merry Christmas, my little cabbage. Betsy stepped to the side of the bed and sat as she set Hannah's morning coffee on the nightstand. The other hand held a long, flat box.

Hannah hugged her mother. "Beatus ferias, Nana." Happy holiday. Turning to the others, she pointed to the large double bed. "Sit."

The two laughed, hugged, and sat as commanded.

"You're late for the theater season. I'm sure you have missed some wonderful plays." She paused and sipped her coffee with cinnamon and cream.

Walter fluffed his immense mustache with his breath. "Pfft. It couldn't be helped. As the summer wound down and we began transferring patients to Dr. Neidumeyer for the winter, a new young doctor landed on our doorstep. So, after he looked at everything, we sold the practice, home, and furniture—lock, stock, and barrel. The new doctor, Dr. Pulz, graduated from Tulane and practiced in the north. He disliked Nashville's snow; therefore, he sought a southern practice. So, we sold him everything."

He looked at Leatha. "Well, not everything. Some things will arrive later this week. The important items are here or within the new Pierce Arrow."

"You sold Black River?" Hannah laid down the unopened package, and then frowned. "Wait. What new Pierce Arrow?" Her eyes suddenly flew wide as it struck home. "Wait! You're moving back here? With us?" She flew out of the bedcovers and wrapped her arms around her family. "I have my family? My whole family? This is the most wonderful Christmas I could have ever wished for."

They all sat wiping and drying tears and smiling like drunken sailors. It was a wonderful Christmas present for all of them.

"Cherie?" Leatha pointed at the forgotten presents.

Hannah threw her arms around the smaller woman's neck. "Oh, Nana, thank you. It is perfect. Thank you."

A tiny squeak escaped the woman's lips. "But you haven't opened it yet."

Hannah laughed as she sat back. "Does it matter?" She batted her eyes and smiled in a way she hoped would pass for cute and innocent.

"Alright, Cherie, we shall play the game. But you must

guess both the colors and the items inside each present." The others nodded, meeting her gaze.

Hannah straightened herself and gathered her coffee cup to her face as she eyed the three packages spread out across the covers. She carefully reached out and lifted the flat, long box. It was the same shape and size as the one she was opening. Only a slight lift, and she let it settle back. With her forefinger, she pushed at the large, cylindrical wrapped package. It rolled easily and silently.

She sat back on her haunches and took a sip of coffee. A smile danced across her face, reflecting the twinkle in her eyes.

"Et?" The doctor asked in Latin.

"In tempore, Papa." In time.

She sipped and then put down the empty cup. She pointed at the unmolested package in front of Leatha, then to Walter, and finally picked up the package with which she had started. "Black, silver, white, and sheer." She smiled.

"Oh, little one! You're as bad as when you were small." Walter sank with a wan smile, as if deflated. "So, what are they?"

"A stethoscope, a lab coat, and sheer silk stockings." She leaned over and hugged her mother. "What play are we seeing that I get stockings?"

Leatha chuckled. "There's another play they would perform on Christmas Day?"

Walter looked aghast. "There is only one proper play today."

"Of course, A Christmas Carol; how silly of me. Hélas, I have been studying too much. My brain has turned to mush."

"Not after your display of correctly guessing the presents. My clever wrapping didn't fool you for a moment?"

She signed to her mother in French, "Silly old father," as she spoke to him. "Oh, no, Father, it had me baffled... truly it did. The rolled oats tin by Quaker is one of the few items I will always remember about you. In fact, when you die, if you wish to be cremated, I will put you in Mister Quaker's oat tin so I can keep you forever in my pantry."

They all laughed. The truth was undeniable. Walter's mornings always started with a bowl of rolled oats from the Quaker company, which came in a round tin.

Leatha narrowed one eye. "But how did you know mine?"

"At first, I thought Nana's was the stethoscope. But then yours is heavier. It dented the chenille spread just a wee bit deeper." She smiled at her powers of observation. "I have been waiting for someone to give me a stethoscope, although I won't really need one for another two years when we do rounds. However, a nice one is always welcome, no matter when. Nez pas?"

"Oui, and it will come in handy as you help me around here. Non?" Walter drew up his mouth to one side in a devilish smile.

"Oui, Papa." She realized what she hadn't noticed the

previous summer. His thinning hair was becoming pure white. It removed any doubt about his bloodline; the whiteness left no questions. She also observed how lightly he sat on the bed, as well as the translucence of his thinned skin. His sixty-nine years were showing. She also knew that under the tricolor of Leatha's head wrap was nothing but pure white hair as well. She could guess at Leatha's age. But Hannah knew Leatha was only a handful of years older than Walter.

LIFE in the large house flowed as steadily as the great muddy river. Seasons went through their cycles of birth, fruiting, and death. The businesses of the house continued and grew with the addition of Nana's voodoo and Hannah's medical expertise.

The door slid open quietly as the two elves giggled at the naked bodies lying helter-skelter on the large bed. Christmas Eve had once again become a time to remember and rejoice. The party of four in the theater box had become a tradition. Even Leatha dressed in holiday regalia, thanks to the relaxed holiday atmosphere and the money paid as theater patrons. Her usual tricolor scarves were replaced by red, green, and gold lamé with sequins of matching gold, rubies, and emeralds about her neck.

The performance was just as excellent as in previous years. However, the party afterward was a source of unexpected joy. Henry, who had managed the theater for over fifty years, was finally retiring. Many of the troupes of past years returned to help him on his way. Even Brennan's sent over a giant spread of traditional Christmas fare, including birds, pig, and venison. The dishes ranged from English figgy pudding to Creole fare that could light the night, if not just your mouth.

The last dessert was, in everybody's opinion, the highlight of the evening. As Henry was leaving New Orleans to retire in New York City, the French Market had sent over a life-sized pastry alligator. Its mouth was stuffed and overflowing with lemon vanilla cream pudding to dip the doughnut pieces in, as they were ripped from the body of the animal. The back lay frosted in chocolate. But as everyone who knew warned others, the chocolate was hot with Creole hot-pepper powder—a genuine surprise for the unknowing.

Betsy set the tray of breakfast treats down on the side table and drew the heavy drapes. Having relieved herself of the tray of coffee, she draped a dressing gown on each of the sleeping angels as she kissed their cheeks.

A dark eye slowly opened. It revealed curiosity, not ill will. A soft, relaxed smile spread across the dark face as Leatha realized it was morning. For the first Christmas of their lives, the younger two had risen before her.

She slipped her right hand under the other dressing gown. Searching, she found a grip on her lifelong friend and partner. Gently pulling him awake, she smiled at the two other conspirators. A snowy white head, finally, swayed, then rose toward the light.

The two youngsters clapped and cheered, "Yes! We have a winner." Years earlier, Walter investigated a lifeless body. When he arrived, he noted the attending policeman smelled just as much of alcohol as the body. He bent over and watched the body's neck for a few moments. Straightening, he kicked the man soundly in the stomach. The dead responded with a lively throwing up of the night's consumption. At which moment, Walter threw up his hands in declaration, "We have a winner." Thus, it became a traditional joke among police and medical practitioners forever after. But also occasionally applied to Hannah falling asleep over her medical books.

The large white mustache, like Walter's new author hero, Mark Twain. echoed the mop of white hair, "Warum so früh?" Why so early? he growled in German.

"Papa, es ist Weihnachtsmorgen." It is Christmas morning.

As the elders went to different rooms for pressing matters, the two younger women bustled around the room. The two pulled the chenille spread flat and fluffed the pillows. They giggled about catching the others in bed like two little puppies thrown about the bed in whatever position took them when they fell asleep.

"Back when you were still a bump, we would occasionally be on the floor or relaxing in chairs in the mornings." Nana giggled at the feigned look of shock on her daughter's face. "One morning, Leatha and I were in bed, but no Walter. Knowing he was most certainly not up making coffee or breakfast, we went looking for him. We found him where the evening party had started. He was in the den. Naked as a jaybird with one hand on a bottle's neck, and the other on his bottleneck."

"Was not." The topic of conversation returned. "I still had my hose and garters on." He climbed, still naked, back onto the bed, unabashed as a child.

Nana looked him up and down and pursed her lips in argument. Rolling her head over to the side to look at her daughter, her mouth puckered as if to say, I rest my case.

Leatha strolled in, still sipping on her large coffee mug with her dressing gown laid over her one arm. Kissing the two youngsters on the cheek, she quietly returned to the fluffed pillows and sat cross-legged like a Pasha waiting to be served.

The younger pair stood watching the older two.

Leatha finally looked over the brim of her mug. "What?" The question quietly echoed out of the mug.

"What do you mean, what? It's time to get up."

She harrumphed. "Do you or do you not see my hair? It's Christmas. Where are our presents?"

"Where are your presents? What about ours?"

Leatha lowered her mug and looked at the youngest in the room. "Hannah Mariah Rose Humphrey, how old is you?"

"Twenty-seven. And that is Doctor Hannah Mariah Rose Cherie Humphrey, if you please." She pinched the sides of her dressing gown and curtsied.

"Well, little miss, for twenty-eight years, we cleaned your poopy bottom, fed your squally mouth, looked after you, and brought you presents. It is about time you started pulling your weight around here." Her face returned to her mug before the others caught her smiling. Her gaze examined the mug's contents for the same reason.

Walter's face never left his mug, but some strange choking burbles were coming from the vicinity of his mouth.

Hannah looked at her mother and shrugged. She reached the door to retrieve the gifts.

Nana called as she climbed up on the foot of the high bed, "Oh Cherie, be a dear and don't forget the little gold envelope in the branches about halfway up."

Hannah spun to face the one she thought was behind her, helping to fetch the packages. She found an innocent face peering out from her coffee mug. Looking at the head of the bed, the other two suffered from minor convulsions. Hannah spun on the ball of her right foot and strode from the room. "Traitor. At least you didn't start getting naked like the others."

The three chuckled as Betsy shrugged out of her gown.

From the middle of the stairs, they caught the daughter's dramatic sigh of disgust, familiar with her mother and the house full of naked jaybirds. "Mo-ther! Really." The three laughed aloud. Too loud to hear the echo from the parlor on the floor below.

The carafe sat empty. The platter, formerly piled with biscuits, lay empty. Bits and pieces of scrambled eggs and grits were the only remaining evidence of breakfast in bed. The spread was a stormy sea of torn gift wrap and naked bodies. Sides ached from laughter, and cheeks were tear-stained from heartfelt joy. They carefully thought out, specially made, or custom-made, each present. This had been a unique Christmas morning. Hannah looked at her new Cartier tank wristwatch. The three had rightfully predicted her enjoyment and embraced its utility.

The troupe's previous spring play informed their design selection. Cartier designed the watch as a thank-you for all the tank combat troops who had helped liberate France. The play recounted the prolonged, ugly trench warfare and the tanks' pivotal role in breaking the hold and winning the war. Hannah looked at the blue sapphire on the stem. The stone originally represented a survivor. She liked to think it portended remarkable things to come.

"Cherie?"

"Oui, Papa?" She looked up and saw the large gold envelope in his hand.

"We have one more thing for you. Whether it's a gift, only time will allow you to be the judge." He handed her the packet.

She opened the end and slid out a passport, a ticket, and two addressed envelopes. First, she studied the passport and saw her smiling face staring back at her. The ticket was for a steamship passage to England. The train ticket to London was attached with a small gold clip. She looked up, quietly. "I don't understand."

Tears were in all eight eyes. The soft morning light glowed in the wet streaks on white and black skin. Betsy reached out and took her daughter's hand.

"There's only a one-way ticket. These letters are

addressed to the Chief of Residents and the Chief of Staff at King's College Hospital. I. Do. Not. Understand." The profession demands god-like decisions with one's hand inside another person, replacing the little girl long ago.

Walter swallowed the frog from his throat, but couldn't look at her. He watched the morning streetcar slide by in the morning sun. "You are being sent away, child."

"Why?" All the playfulness of obfuscating languages dropped. But she backed down on her tone.

Walter glanced at the other women. Nanna squeezed Hannah's hand. "Because it is for the best. Best for the times... and best for you, Cherie." She moved to stroke her daughter's cheek, but Hannah pulled away. The fire still burned in her eyes.

"I understand the depression and all, which is why we take supplies to the Tenderloin. We help those who cannot help themselves. But what do you mean it is the best for me? Why do you believe you understand what's best for me?"

Quietly, Walter's watery eyes rose. He watched one of the most precious things in his life being hurt, but he had no choice this time. "Sweetheart?"

"What?"

He stopped. Silently counting to five. In a whisper, he asked, "Have I ever raised my voice to you? Have any of us?"

"No," Hannah grumped.

"Have I ever taken a belt to you or struck you in any way? Has any of us?"

She calmed. "No."

"Have we always looked out for you? Looked out for your best interest?"

"Yes."

"Then why don't you trust us now?"

The young woman slumped back against the iron footboard. The metal was cool on her naked skin and gave a focus point for her mind. She thought about the four of them sitting on the large bed—naked. She thought about all that had happened inside the walls of this house, this family. How different they were from the rest of the world. The secrets they shared from the gold cast soldiers to the blood running through their veins.

The streetcar rolled by. She thought about how she and Nana could ride it up town with Leatha. But if they tried to take her into a café or even a bathroom, Leatha had to use the colored facilities. Even though she and her mother were no less colored, just in a lighter way, she thought about their secret conversations in public that others just didn't see. People believed conversation was only something one could hear.

Her gaze fell upon the small scar beside her kneecap. She remembered falling while jumping rope on a balmy day, right before her family moved. Walter had walked her back into the house, cleaned the laceration, and stitched it up with five of the tiniest stitches he knew how.

There were so many memories here.

She slowly opened her eyes and watched the silent, still ceiling fan. Finally, she lowered her head and sadly looked at her family. Naked as jaybirds, on Christmas morning. Nothing would ever be as strange or as perfect.

"I'm sorry, I was angry." She licked at her thin, tight lips. "England... It just sounds so extremely far away." Her voice took a jump, and it quavered as the tears overflowed down her cheeks. "And I know... this time... you won't be coming with me."

7

WELCOME TO ENGLAND

THE TRAIN RUMBLED STEADILY along the tracks as Hannah attempted to immerse herself in the travel book. The rhythmic clack of the rails blended with the static of the words on the page. She found herself reading at a pace half as quick as her usual speed, yet it was just slow enough to muddle her understanding of the text for the fourth time. With a sigh of exasperation, she placed the book face down on her lap. The soft cover creased slightly as she turned her gaze out the window. The landscape busily passed in an artistic hue of green fields and distant hills. Blue stretched endlessly above, as if urging her thoughts to drift away with the passing scenery. As a part of her brain picked out the familiar shapes of clouds, she heard Nana's voice identify the types of clouds. Another part of her brain was at war with what she had just read. She muttered some vulgar terms in Latin; something highly specious for a refined woman alone on a train crossing the south of England. But altogether, it also had a certain satisfying earthy gut feeling by swearing in the almost obscure language.

"You have mixed your tenses, dear."

Hannah looked up at what she had been thinking since Southampton, as the bird lady. A tight hat with a mere inch of veil covered her entire head of hair. Her soft blue-gray tweed suit distracted from but didn't entirely hide her severe varicose veins, even with the orthopedic stockings and boots. The difference in heel thickness—almost a full inch—didn't go unnoticed by Hannah. The woman's hands never stopped knitting. It was as if she never spoke.

"Excuse me, but did you say something?"

The hands continued, and the eyes never rose. "You used the wrong tense." The hands reached the end of the row, then started back the four inches. Knit one, cable one, knit one, cable one; four inches wide of stretchy wool bandage. "You said *fucked*, as in the past tense. It is impossible to have a past tense for an active verb. It must be—to fuck the world. Active and present tense: Pedicabo ego mundo. The ego, or I, while implied, is best pronounced. It lends a little muscle to the sexual umph, as it were." She looked up with bright, sparkling, powder-blue eyes and a wry smile. "Don't you agree, dear?"

Hannah laughed. "And here I was missing my family horribly, and up you pop. My father would have adopted you to our dinner table on any given night."

The woman fed the knitting into her left hand. "Then you agree." She stuck her right hand out. "Mrs. Lucinda

Daisy Holt, Languages, second form, retired; and your father sounds like a sound fellow."

Hannah took her hand. "I'm pleased to meet you, Mrs. Holt. I'm Doctor Hannah Maria Humphry, new to King's College Hospital's surgical ward. Father is sound, but with some quirks to keep life interesting. Are the bandages for burn victims?"

The woman leaned back, tightening her puckered lips with barely a hint of coloring on them. Thinking, she studied the young woman. "Hmm, Surgeon, the lowest and meanest of the medical profession. You have a wonderful manner about you. You should have worked harder and become a regular practitioner. Truly... hmm, and a Yank to boot." She chuckled. "No, dear, these are for the people with leprosy. The Ministry operates a hospital near Bath, and as a result, the auxiliaries knit approximately fifty thousand bandages a year. Our churches purchase the skeins of wool and provide them to us. All we must do is remember to stop at the tenth centimeter. One skein makes one bandage."

Hannah's eyebrows rose. "An exemplary endeavor."

The woman glowed brighter. "So, what was all the swearing about?"

Hannah held up the book. "I am trying to get a sense of what Victoria's Station will look like. However, this author simply focuses on lengths, widths, and heights. It's all just numbers, and it doesn't make a lick of sense."

The teacher reached out. "Let me see this tome of edification." She turned to a couple of pages, then handed it back. "You may as well just open this window and pitch the blighter out to the tracks. It's tripe, written by a stupid..." She stopped herself as she realized to whom she was talking.

"Yank?"

The woman blushed and smiled. "Yes, well, I guess one should not rush to judge. But you are entirely correct, dear. He makes no bleeding sense. Vicky's Station is a grand marvel. All the trains come into the building, and there is a grand bustle of people going here and there. The noise is a barnyard of culture, marketing, and people in general. Along with the trains coming and going, of course."

The woman's open right hand passed dramatically in a wide arch over her head. "High above you, the roof is of glass and iron. Flocks of birds take refuge from storms there. Some say a crazy pilot once flew his airplane into the station. Flew a lap about the building and flew back out. Some say it was a publicity stunt for a new way to travel, but I think he was just lost."

"The largest building I have ever been to is the theater in New Orleans. It accommodates over a thousand people with three levels of seating. I can't imagine a building large enough for a single train, much less three or four."

"Eight." The woman patted her hand. "Don't try to imagine it. Just show up and enjoy the wonder of something new and amazing."

Hannah leaned back, considering the woman. "Are you sure you aren't my father's twin and the lost sister to my mother and..." She stopped. Defining Leatha, even to herself, hadn't occurred to her; neither had explaining her family. Twenty-eight years, and Leatha was just... well... Leatha.

"Are you alright, dear?"

Hannah shook her head and refocused on the woman across from her. "Yes, I'm fine. I just had an epiphany."

"Epiphanies are good, dear. They remind us we are thinking human beings and are still alive."

Hannah smiled as she turned and gazed out at the lush green countryside passing by. Everything looked different, yet it felt so comfortably the same. Cows grazed, narrow roads wound, a man drove a tractor, a woman hung laundry, and the sun shone. She felt torn between a longing for home and finding comfort in familiar surroundings, despite being far away from her loved ones. Turning, she studied the bird-like lady who pecked at the yarn with the long needles in her arthritic hands. "Do you live in London, Mrs. Holt?" Hannah reached out verbally.

Without looking up, the woman replied. "No, not since the market crash; I live near Southampton with my younger sister and her family. I keep the house, and she looks after the small farm. Her husband works on the railroads as an oiler. I just like to escape to London a few times a year and spend a few duckets on a play or two. I have an old friend with whom I bunk. She taught English and literature. Poor dear never married. There's no time once you start your career in teaching. I was lucky to meet my Charles when we were in second form. He became a boilermaker and helped me make my way through my schooling to be a teacher."

"Mr. Holt passed away?"

"No, dear, a jealous husband shot him during the Great War."

Hannah's shock was obvious. The woman dropped her knitting, then took Hannah's hands. "No dear. I'm sorry, we use such awful terms for you poor colonists. He was in the trenches in France. He was sleeping in the trench the Huns had been in the day before. The man probably thought the bed was still his. Poor Charlie never knew what hit him. I prefer to think that he reached heaven before the devil found out he had passed away."

The woman's lips tightened, her glance sidelong as she murmured. "When you really think about it, it's not a bad way to go." She looked back at Hannah and changed the subject. "Attend theatrical performances, my dear?"

A thin smile crept across Hannah's face as her eyes drooped half shut. "My mother was in the theater when she was young. We lived for the season."

Her eyes slid closed as her head rested back, and she leaned against the window jam. The country green rolled by as the clouds hung in the sky. As if waiting for her to speak.

"I led them on in this distracted fear. And left sweet Pyramus translated there, when in that moment (so it came to pass), Titania waked, and straightaway, loved an ass."

The elder woman clapped softly as she smiled with a tiny, giddy squeal. "So well, so well done. You honor our sweet Will."

Hannah mock bowed, "Thank you, dear sweet Mrs. Holt. You honor the memory of a nine-year-old who played Puck one summer in a backyard production in Black River, Mississippi."

"Well, you must have been smashing, my dear, and please, call me Daisy. Everybody does, and I'm losing those who do."

"Let's plan to get together, Daisy. We'll enjoy a play together, the three of us—my treat. Come round the hospital, and together we'll choose the top troupe and play in town. It will be a smash."

Daisy tutted her teacher's tongue. "The word you seek is smashing. As in, we will have a smashing good time. And I cannot agree more."

8

WELCOME TO LONDON

THE MAGNIFICENCE of Victoria's Station was more than Hannah had been prepared for. It was all a laughing Daisy could do to tug on her coat and draw her nose away from the train car window. As their shoes landed on the platform, Hannah's head was in the glass clouds high above. Still laughing, Daisy took her arm and guided the gap-mouthed child along the way. To avoid harm to either themselves or others, the neophyte Yank could run over.

"Daisy, you didn't warn me."

"I did, child. You just didn't listen with your head."

They cleared the platform and headed for the station to gather their luggage. Hannah could barely bring herself to pay attention to the business of being an adult. She was more enamored with the business of being a gawped-mouth child again. As Hannah collected her bags, her empty stomach reminded her of the biscuits and coffee she had quickly had before leaving the ship.

Turning to her new friend and aide, "Daisy, I just realized it has been a long time since I have eaten. Is there any way we can get some fish and chips? I did say it correctly, didn't I?" She glowed with the eager-to-please look the teacher had not seen since retirement.

The slight woman leaned toward Hannah. In a conspirator's whisper, she shared her secret. "You don't buy fish and chips inside the station. The king will take his due. But if we walk through the large door over there, turn to the right, there is a sweet gentleman who will satisfy you, me, or even the king's wife—if she knew where to come." She leaned a little closer and turned her head up sideways to get closer. "He's not my dear Charlie, but I do hold a fancy for him. His name is Rupert, but I call him Percy, because some days, I think he is searching for my heart."

True to her words, they had no sooner cleared the portico of the building than a big smile of gaping holes and a few brown pegs of what was left of his teeth greeted them. "Eeear now, is that the finest flower in all o' 'nglind?"

The little Bantey of a man with a beaten-down snap cap and trawler's coat over his workman's pants and boots, sparkled with his delight at seeing Daisy.

"Good to see you, too, Percy. The time has been like a yoke upon my shoulders since I last saw you." She offered her hand, and with his heavily armored long rubber gloves, he raised it near but not to touch his lips.

Half turning toward Hannah, she continued. "Percy, dear, I want you to meet one of the new doctors up at King's College. Her name is Hannah, but you must speak the King's English correctly. She's a Yank."

The man whisked his hat from his almost bald head and gave a slight bow. "It is a pleasure to make your acquaintance, miss, and welcome to England."

Hannah could tell immediately why he was completely covered with clothes and had an assistant serving the public. Under his clothes, he probably had one of Daisy's bandages wrapped around an arm or a leg. "Percy, the pleasure is entirely mine. Daisy has assured me there is no finer dining in all of London she would care to taste."

The man drew back as he fumbled to put on his hat. He studied the sincerity of Hannah's words. The hat slid to one side. Hannah guessed it was the lack of feeling in his hands, if there were full hands left in the large gloves. As it fell, she caught it.

"Here, Percy, let me help with that." He tried to protest being touched, but Hannah stepped in, whispering, "It's okay, Percy, let me help. The kind you have isn't catching, or you wouldn't be here feeding the best to us undeserving." She squared the hat in a nice rakish look, then kissed her two fingers and pressed them lightly on the tip of his nose. "We will talk in a few weeks after I have settled in."

The man was embarrassed, but also grateful there was one more person he didn't have to hide from. "In commemoration of our meeting, and London gaining a new fine doctor, the meal is on the house." Turning to his young helper, he softly commanded, "Gus, two trenchers for the fine ladies. And mind it's the Turbo, not the Skate." He turned back with the packets and smiled, a gesture of friendship and pride. "Welcome to our little piece of 'eaven, mum."

"Percy," Daisy warned.

He saluted her with the touch of two fingers to the brim of his hat. "Yes, mum. But bugger all, it's in the blood." A young man, caught stealing cookies, smiled. Hunger, not shame, shone in his eyes.

As Hannah and Daisy sat on their luggage, eating the fare from the wrapping of newsprint, they smiled, listening to the worst of the Cockney accent as it berated and cajoled the walking mass of humanity to come and eat or be cursed for not doing so.

Hannah pursed her lips to keep from laughing as she almost understood one string of cursing after a swell in a fine suit. What surprised her were the Latin swear words he intermixed in the tirade. She looked at Daisy, who just rolled her eyes.

"When he first came to me, he was worse for the living. I was just starting my second year teaching and could only understand one word in every three. By Christmas, he was talking like a Seville Row prince. By the summer, he had mastered two years of Latin. It's a bleeding waste. A sharp mind like his, trapped in a wasting body. But he is a trooper. It is always special to see him still this side of the iron fence."

"An iron fence?"

Daisy nodded. "A church's graveyard."

She looked back at the man, watching. "I dread the day I arrive to find he can no longer find his way here."

Hannah laid her hand on the woman's leg. "I will check back with him. I'll see what I can do to delay that day as long as I can."

The woman couldn't speak. Her eyes were clouding with mist as she watched her former student go about his day. Her left hand dropped onto Hannah's and gently squeezed a thank-you.

Percy had gallantly whistled for a taxi, and the large boxy black automobile had glided to the curb. An older gentleman was bound to the curb, and before Hannah could say anything, he stowed the bags. The man bowed with his soft cap, almost sweeping the sidewalk in an arc as he held the door open. "Ats 'lways a pleasure ta be o' service ta any fren' o' the Governor Rupert."

Hannah turned and frowned at Percy in question as she edged toward the door.

"He said it would be his pleasure to serve you, miss. He'll take you the best way to Denmark Hill and the King's College Hospital and only charge you a farthing for the trouble." Percy winked at her. "Harold, you see well toward her. She's my new guardian angel, she is. A fine look, but a surgeon, ta boot."

The man's face lit up. As he swept the door closed and squared his hat on his head. "In that case, Rupert," As he stepped over and grabbed a large piece of fish from the stand, "The carriage is on the king." The two old friends laughed as the motorman slid into his station of life, whisking the new doctor to hers.

Hannah studied the man's face in between, catching the

sights and sounds of a vast, bustling city. "So you are a Cockney?" Hannah asked.

The man watched her in his mirror as he navigated the traffic. "Me mum was born and raised in the sound of the bells, but me da was born and raised in Brighton. They met in Liverpool, and I came along when they was camped in Blackpool. But most me young life was in Wales, a small town just across the wall from Chesta. So miss, what do you want me ta be?"

Hannah laughed, "I don't have the faintest idea what any of that means, but I think I want you to be a friend, same as Percy."

"Percy? Percy, is it? That would mean you are friends with our school mum, Daisy."

"Right you are, Harold. It is Harold, isn't it?"

"Yes, mum. Harold Alfred Charles Kentmorr. I respond to either Harold or Hack. Mr. Kentmorr was my da, and he passed low these past ten years or more."

The taxi swept into the large, sweeping driveway and stopped in front of a large, imposing, dark brick building. Nurses in white scurried to the door as Hack pulled the bags from the back of the car. "Which way, miss?"

"It's all right, Hack. I can take them from here." She drew some bills from her purse.

He stood holding her bags and ignoring the money. "We don't want to get you off on the wrong foot your first day in London, do we, mum? So, which way?" His face was dead-pan, but the slow, dull twinkle in his mirthful eyes was pure Leatha having her fun and her way.

Pulling on her mother's drama lessons, she took a deep sigh, drooped her shoulders in surrender, and turned on the ball of her left foot. "I suppose... maybe through these doors."

A smile of approval lit her new friend's face as she turned.

9

WELCOME TO KING'S COLLEGE HOSPITAL

My dearest Father, Leatha, and Mother,

I have arrived in London with none the worse for wear from my journey. Father, your choice of traveling by merchant ship instead of a steam liner was an incredible stroke of genius. Of course, I should not have been surprised by it coming from you.

I had the opportunity to experience the local food and attractions at various stops while the ship was loading or unloading. Most days, I had at least a full day's worth of walking about. In Havana, Cuba, we tied up for a full three days. I hired a man to take me on a safari. We were in the middle of the country on a coffee plantation. If I hadn't loved coffee so much before, I would love it now. I was allowed to pick some beans, and then they showed me how they removed the outer layer of the fruit. The beans are then dried in sheds. The farmer's wife showed me how to roast the beans, grind them while they were still warm, and finally make them into coffee using a French Press. I must find one here, as well as some decent coffee.

Leatha. There was a man on the ship. He worked in the engine room. His name was Clearwater, Hugo Clearwater. He thought you might remember him, as you once saved his foot from being cut off. His payment was a small dagger. He traded with the blacksmith for it in the ancient city of Damascus, now part of the French Colony of Syria. He is a soft-spoken man who adheres to the Muslim religion, but he said that if he knew what religion you believed in, he would change. I tried to explain voodoo, but I don't think he will come to church any time soon. But he's still a delightful man, and it was kind of him to remember you. I just don't remember the small knife he spoke of.

Once we were free of the Caribbean islands. We steamed due east for the Spanish Canary Islands. The entire time, I thought we were traveling to islands that would be filled with tiny yellow birds. Imagine my embarrassment when I found they named the archipelago for dogs, not birds. Canine, not canary birds. We laughed about my faux pas for days while we waited in a port devoid of any vegetation or interesting places to walk to.

I derived a diversion by walking with the harbormaster's four canines. To call them dogs would be to call the tiger in Mr. Kipling's jungle story, a kitten.

Mr. Aliso's four dogs are Spanish mastiffs. The three males are brindle colored. The female, Blanca, was my love. She was a constant presence at my hip. She had slightly longer hair, which was almost pure white.

The third day, I was pressed into service as the ship's doctor. One of the crew had taken quite the tumble during a storm. Luckily, nothing broke. But he suffered a severe concussion, which had him vomiting for four days. I enforced bed rest for eight days. But, as he was the cook, I had to release him to duty early. The crew didn't like my taste in food, and I don't know how to cook Turkish food—yet.

On the train from Southampton to London, I met a lady named Daisy, whom I have dearly taken to my heart. She is a retired schoolteacher, well-versed in Latin, and enjoys the theater. So we promised that when she's in London, we three will take in a play or two. She also introduced me to a man with dry leprosy. I promised to help once I have settled in.

The hospital is all a mix of feelings. It is an extensive building, I think, that could swallow at least a quarter of the French Quarter. I'll carry the little map for the next five years, I am sure.

I'll feel blessed starting work in that exceptional surgical wing. As expected, a qualification follows. Her name is Nurse Hemplewhite. When I inquired naively what her first name was, a much younger and nicer nurse whispered it was the name "Nurse". Nurse Hemplewhite reminds me much of the ancient anatomy professor Dr. Theodore Jefferson Jackson IV. The one who ruled the anatomy department, but wasn't the department chair. Father, he was probably there when you attended and suffered under his stone-cold glare.

Well, I'm sure there beats an icy heart of stone in her chest somewhere. I will just have to hire a fireman to bank the coals against her armor to warm her so that we may see the cold beat. Until such time, I'll remember the famous quote, "One suffers shortly for the pleasure of the life so long."

I must now trim my wick and toddle off to my chamber. They found me a flat only three short blocks from duty and call. The surgery starts at the earliest crow call. So to eschew the cold appraising glare of Nurse Hemplewhite, I must get my sleep and be in before the cock knows morning is coming.

With all my love, and I miss you something fierce,

Cherie

THE LONG HAND on the large clock over the main surgical nurses' station ticked past the one. The small pointed at the five, when the right eyebrow of Nurse Hemplewhite rose. Her face floated upward as she watched the new surgeon, a woman from America, no less, arrive through the half-glassed doors. She turned her face toward the electric clock when she knew the young woman was watching her. Slowly, her face retraced its path, and as the woman tried to walk past without comment, Nurse Hemplewhite mentioned the time. "I didn't know the living accommodations we had arranged for, made for such a late arrival, Doctor Humphreys."

Hannah regretted her smart rejoinder the moment it slipped from her mouth. "There is only one of me, Nurse Hemplewhite. Therefore, the Humphrey is singular, not plural." She kept walking as she swore under her breath in Latin. She muttered as she walked. "I know, just know, that will come back to bite me in the Gluteus Maximus someday."

The redheaded doctor named Steve something, who was only there to finish his residency and move to the north end of London, swung into march-step with Hannah. His white smock's wings were flapping like a doctor with decades of Devil-be-Damned. His red hair was tousled like he had just gotten out of bed, and his shirt and pants looked like he had been sleeping in them for a week. Hannah thought for a second and realized it was all probably true.

"Stoking at the coals of Hades this early?" His chuckle was soft. "I'm shocked you had the guts, or were just stupid enough to tell Nurse Hemplewhite such." He smiled at the surgeon as they walked, all the while, gyrating his eyes and face—trying to focus and stay awake.

"How long have you been on duty?"

"What day is it?"

"Thursday."

"Is it still June?"

"Stay out of my operatory."

"A spot of tea, then I'll be fine."

"Show me your hands." They stopped walking.

He held up his hands to show her they were steady. He smiled wanly.

"Name the minor facia from the second phalanges to the top of the brachial radial."

He stared at her numbly, thinking.

"Time is up. We have three operations scheduled for this morning. The third is the tricky one. I will start it at about ten o'clock. I don't want to hear you leaving the steam room hidey-hole until then. Get some sleep. Who is the scrub nurse you can trust?"

"Steam room?"

"The secret room where you junior doctors hide to get some sleep. Who can you trust?"

"Perkins. Nancy Perkins. She's the young redhead with the... umm, freckles." He blushed.

Hannah thought for a moment. "Hmm, yes, I remember those, umm, freckles. Alright, now off with you. I'll have Nurse Freckles come wake you about nine, so you can get some tea." She turned on the ball of her foot and headed for the doctor's prep room.

The redhead started down the other hall, then stopped, snapping his fingers as he turned. "It's five."

Hannah stopped and swore a little more. "Five what?" She asked with dread.

"Flexor, Abductor, Palmor, Supinator, and Pronator... five, but there are also five surgeries this morning. I'll be scrubbed by nine sharp. Cheers, Doctor Humphrey. You're the pip."

Hannah's eyes closed as she went into a slow burn. She could only guess who oversaw the added surgeries. As she opened one eye with pure malice, she looked back down the hall she had just walked. The person on her mind was standing in the middle of the linoleum hall, watching with a clipboard crooked in her left elbow and jammed lightly on her hip. The stance was pure tempered steel.

Hannah's Latin left her. She switched to the more collo-quial Creole. Turning, she stormed the rest of the yardage into the doctor's quarters to get changed and scrubbed. The opening volley had gone to the woman in surgical greens. Hannah swore the nurse would not take the day.

Soon, the routine of skin, muscle, organs, fascia, cuts, bone, sutures, bandages, and repeat took over her mind. In a busy operatory, a surgeon has little time to review what is next. Transitioning from the used, unsterile operatory to the fresh sterile operatory, hopefully with a bit of water, maybe some coffee, and a cracker or two to sustain you during the highly demanding day.

After overcoming a tumor the size of a football, or, as the nurse described it, a rugby ball, Hannah proceeded to the scrub area. Standing leaning against the prep counter was the young, redheaded doctor, sipping his tea and eating a sandwich of kippers and brown mustard. Hannah felt overwhelmed and threw decorum to the winds, as she knew they were alone. She reached out and grabbed his left wrist and guided the sandwich to her mouth. Taking a large bite, she released the left wrist and gently guided the right hand with the tea to her lips. The young doctor laughed and drew back.

"A rabid dog would have more manners. St. Crispen's dainties, I made you your own sandwich, and I even fetched you some of that foul-smelling coffee." He pointed at the snack laid out at the other end of the counter.

Hannah seized the coffee and drank half of the cup in a single gulp. As she chewed on her first bite, she thought. Then she reached over with her head, stealing a nibble from the other doctor's sandwich.

"Cripes. Again?" The doctor howled.

"A bite stolen from another's sandwich is always spiced sweetly by the honey of a stolen kiss."

"So now we have to share sandwiches with Shakespeare?"

"Certainly not." Hannah laughed as she chewed. "That was pure Leatha Humphrey, Voodoo Queen of New Orleans."

"Voodoo? Humphrey? You're telling me you're related to a Voodoo Queen?" He stared, eyes wide open. "Voodoo... As in sticking needles in little dollies? That kind of voodoo?"

Hannah giggled silently. "Certainly not. They are small knives. The effigies are much larger; the larger the effigy, the stronger the curse." Hanna rolled her eyes and showed her contempt for poor education. "Voodoo is about aiding balance within the human body, so it matches the spiritual world as well. And yes, Leatha helped raise me no less than my mother and father did. Every soul in a household raises and influences a child. Nez pas?"

"Nose who?"

"Nez pas. It is French for do you understand." She looked at the young doctor. "You are this close to France, and yet you don't speak a word of it?"

"I struggled to master German and Latin for my exams."

"Well, I guess we won't be having any fun by doing the surgery, all in French or Latin today. Now, will we?"

The young nurse's freckled face paled; she'd arrived just as the conversation ended. "You wouldn't really do a surgery while speaking French or Latin; would you?"

"Cert. Back home, we performed surgeries in Latin, German, Creole, and sign language all the time. When it was an especially wonderful day, we spoke in lines of your William Shakespeare, or at least in the iambic pentameter."

The young woman giggled. "I would love to hear you ordering tools in the tone of William Shakespeare."

The other redhead just rolled his eyes as he prepared to scrub for surgery.

Hannah winked at the nurse as she, too, turned to scrubbing. "Away, you trifler! Love! I love thee not, I care not for thee, Kate: this is no world to play with mammets and to tilt with lips: We must have bloody noses and cracked crowns. Staves of barrels where ribs of man wouldst be; switch which cuts for which binds, and we shall be as merry men and drunken be on Saint Crispen's Day, or we are not worthy to hold the beat of man in our hands."

The nurse frowned at the turn of the quotation. Her gawping mouth pursed. "I don't think those were Willie's words."

Hannah looked around the young doctor's shoulder. "And yet, you admitted you had never heard Shakespeare spoken in an operating room."

"Well, no... but still..."

"And I will assume you've never been to the fine city of New Orleans?" Hannah winked at the other smiling doctor.

Freckles leaned behind Hannah as an excuse to grab a sterile towel and whispered with a smile. "You are most wonderfully evil."

This made Hannah smile even more. Turning, she faced

the young nurse as she dried her hands with the sterile towel. "Young lady, I can see your education has been sorely lacking. But before we continue this education, you will need to change out of that bloody smock and scrub before you enter my domain of blood and knife." She pushed backward through the doors, following the younger doctor, calling out. "What have we here?"

10

THE PIG AND DUCK

GENERATIONS OF LOVERS, and beer lovers, left their marks—carved messages and stains—on the table's surface. Hannah wasn't sure if coming here was the right thing to do. She knew, though, that sitting in her flat and reading, as she had for the past three months, wasn't what she wanted. Her life had become a routine of eating, sleeping, working, and quietly reading alone in the evening. Only her Saturday night letters home interrupted this each week.

"What are you drinking, Love?" The barmaid was not the large, friendly, big-bosomed gal Hannah had expected in an English pub. Instead, she was more on the diminutive side, almost small. The woman would barely come to Hannah's bosom if she were standing up. The smile was a little wryer, but still there. It fit nicely under the mouse-brown hair, pulled back into a looser version of the French curl bun, which had become Hannah's signature hairstyle. The humidity had turned her hair more aggressively curly, instead of just being wavy.

"Hello." Sticking her hand out, "I'm Dr. Humphrey, but I respond well to…"

The rag-holding fist was buried into the out-swung hip. "Look, Love, I have fifty flipping idiots from the hospital on the hill. Everyone wants a beer and tucker. You're the new Jack from the States, but it doesn't tell me how you want to get fed, does it?" The woman shifted from one foot to the other. Hannah could see she still had a bit of a twinkle in her eye. But a much-harried eye.

"Right! Pour it, slop it, plop it, and I'll eat it. I want what you would have if you could ever get a break around here." Hannah's deadpan mirrored the woman, the same as the competitive sport at home.

The woman took one last look at the new surgeon from America and turned on her heel, heading for the barman. "Willie, sweet, neat, greased and squealing."

The barman looked up from processing a half dozen pints of beer. "Core, Penny, I kina 'ave ya goin' oot the back way right now."

The small woman threw her head as she pointed the back of her pencil over her shoulder. "It's fur the Yank, Jack, ya daft weasel."

The barman looked across the pub and saw the high-backed booth near the corner. He spoke softly to the small barmaid as she walked by. "That one ought let 'er 'air doon."

"Mind your Pees and Ques there, boy-o." Glancing back over her shoulder quickly, "At one kin cut your 'art out in a beat, ana still no spill ya beer."

"I'm nonna lookin' fo' a shag on Frida' ni'. I'm just sayin' she looks like she needs ta take 'er shoes off."

The two watched the slender woman in the dust-gray wool suit as she unfolded an envelope and took out what appeared to be a letter. The two shrugged their shoulders like twins and went about their work.

Cherie,

This summer's heatwave has us firmly in its grip. We moved some of the lounging chairs into the basement. It's created a cooler parlor to repair to during the heat of the day. None of us sleeps well these evenings. Even without clothing, we prefer to stay up and play three-legged gin until after the stroke of one or two.

Your letter regarding your adventurous trip to England arrived. I stare at the moon over the French Quarter and think how you seem even farther away. We all miss you so much. Walter is cheating more and more, but Leatha either doesn't care or doesn't know. I was never as good at catching his magic shenanigans as you.

Leatha has a cough, but she says it's just from the summer dust. Walter rolls his eyes, so I know it's more than just dust. But they have their secrets, and I am only privy to most, so I don't begrudge them the few.

They are both sleeping or dozing more these days, and I don't know if it's due to missing you or simply aging. Maybe it is the combination of the two. I know that as Walter nears his monumental (his words) milestone, he forgets that Leatha is about ten years his senior. But then, there are days I think she will outlive the three of us.

I have taken on most of the cooking duties, with occasional help from one or both of them, as the spirit or energy moves them. We have taken to eating more gentle fare, with most coming from a local truck farmer who comes by with a small pony-drawn cart of the day's fresh pickings. Walter has taken a fondness for the man's brown eggs and won't eat any others for breakfast.

Clarence Porter, the friendly butcher, who you sewed his thumb back on, says hello. I laugh because he sticks the thumb in the air and says hello, but he says it in a soft, slow, breathy sort of way. You would think he might believe that if he makes love to my ear, you will feel it through the ink on this letter. If you think it might help the poor man out, take this letter and rub yourself where you think it might do some good. Just don't tell me where. I'm a delicate, innocent young lady, you know.

Speaking of naughty and sexy, the troupe of all-female players from Spain is here this summer. If the weather breaks, Walter says we should have them over for dinner and a sleep-over. Some days, I don't know if he remembers who he liked most before, but for these latter days in his life, he certainly has something for naked women. And with this heat, he has been getting weeks of his poor eyes filled to the brim. But it puts a smile on his face. And Leatha and I love our man.

Speaking of Leatha and her nakedness, I have noticed lately that she has lost a lot of weight. Her upper legs are just sticks inside of her skin, and it seems to just hang from the bone. I can almost hold one of her buttocks in my hand, some-

thing which used to take me two before. I don't know if I should be worried, but she seems to eat all right.

Well, I can hear the children rumbling in the cellar, and any moment, Walter will call on the Bell, asking about supper. So, I need to slice up something and be ready to take it down to the naked ones, more so, as I can slip out of this chemise and join them.

Je tem,

Nana

"Who's the letter from?"

Hannah looked up into the bright green eyes sparkling above a sea of freckles. She then turned slightly and closed one eye as she gave a hard look at the other redhead. Steven's cat grin had a canary feather stuck in the corner.

"You two should be ashamed of yourselves. You barely have a minute off, and you run off to the steam room and do nasty disgusting things."

The three laughed as the barmaid brought Hannah's food and beer. "Oh, that looks good." He reached over and stole a bite. Looking up at the barmaid, he blushed. "I'll have one of those as well." Freckles licked the tiny tip of her tongue over her lips and nodded.

The barmaid turned and called out. "Two more, corrupted and goin' to 'ell."

The publican pulled back on two tall wooden beer pulls and replied. "Ring th' grave digga, we hay a bita twins."

Dr. Steven tapped on the letter. "From across the pond?"

Hannah, caught in the middle of a sip of the strong dark

beer, almost choked as she stifled a laugh. Wiping her mouth with the napkin, she folded the letter to move it out of reach. But the young doctor was too fast.

"Ah, we have a love letter here." He read only the salutation. Teasing, he feigned a flouncy voice. "He writes not to his dearest Hannah, but to his Cherie." Nurse Freckles giggled as she played along. Respectfully, Steven folds the pages closed around his thumb and continues the teasing, but without invading real privacy.

"It's not a boyfriend. It's just my mother being a little naughty. Much of that seems to be going around lately." The nurse squirmed, but also giggled. Steven gave her a stern look, then a giggle slipped out of him as well.

Reopening the letter, "Truly, you have a mother who knows how to be naughty? Is that poss ... without clothes ... Three-legged gin?" He looked up. "What, pray tell, is three-legged gin, and do you have to play it naked?"

Hannah blushed. "You have a very naughty mind. Three-legged refers to a game played with only three people instead of four. You deal two extra cards into the hands."

Steven looked at the laughing Nurse Freckles with wide, wild eyes. "Which, you can only play while being in the state of dress where one can obviously see your third leg."

The splatter of freckles disappeared in a flash as she slapped at his shoulder. "Oh, you are horrid. Why did I even agree to come here?"

"Because without you, he would risk being arrested," The barmaid laid out the other two's drinks and food. "When it were jus' 'im and 'is mates, they were ready fer the nick mor' nights than no." She rolled her eyes. "So, now a new Jack, and ya hay ta work wid 'im till he leaves or some 'usban' nicks 'im?"

Hannah smiled and opened her eyes wide, and then frowned at Steven. "I speak nine languages, but only got that you are a naughty boy most days." She looked back at the barmaid. "What is a Jack?"

Steven and Freckles started laughing. "It's a doctor, but more directly, it is a surgeon. You know, Jack the Ripper... he was a surgeon. Well, or so they say," Looking at the barmaid in a wild face. "I personally think it was a crazy barmaid, out for revenge."

The barmaid leaned in, her nose coming inches from his. "I tol' ya, I'd best be oot wid the likes of Willie, then you. So, boy-o, ya n'ver stood me up." She held his stare for the count of three and turned her smile toward Hannah. She extended her hand, "Penny, Jack, and I pity you fo' puttin' up wid 'im day in 'n day out."

Hannah shook her damp hand and felt the strength. It was warm and reassuring. "Hannah, and I like your taste in food, beer, and men."

"I'll stick with Jack. Hannah is for th' woman who's 'air is down abou' 'er shoulders, wid three empty pints a fron' o' 'er, and still kin tell a boy-o what 'e kin' do wid the pistol in 'is pocket. As fer me taste, we'll see, lassie, 'ow ya like me taste in me, wiman."

Hannah laughed. "Fair met, Portia, fair met."

As the barmaid danced away, "And she knows good Will, as well."

Hannah turned to find Steven just finishing the letter with a serious look. He quietly laid the letter on the table and slid it across. "I never should have intruded. It was most impolite of me. I'm sorry."

Hannah thought about how right he was. Then, realizing she was thousands of miles away from her family, and this was as close to friends as she would get right now. And they had invited her into their friendship. "No, it is quite all right. Yes, it's wrong to snoop, but then how would you learn about me or my family?"

"Leatha is... how old?"

"Probably close to eighty or more. My father was born just before the War Between the States, which makes him close to seventy-five or so."

"She had a cough during the summer, combined with her losing a lot of lower-body weight. You know King's is the premier hospital for tuberculosis and other infectious diseases?"

She nodded as she sipped the beer. "I was thinking along the same diagnosis. But, in the Deep South, we have even other problems which don't have real names in medicine, so we just use the all-encompassing names like ague and consumption."

Steven tilted his head. "So, Doctor, what is your snap judgment?"

Hannah looked at Nurse Freckles, who was quietly eating and listening. "You can jump in here."

She looked up in horror. "I didn't read the letter."

"No, but you have been listening. And when Steven

described the symptoms, you got extremely interested in your sandwich."

The young woman's face was a war of emotions and thoughts. "I had an elderly..."

"Snap judgment."

"Consumption."

Hannah held her stare, and then slowly turned to Steven. "I concur."

Steven drew his lower lip between his teeth. It was one thing to deal with in people you didn't know, but when it is close to home, or someone who is this close, it takes on a more distinct feeling. "Hazard a guess?"

Hannah nodded. Her voice was husky. "Probably by the next letter... certainly not as long as the holidays."

The three thought as they quietly ate their dinner.

11

SURGERIES AND PERCY

THE END of the summer heat did little to diminish the simmering tension emanating from the head nurse's station. "Doctor Humphrey... a word, please." The words were as sharp and chilly as the icy water trickling down Hannah's back from her tightly wound French roll. Outside, chilly rain cascaded down the windowpanes, blurring the world beyond with its relentless drizzle. Hannah mused to herself. *Winter arrives early in England, especially around the nurse's desk.*

She halted in her tracks and turned slowly, her movements measured and composed. "Certainly, Nurse Hemplewhite," she replied, her voice steady despite the inner sigh she suppressed. She had calculated that by passing the nurse a full thirty minutes before the five o'clock shift began, she might sidestep the routine vexations. Yet, it seemed, her efforts were in vain. "It would be about your requisition forms... again." She locked her stare on the much younger doctor's eyes.

Out of the corner of her eye, Hannah saw the woman's hat, coat, and umbrella. They still dripped where the woman rapidly tossed them on a chair or leaned against the corner. Hannah glanced at her watch. It was only a quarter to five. She smiled. Her hunch had been correct about the half hour being the magical time to bypass her morning dose of heartburn and ill will. "Yes, Nurse Hemplewhite, I have been trying very hard to fill them out completely instead of the sloppy American way."

The senior nurse stood stone-faced as if she were dead. Gradually, her left eyebrow crept toward her hairline. "Completeness isn't the current issue or the concern at this time." She waited for the doctor to step out into the open air and plunge into the abyss of her own making.

Hannah knew this game backward and forward, having wheedled things from her father or lifted extra from Leatha's kitchen. First to blink, or offer an explanation (typically false), forfeits. The winning strategy her father taught her was always to deflect and change.

Making a large, grandiose sweep of her arm to expose her Cartier Tanker's watch, she looked and thought about the time. "I'm keen to discuss this more, but I have a tight schedule today." Turning as she spoke, "Starting with a nasty amputation I must get ready for." Her hand waved above her head.

"The leg is number four this morning, and you know it." Nurse Hemplewhite knew she had lost the battle as the doctor was already a dozen meters down the hall.

"Nope. Changed the schedule last night. Remove the

limb before the heart and humors are awake, and you end with a happier outcome. We will talk about this anew." She waved over her head, but under her breath she said, "Unless I see, hear, or smell you coming first."

As she passed the scrub room, she spied Nurse Freckles. Glancing back over her shoulder, she ducked into the room. She hissed, "Nancy."

The young nurse looked up, beaming. She pointed to the large chalkboard, now covered with new red-colored lines and arrows. "I sent Judith up to the third floor to warn the nurses to get the leg ready." She almost laughed as she looked around Hannah. "I heard you down the hall and took care of it."

The young nurse held her finger to her pursed lips and stepped around Hannah to close the door gently after checking the hallway. She guided Hannah to the far corner and the large metal sinks. Turning on the taps, she ran the water into the galvanized sink. The nurse spoke just loud enough to overcome the deep rattle of the water on the metal drum. "She knows you're taking supplies to Percy and his friends." She drew her lips tight against her teeth in consternation. "I spoke to two others, and we can start spreading the hard items around where they won't be missed so much."

"Nancy, I appreciate that, but you just can't be getting other innocent people involved." Hannah leaned her back against the large metal tub. Her shoulders rolled in as she looked at her new friend. "If I get in trouble, I simply go back to America. But if you get caught, they might ship you off to Australia or something."

The two laughed at the criminal history of the English colony as they changed clothes.

The freckled nurse rinsed and grabbed the bar of soap for the second round of washing. Her voice rose as she covered safer territory. "You know, Doctor, this hospital was originally much closer to the center of London. It was known as the pauper's hospice, where you went to visit or die. Hopefully, we are getting better at sending people home the better for their visits instead of passing them on to the dustman."

"Dustman? Do you mean the garbage collectors? Surely you don't mean they put the dead out with the garbage?"

"Aye. I dooo." Her Scottish upbringing slipped out as she relaxed. "In the bad old days, if ya could no' pay, you got buried in the heap with last night's tainted herring, and Mrs. McDonald's worn-out dainties."

Hannah snorted softly. "Oh, now I know you're pulling my leg."

The freckled face split with a mouth of small white teeth. "Aye," she laughed. "Mrs. MacDonald would use them for a dust cloth before she would throw them into the dust-bin." She grabbed two sterile towels, and they held their hands up and dried them.

Backing into the swinging doors, Hannah asked. "So, I suppose it is on for tonight?"

The nurse rubbed shoulders with the doctor as she leaned over. "The boxes are already at the Pig & Duck, and

Hack is due to arrive at six sharp for his supper. You know, boxes are one thing. But when it's just us, we can take the tube."

Hannah froze. "The tube. You mean the underground train?"

The freckles scrunched as the prep nurse pulled the mask over her face. "You make it sound so... going to hell. It's just a train. A few coins will buy a round-trip ticket."

She wiggled her fingers in the gloves. "Don't get me wrong. I love Hack, but I know he can't trot us around for free every time. Petrol alone is expensive. But with the depression and all, it's downright painful on him."

Hannah realized that what the young nurse was saying must be true. "Well, then, we amend that tonight. Hack gets paid, or we will take the bus." The prep nurse pulled the surgical smock snug on Hannah's back and tied the straps.

The green eyes danced as she surveyed the operation area, taking in the layout of everything. She nodded at the transport nurse to bring the patient in. Turning back to the deep brown eyes floating over the white mask, she continued to probe. "Bus. That is your answer. One would think you're queer about going underground."

Hannah wasn't ready to face her biggest fear and became defensive. "In New Orleans, they respect the dead enough to be buried above ground. You push seeds into the ground, plants get buried... but people do not." The door banged open as the gurney wheeled in with the patient. "And that is the end of this subject." Turning to the secretary nurse, she asked. "I'm assuming this is the spleen?"

"Yes, Doctor. Male, fifty-one, eighty-seven and a half kilograms. No previous call for concern, but he started suffering pains last month." She continued to read the rest of the intake file as Hannah examined the man lying on the gurney.

Quietly, she queried the groggy man. "Can you help us get you over onto the table?"

"Yes, mum. Certainly, mum." The man rose on one elbow and started the small jerks of his body to transfer to the operating table.

She smiled, even though she knew he couldn't see her face. To put the man at ease, she leaned in close as she helped shove him over. "It's all right, Alfred. Mum was my mother's name. Mine is Doctor Humphrey, but you look like a friendly sort of bloke, so you can call me Hannah."

"Certainly, mum," the man replied.

Hannah nodded at the anesthesiologist. The pill he had given the man to relax him had worked its magic. He was working by sheer rote learning and would never remember a thing. To lighten the mood in the room with the staff, as the anesthesiologist slipped the mask over the man's face, Hannah patted the patient's hand and assured him. "Don't worry about a thing. I'll take the dog for a walk, and we'll have you home for Saint Crispin's Day supper."

Through the mask, they could all hear the man reply, "The dog is done passed, but thank you anyway, mum."

Their shoulders shook as they began the seventh operation of the day. The workloads were getting worse as the year ground on.

Hannah performed the surgery's initial steps routinely; however, her mind wandered far, to the letter in her handbag.

My Dearest Cherie,

With profound sadness, I share the news of the passing of Walter and Leatha.

I'm sure you had guessed our dear Leatha wouldn't make it to the plum pudding she loved so much. But I had expected them both to at least celebrate one more Thanksgiving.

Her weight loss this last year surprised me. I felt helpless. Our dear Walter just patted my hand and told me not to worry. When the old girl lay down the evening before last, she looked like tired bones bundled up in loose skin. She kissed me gently on both cheeks and told me to give you her love. I suppose she knew it was going to be her last sleep.

I think Walter also knew because, as he waited in his chair for her to drift off to dreams, he climbed in under the covers with her. Over the last few weeks, she had been testy, and Walter was sleeping with me instead. Leatha couldn't stand nighttime touching anymore. We treated her delicately, even in daylight.

When I woke up late yesterday morning, I found they both had passed. Walter rose to use the plumbing just before daybreak. His coughing woke me. I think he returned to bed and realized his love had passed in the night. I can only assume he passed right there from a broken heart. He just could not imagine living without her.

Their absence leaves me at a loss. But I know I'm not ready for any other changes right now.

I called Harold Jax, that nice man at the bank, seeking guidance. He came round, making all the arrangements for the bodies. I requested the ashes be returned to me. I will take care of the remains. There is an old, tin-enameled urn from China. We three agreed that their ashes would be stirred into and contained within it. So, I tell you now that I am to be treated likewise, and then you can think of what to do with us. None of us could stand the thought of voyaging for eternity alone in some box somewhere. We may be a strange bed of a family, but we naked little jaybirds want to be together in death as we were in life.

We don't want you to be sad. Their lives were a celebration of living in joy and love. You are a product of our love, and I was graced to join it at the best possible time.

Cherie, know they loved you beyond all else. Please, rejoice in their being beyond pain, suffering, or old age. They now rest in a place where they can watch over you.

I would come to visit, but you know I am deathly afraid of crossing water. Every time we ever crossed the Big Muddy, I would close my eyes and just faint straight away. I accept your current inability to visit; however, I will await your homecoming, whether short or long-term.

Your ever-loving mother,

Nana

12

SOHO

A BUSTLING PUB is a wonderful thing to behold. The Pig &
Duck was wonderfully busy when Hannah and Nancy
walked through the heavy glass-paneled door. Windows in
the door depicted a duck lewdly stuck in the backside of a
very unhappy squealing pig. The windows were so old that
the glass was pulling away from the lead came, holding the
window together. A preferred theory depicted the duck as a
lowly worker fantasizing about doing so to the powerful.
The letters "MDCAAI" carved in the mantle over the back
bar represented the history of the bar dating from the seven-
teenth century.

In 1621, a local woolen mill had been the center of a riot.
The workers had their wages cut once too many times. The
weavers called on the owner to see the broken-down condition of the looms. His refusal was that they were to double
their production.

The weavers and spinners rose, man and woman, and
stormed the lord's house. They razed the house to the

ground with fire, represented by the orange and reddish glass around the animals. Someone found the fat pig sneaking out of the conflagration and dragged him back to the fulling mill.

With the water wheel at full free run, the heavy hardwood fulling hammers were hitting the fulling table with such force as to leave dents. They dragged the owner to the start of the run, tied him to a run of yardage, then dragged it all through the mill. What oozed from the other end wasn't worth burying. It washed away into the river. Over time, they dismantled the mill and repurposed the dented fulling tables as serving tables for the local pub. The black stains from beer and meats served directly on the tables lent a sense of the gore of the story.

Hannah wasn't sure of the truth to the story, or whether a story grows over many centuries. The truth hones away from the telling. Either way, she always loved coming for the energy of the people. The doctors and nurses were the anomaly on the social scale. Most of the patrons' fingernails were cracked, split, broken, and dirty. The mix was dustmen, longshoremen, draymen, cabbies, ditch diggers, seamstresses, cleaners, and other people who worked under the stairs, behind the walls, and away from the view of society. What Hannah found interesting was that these people were all the same color as their masters. But even in this oasis, another group ranked below them.

Freckles smiled at Hannah as they bustled their way through the crowd toward the back room. The freckled nurse pulled at Hannah's shoulder. She mimed eating, then signed the *beer* by bouncing the inner side of her hand against her jaw. Hannah nodded and turned back to swimming through the jolly mass.

The Scottish nurse stuck her curled thumb and middle fingertips between her speckled lips and blew an easily heard, shrill whistle. The barman looked up just as Freckles raised her right hand with two fingers facing him, then flicked them toward the back. He mimicked the sign, then pointed toward the back room.

Her hand sank into the sea of humanity as she swam after her friend.

"Well, as I live and breathe, two wandering kind souls in green." Steven leaned back in his chair with his arms thrown outward in exclamation. The pint in front of him belied his being there long. He had probably arrived only a few minutes ahead of the two women.

The men's toilet door swung open as Hack stepped into the room, finishing the buttons on his trousers. "Bugger these pants. They make the buttons smaller every year..." He looked up and blushed around the white stubble of the day's growth. "Core, the medicos have caught me with my trousers halfway to me knees." He smiled and hugged the two.

Pointing to the young doctor standing there with outstretched arms, he confided, "I was up in the Posh acres and got waylaid. 'E forced me po soul to carry 'im along 'e did."

Hannah rolled her eyes and widened them. "Oh yes, forced you." She laughed as she turned to hug her old associate. "Hello, Steven, it's so good to have you come down and help."

His hug lingered, releasing gradually. Turning to his old flame, he buried his face next to her red hair. "It is Christmas, Cherie. I just cannot imagine waking up in a couple of days, having not been with you in SoHo. You have taught me the true meaning of the season."

Karen hugged him a little tighter.

"Hear, hear," grumped Hack.

The door swung in as the barman himself delivered two pints of dark ale. His right arm was full of trenchers filled with fish and chips, done crispy, just the way Hannah loved them. "You'd best eat fast. The truck just pulled up across the street. I'll stall the boys with a pint, but you know they don't like being down there when it's dark."

Hannah put her hand on his shoulder. "Thanks, Bert. You're the bee's knees."

They all fluffed their coats off and sat at the table. The salt and vinegar flew around the table as they sampled and blew on the hot morsels of delight.

"So, what do you hear from your mother?" Steven asked as he shoved a couple of chips in his mouth.

"She's doing grand. The theater season is in full swing. She has a friend to go with. She still maintains our box at the Royal so that she can take up to eight people. Lately, for matinees, she has been taking some young children to see Shakespeare."

"Is she still doing the herb and spice stuff?"

"Voodoo? Certainly. The kitchen door never turns away

those in need. I know she misses Leatha with her wild, high-priestess clothes and spinning eyes act, but these are changing times. So the quiet woman on Saint Charles Street is just as powerful. It's the medical end of things she can't do."

"So, what is she doing about that?"

Hannah swallowed and washed her mouth with another hurried sip of the beer. "It's been something of a struggle. Abortion is something people don't talk about. There was a doctor across the river in Gretna. But some members of the Ku Klux Klan caught wind of a white doctor performing abortions on not only white women but blacks as well. They took him out and beat him to death, doused him with kerosene, and then threw him back in his home, and burned it all to the ground."

The others knew Hannah had no bone of exaggeration in her and just stared at such an inconceivable event. Nancy was the first to close her mouth back around her food and slowly chewed until she could talk. "That is horrible."

Steven took the larger view. "It gives more meaning to what we are doing this weekend."

Hack raised his pint. "Hear, hear." He sipped and raised it again. "An 'ers to the young miss 'oo shows us the way."

Hannah blushed as the others joined in the toast.

Hannah raised her glass. "And here is to those in need who give meaning to our lives." Four pints were upended as the meal drew to a close.

The crowd had grown in the main room as they were making their way out—a sea of bodies washed across the room with its own rhythms and waves. The movements only seemed random, but to Hannah's eye, the slight movement stood out. She reached out and grabbed Hack, hauling him back.

She leaned her head forward over his left shoulder, so her mouth was right near his ear. "Hack, see the man at the end of the bar?"

"Dugan... the one with the broken tam?"

"No, the next one over. The one with the black curly hair in the leather jacket."

"Oh yeah, I sees him, miss. What about 'im?"

"Do you know who he is?"

"No. No, I don't, miss. I've seen him 'round a few times, but know nothing 'bout 'im. Bert might know." He turned around and looked at her. "Ya sweet on 'im?"

She pulled back. "What? No. I just saw him say something to someone... but in deaf sign language."

"Weel, there you go, miss. 'E's probably deef."

She gave him a stern look. "Hack, his signs were French, not English."

His eyebrows raised, and he smiled as his light bulb lit. "Weel, there ya go, miss. He's a Frog." He laughed and turned toward the door as he called out. "Mark, Rupert, time to go."

The two men sluiced the last of their beer down home throats and saluted Bert as they spun off the bar and made their way through the sea of people. The twins looked like Romulus and Remus, roughhewn and large, through the shoulders and chest. As Hannah observed once, it was better to house the large hearts beating there.

The passing of the six from the public house didn't escape the notice of the man at the end of the bar. He ran his fingers through the thick black curls of hair as he thought about where he had seen two faces before.

The crisp night air smelled of the burning of soft coal in stoves. They knew the thick fog would be upon them before the evening became a solid night. The only two worried souls were in the large lorry following the black taxi.

Steven had been quiet since their leaving the Pig & Duck. The brooding hadn't passed Nancy's notice, as she was used to his moods. She recognized this to be his deep-thinking, silent mood.

She nudged him with her elbow. "Really, Steven, must you prattle on so? It is getting to be downright painful on the ears."

"Hmm?" He looked up at the women as if he had just noticed them come into the taxi. "I'm sorry. Did I miss something?"

Hannah jabbed in with an off-hand verbal blade. "We were just talking about the new guy, what's his name, Eddy Something..."

"Edward the Eighth?"

She snapped her fingers in the air, "Ah, yes; that would be the chap. A shame him dropping dead like that and all." Nancy hid her face by looking out the window at the passing street. Hack harrumphed in the front seat. It wasn't often someone played so loose with a royal's name, at least not in public.

Steven sat up and frowned. "Dropped dead? What are you on about? He didn't drop dead; he abdicated to his brother." Steven frowned at Nancy, who could barely keep herself contained. He looked back at Hannah and cocked his head, giving her a stern eye.

Nancy snuck a peek and then slapped him in the chest lightly. "Core... a virile man in a hansom with two good-looking birds, and all he does is sit and stew. What did you expect from us?"

The man whined, his hand on the wound. "I was thinking."

Hannah reached across from the jump seat and patted his knee. "Steven. Steven, it's all right. We were just teasing you. This weekend is always serious enough. We didn't want the ride to start from a pensive perspective, did we?"

"No. No, I suppose not." He leaned back in the seat as the automobile slew around a broken-down lorry in the street.

"Sorry," Hack called back.

"It's all right, Hack. Just get us there safe and sound, please."

Nancy leaned over and rested her hand on Steven's arm. "I know that mood. What were you thinking about?"

His gaze lingered on her, tallying each freckle while the streetlights danced across her face like a zoetrope. His eyes softly closed, perhaps envisioning possibilities, before he turned to Hannah. "The house in New Orleans is what, three stories and quite large?"

"Yes." Her brow furrowed at the question, as it seemingly had no context. Her hands lay relaxed on her crossed knees.

"And she is there all alone."

"Do you have a point in all of this?"

Gazing out the window, he thought. He murmured, uncertainly, "I'm not sure." He softly squeezed the pale, slender hand on his leg. "I had not thought that far." He drew in a deep breath and let out a half-caught sigh. "The idea concerned lodging a boarder, possibly a doctor, providing medical services."

Hannah thought about the idea. It wasn't the first time she had also thought about someone living with her mother. She wasn't in her dotage, but just for companionship, and now maybe the medical argument made sense.

"We're here." Hack turned in his seat. His left arm lay beefy in his winter coat along the windowsill that separated the cab from the passenger section. I'll be back on Monday morning at the second strike of Ol' Ben in his four of the morning chime."

The three clambered out. Hannah turned to the window that was perpetually rolled down. The man's right arm relaxed along the door's windowsill. She took it in her hands. Leaning in, she kissed him on the cheek. "Say hello to your lovely wife and thank you again for doing this." Her right hand slid a small wad of money into his coat pocket, where she knew he stuffed his hand.

"Right, now off with you. Message to the Trouble and

Strife, and then there was somethin' else." He smiled his crooked grin as he teased.

"Stop maligning your wife, Hack. Mary is neither trouble nor strife, and you're a better man for her suffering to marry you."

"Right you are." He laughed and put the car in gear, easing away from the curb. Eager to be away, as well as to get back to where he wouldn't be afraid to pick up a fare this time of night.

Hannah knew from past years that he wouldn't stop for the next few miles. She smiled weakly as she thought, *"Probably head straight away to Vickie's Station."*

At the sound of the lorry, the doors of the church opened. The young man in a black dress slipped down the three steps and hurried out to the three on the sidewalk. "Welcome, welcome." His hand extended as he walked.

"Father Joseph, so good to see you." Hannah took his hand in hers. "We have an extra tonight." Turning. "Joseph, this is Steven. He is also a doctor, and I'll vouch for his steady hand. He was at King's when we started this skulduggery."

"Steven, so good to make your acquaintance; any friend of Hannah's is welcome at the Redeemer." Turning to Nancy, "And it is so good to see our spotted angel of mercy and loving care is still willing to come down into the bowels of the city. And how is your father's hand?"

She laughed at Steven's confusion. "Dad's hand is doing fine and is back where it is supposed to be. He returned to work last week. His probation, on the other hand, will last for as long as my mother's memory holds out." She turned back to the others. "My father was caught with his hand where it should not have been. At least it was only his hand." She hung her head and glowered. "He's the dean of a girls' academy—and should know better. Thankfully, it was not the student, but her mother instead."

Rupert appeared from around the corner of the church and walked over. He washed his cap from his head as he approached them. "The crates are all unloaded, miss."

"Thank you, Rupert. Are they inside or out on the stoop?"

The man nodded at Hannah. "Inside, miss. The menfolk have taken them all in for safety, miss."

"And you are all taken care of?"

"Yes, miss."

She could see his right foot had already turned to retreat. "Well then, no dilly-dallying, you need to be off before this fog becomes beef stew. Get back home and kiss the wife for me. Oh, and Rupert, tell her I will need another loaf of her dark bread before the mid-week."

He bowed slightly. "Very good, mum." He dissolved into the night like the whisper of a past lover. The thin gathering fog swirled in his wake.

Hannah turned. "Right, to work now."

13

GOD'S WORK

UNDER THE SANCTUARY of the church were clusters of many rooms. Some with permanent residents, while others are more communal, and some are more set apart. The original purpose was to hide. Whether it was people, reliquary, or treasure, such as books or scrolls, was anybody's guess. Tonight's use was a refuge for those in need. On this occasion, it was to become a rotating carnival of care and blood.

"Tonight will be a repeat of last Christmas," Joseph observed as he pointed out the rooms and areas packed with people waiting in the catacombs they strolled through. He pointed to the large sinks and other counters, laden with equipment. "We have learned over the years, and we now have a central cleaning area. So, come here to wash and change, please."

Hannah stepped over to one counter. "Where in heaven did you get not one but two sterilizing autoclaves? Or do I even want to know?" She marveled at the equipment which was only available in some of the better-equipped hospitals in the more affluent parts of the city.

There was a soft step from an anteroom. "I may have only been a schoolteacher, but over the years, my students have gone on to their own glory."

Hannah smiled at the voice she loved, and yet, only associated with going to the theater and other girlish frivolities. She closed her eyes as she turned. "Non nobis solum nati sumus. (Not for ourselves alone are we born.) Daisy, what a gift of a surprise." She stepped over to her friend and embraced her. The two hung on each other, silent, and saying so much.

Finally, Hannah pushed her back and held her shoulders. "Why aren't you at A Christmas Carol with Ethel?"

"Because..." The voice came from a smaller room. "She wouldn't be here with me." A towel wiped her hands clean as she came out. She smiled as Hannah took in the nurse's clothes from a past decade.

"You never told me you were a nurse."

"Cherie, you never asked."

Nancy and Steven stepped over to be introduced. "Cherie? Are we using code names now?"

Hannah rolled her eyes and groaned. "No. No, we're not. Nancy, Steven, these are my dear friends Daisy and Ethel. Daisy lives near Dover, but comes up for the theater and stays with Ethel. We all go out and act like schoolgirls and make lewd comments about the actors."

"Now that sounds like fun. Why haven't you ever invited me?"

Daisy took her hand. "So we finally meet the famous Nurse Freckles."

Nancy blushed well into her prodigious breast and turned to Steven. "Sounds like the code names started long ago." Steven blushed even worse.

Father Joseph cleared his throat.

"Yes, to work." Hannah turned to take a better stock. Joseph waved two fingers for the doctors to follow.

"As I was saying, this year we have a few changes. Hannah..." He peeked back. "Or should I say, Cherie?" He pointed down the one hall, which ended at a door leading directly to the outside. Off the hall were six rooms. "You'll have two operating rooms and four recovery rooms. This is your sole focus this year because of the specialized surgeries. Steven, we will use your skills elsewhere. Please do not come down this hall. We don't want to mix the wet leprosy with the other patients."

"What?" Steven exploded. "Wet..."

Hannah spun him around and backed him against the wall. Her index finger pressed against his lips. With her nose within a couple of inches of his, she whispered in a low tone. "Yes. Wet leprosy. Now. In nineteen hundred and thirty-six, we still have leprosy in England—both dry and wet. You signed on to help people experiencing poverty who had nowhere else to go. What did you think it would be? Just syphilis and carbuncles, with a stitch or two for strong telling when you get back to your man's club? Standing by the stone mantel, sipping old brandy, and smoking smelly cigars and pipes. While you prattle on about your virtuous deeds in So Ho during your vacation? Well, if this is too much for your Kensington Gardens manicure, you know where the door is. Otherwise, you little pissant, suck it up and show these ladies you have some actual balls in those trousers." Her brown-green eyes burned into his blue as she looked for any squirming.

Turning, she walked past the priest. "Throw him out the front door. He can find his own way home. We have people needing my time and breath more."

The two men watched as she slowly stripped as she walked down the hall. Near the other end stood a nurse in operating garments, holding the doctor's garments like a squire waiting to dress her knight. Ignoring all decency protocols, she mirrored society's abandonment of the patients she would now do battle for.

"Hello, Mary. It's so good to see you back this year. And thank you for volunteering for this wing. How is that boy of yours? Did he pass his interviews for Nordington?" They stepped into the make-shift surgery room.

The two men, alone in the hall, turned. The young priest wore a crooked smile as he looked the redheaded doctor up and down. "How are your balls?"

Steven felt himself. "Still there, but wounded." Glancing back over his shoulder, he looked at the priest. "But I think she grew a pair the size of Manchester."

The man in the dress nodded. "You have no idea. Her's came only in brass-coated cast iron."

"Not the same squishy Yank she was four years ago when she first showed up at King's College, I can tell you."

The young priest hummed. "She has mentioned a certain woman named Hemplewhite?"

Steven put his arm around the shoulders of the priest. "There, my good man, is a woman who wasn't satisfied with just a pair of cast iron balls. She has the full set, and she lays them well, too, on Hannah, something fierce. I offered to just run the cold bitch under the knife and cut her heart out if I found one, but Hannah said it was her test alone. Excuse me, Father, but bloody hell, the shit has to stop sometime. That woman is the devil's own."

They looked about the large central room. "So, where do you want me?"

Joseph stripped off his jacket, leaving just a black shirt and skirt. Taking up a white coat, he turned and handed another to Steven. "Let's start in the puss room, shall we?"

Steven rolled his eyes and left one crossed as he humped over, putting on the smock. "Ooh, Master, boils and carbuncles are Igor's favorite." He made slurping noises as he flicked his tongue in and out, lapping at imaginary tasties.

"Please, hold off on such humor for a while. We have a few patients who resemble..." Turning, the priest walked toward the long hall. "Come along Igor."

The walls were thick stone and masonry, which sucked the conversations and activity away to a low general moan. They mostly stayed put, providing the same service repeatedly, although some moved around. At the back of the room, near a door that led to the cemetery, several people huddled in partitioned areas. They quietly waited for their turn to be seen by a nurse, if not a doctor. From his doctor's perspective, Steven could see that many of the souls had received no medical treatment in years, even under a system of socialized medicine.

Turning, he nodded to the priest, who was rolling up his sleeves. The long weekend had begun.

In another room, the freckles floated above a kind smile as Nancy dressed a freshly washed wound. The child was no longer crying, but was more stoical than quiet. The nurse watched the mother, continuously comforting her young daughter.

"You'll need to change the bandage every day. I'll give you some more bandages, but you must boil them to clean them. Do you understand?"

The Hindu woman in the ethnic garb nodded. "Yes, mum. Boil the bandage to clean them. Put the clean one on every morning."

"Good. If her arm even slightly reddens and swells, you need to come back here. Father Joseph knows how to get in touch with us."

"Yes, mum. Come back if red."

The freckled smile peeked up to face the little girl with enormous eyes and a mop of black hair. "And you, little moppet, must help your mother by keeping this arm very clean, you hear?"

A tiny "Yes, mum" escaped from the little mouth.

Nancy studied the mother. "What about you? Anything wrong?"

The woman shook her head slowly. "No, mum. No pain."

Nancy held her gaze momentarily. She was sure the

woman was hiding something, but knew not to push. Patting the tiny hand one last time, she rose from the small stool. "Well, then. Off with you two. It's past bedtime." She watched as the two left, hand in hand. At the door, they stopped as the little girl turned and waved at them. Her mother smiled wanly and nodded. The nurse nodded a slight bow in return.

A gray dawn was lighting the Rose Window over the altar when Steven collapsed on the pew with a heavy sigh. "It's never ending..."

"At least they know to come here." A weary voice drifted from a nearby pew.

A faint voice echoed through the sanctuary. "Shh, the next shift arrives just after noon." Four voices groaned nearby.

Steven stretched out as he mussed, "Whose idea was this, anyway?"

Seven voices chorused. "The Yank."

Minutes later, a weary young man in a black dress turned from the small altar door as he heard the muffled sound of snoring. Finding his bed too far, he rested on the foyer's bench.

The next shift came and went. The day dragged into night, and they continued.

"Where should we set up shop, Father?" The three young men stood in the hall holding cases.

Father Joseph became erect as he blinked. He frowned, "And you would be...?"

The blonde and tallest of the three set his cases down

and stepped forward, presenting his hand. "I am Winkum," he stated, gesturing toward the others. "Blinkum, and Nod —is the fiery-haired one. He is the gas passer. We are... well... next year... dentists."

Joseph blinked. "Dentists?" He shook his head. He knew it was Christmas Eve, but could there just appear three wise men... who happened to be practitioners in the art of teeth? "... On Christmas Eve? Three smart fellas?"

The redhead nodded with a chuckle, "It struck us as appropriate, sir."

The leader nodded and smiled. "It doesn't really matter, sir. We're not really here, you see. Not being true dentists and all."

Father Joseph would not argue with providence. "I'm sure I shouldn't see." Turning to his left. "But I do have this room over here... but not the kind of chair you would require."

The three peeked into the room and conferred. Nod snorted. "Perfect, we can slab 'em on the table, and I won't have to worry about them falling out of the chair."

The blond laid his hand on Nod's back. "Don't be so hard on yourself, Nod, you old sod—it only happened the one time."

The quiet one wheezed. "Yeah, and it was only the head-master's wife..." The two smiled at the groaning gas passer as the wheezer continued. "I'm sure there won't be any governmental types here on Christmas." Turning to the father. "We'll take it. Can we find a second or even a third table to put the bodies on?"

"Oh, good, William." A cheerful yet weary voice, Daisy, chimed down the hall as she headed toward the four. "I wasn't sure Hack could find you on Christmas Eve." She walked into the tall blonde's hug. "How are you, dear?"

"I'm fine, Aunt Daisy, but you look tired, I'm afraid."

She gently slapped at his chest. "Oh, pish-posh, you're just flattering this old gal. I can still look in a mirror. It shows that I look like hell warmed over, but we only have a few hours left in this year's goodness. I'll rest when we're done here." Turning to the others. "And I see you brought troops as well."

"Aunt Daisy, this is Blinkum and Nod."

"Which still makes you Winkum." She smiled and shook hands. "Thank you, gentlemen. Your rewards are small here, but be aplenty at the hands of the maker."

The redhead shook his head. "Nay, our greatest rewards are here and now. We would study by falling asleep over books. Here, we experience both pain and much good. And there is no better learning than by doing."

"Wise beyond your years, Nod. Wise beyond your years. And a good heart to boot."

The blonde kissed Daisy's cheek, then turned toward the men. "Right, let's shift the bags and get to it."

Daisy called after the retreating four. "I'll start lining up the customers."

Three right hands waved at her in reward, along with a left one.

14

1938

Cherie,

I'm devastated; the season has started, and you're absent from our box at the Royal. The female troupe I mentioned previously performed Othello's opening last night. It was unique to see Othello bouncing around with large breasts instead of a barrel chest, but the actress was nonetheless adroit in her portrayal.

This summer I took in a boarder. Even though she is a certified nurse, she is of color. She works at a hospital in the Tenderloin, but they don't pay her nearly enough. Our arrangement is for her to help me continue your father's and dear Leatha's work here.

I did not advertise for her; she sought out the back stoop on her own. I hope you remember her, as she remembers you. Her name is Edwina May Holder, from the other side of Black River. She confided that her scholarships said they came from elsewhere, but she knew who the true patron of her rise from the dirt side of that horrid main street was. She said to tell you the clothes you provided always fit, and you would always be in her heart. Cherie, she truly feels like a second daughter. And you finally have a sister.

Her language skills are sorely lacking, but at least she learned Latin and French in school. I found it surprising. Nurses, unlike doctors, studied in English instead of German. As for the language of the hands, she has proved to be a deft student. We even eavesdrop on the stagehands when we're at the theater. As my hearing is not as good as it used to be, I traded the premium box for one closer to the stage, which provides us with an oblique view. This view allows us to watch the prep and conduction in the opposing wing.

We read in the papers where the nasty man Hitler and his gang of thugs have annexed Austria. I suppose they didn't go willingly. It is a shame he has chosen that facial affectation, as we so loved the comedian Charlie Chaplin when the talkies were silent. However, Austria is just an aside to what we fear is truly happening in Europe. I know it is a long way from here, but I fear for your being so close.

Last week, the city elected Robert Maestri as its new mayor. You may remember him as one of Huey P. Long's thugs who controlled the oil drilling. After Mr. Long's assassination, he didn't learn or become any better of a man. I fear for the health of New Orleans.

Mr. Turpin, the truck farm man who always came around with the wonderful wagon full of fresh vegetables, passed away. His son will continue with the old Locomobile truck for as long as he can. But he was schooled to be a teacher, and such is where his heart lies. I am sure Winnie or I will soon shop for our fresh food at a local market. I'm not sure I am truly taking to the modern ways of things.

The new roof and rebuilding the back stoop took their toll, along with the new higher land tax. Four men and a cannon died from melting because of the draw in banking this year. I regret to report that General Lee will no longer take the field. I won't miss his ugly face.

Because I know you will want to know, I saw Doctor Thompson last week. He did a complete exam. And I can tell you here, if the man doesn't stop smoking, he will cough up his left lung by spring. I'm eight years older than he, and I will outlive his son Randal—who also says hello.

My health is vigorous, and occasionally I have a craving for a younger man. The Vieux Carré has become a dangerous place when Winnie and I go visiting. I know you find it shocking of your mother, but at forty-seven, I am still ready, willing, and able. You can tell your young doctor friend, Steven, that he should indeed come for an extended visit. And, if he sees his way clear, to bring along his two cohorts in medical crime and compassion—so much the better. Eah, Cherie?

I haven't received a letter from you since summer's end. I'm guessing you're busy or Nurse Hemplewhite has taken you hostage. And I am awaiting a ransom note for three pounds of flesh or sterling. (I have marked my pun on the chalkboard and await your rejoinder.)

Take care of yourself. Convey my regards; your letters made them feel like family. Give my special hug to Daisy, as I am so sorry for the passing of her dear friends Ethel and the sweet man Percy. You must make extra time for her now, as she is all the family she has left in London.

I trust you will once again enjoy your special observance of the Christian holy time. Be careful, but show no less compassion and thoughtfulness than you do.

Your loving Mother,

Nana

NURSE FRECKLES FOLDED the thin paper and raised it to her nose. "Lilacs?"

"Lavender; it grows in long rows down St. Charles Street. At times, the heat and lavender could put the streetcar drivers to sleep, and they would miss your stop. Laughing, we walked back just a block or two. I think every woman on St. Charles Street scents their stationery, if not their woman parts, with lavender oil or perfume."

The freckled hand presented the letter back to Hannah. "I think of your mother as the aunt I have never met. Her letters are so chatty and amusing." She blushed slightly. "Does she really shop for a young man at that carry place?"

"The Vieux Carré is the French Quarter of New Orleans." Hannah leaned her backside against the large scrubbing sink. "I suspect her nastiness aimed for either shock value or amusement. But—as a young girl—she was very sexually active. At forty-seven, I see no reason she would restrict her nature."

"But you know this Winnie person?"

"She was a colored girl my age. Maybe a year or two

behind me. I knew she would never have a chance to leave Black River unless she could go to school."

"And so you helped her."

Hannah nodded. "We had more than enough. It was something we could do."

"And now she looks after your mother…"

Hannah tapped the corner of the letter against her lower lip. "I wouldn't call it looking after my mother as much as it would be—she has joined the family tradition of helping others."

The small noise of the slight limp on hard-soled shoes sounded in the hall. The two ladies turned to the sink and twisted the hot water taps. Using the new liquid antiseptic soap, they lathered their hands and arms.

As Nurse Hemplewhite turned into the scrub room, Hannah took to the offensive. "Ah, Nurse Hemplewhite, we were just wondering where you were. The gall bladder should have been here a full ten minutes ago. Is the appendectomy across the hall prepped?"

The older nurse opened her mouth wider, froze, and then closed it. She looked for something that might have been out of place, but there was no evidence of a crime to point to. She closed her eyes as her head rotated toward her nemesis. As her eyes opened, they also contracted into her trademark hard stare. "Doctor Humphrey, there has been a change of order. The leg wound—"

Hannah cut her off. "Yes, I know. The man has gangrene. He's going to lose his leg in the same spot at three this afternoon as he would if you brought him along now. I will not tolerate changing my schedule on the day of the surgery. I plan the work to create a flow which is conducive to my strengths and humors. Unless you have studied the dark arts of voodoo and can cleanse the spirits lurking in the shadow holds of the operatory, then I strongly suggest you fetch the correct recipient of my scalpel." She stared the woman down with the darkest of looks she could muster.

The nurse blinked. "I'll check on the appendectomy."

As they listened to the sound of her hurrying back down the hall, the freckled face buried itself in the right shoulder of the good doctor. Hannah had only a slight bit more control than the giggling mass of the nurse now smothering her laughter.

Much later, under the fiery glare of the surgical lights, the leg didn't appear as salvageable as Hannah had hoped. The gangrene had gotten into the bone itself and infected the marrow. She closed her eyes and laid her hands along the man's thigh. Gently, she felt the muscle mass. Finally, she opened her eyes and glared into the freckled face and green eyes of her friend. The tough decisions a surgeon makes are life-and-death and are never made frivolously. Hannah looked for reassurance from her friend.

The voice muffled slightly through the thin fabric of the mask, under piercing green eyes. "Whether you use voodoo or the skill of a surgeon, this man will never know. Whether he lives out his days in a long arch or is struck short in his prime, this is in your hands. Only you can make that call. But in my heart, I will always trust your hand more than any other, considering the lives you rescue annually from society's discard pile."

Hannah stared silently into the other's eyes, counting her own breaths.

"Besides, Doctor Humphrey, today is your best day. You reached out and bearded the lion in her own den. You faced her down and sent her back through her kingdom with her tail between her legs. Every single patient has been waiting at the door ten minutes before their scheduled time... every single one. Except for the first."

Hannah sighed. "Let's move the tourniquet."

THE PIG and Duck hadn't started working up its usual head of steam yet. The whistle down the hill was still ten minutes away from blowing. Only Mick and Trevor were at the end of the bar, talking about the awful team Manchester was mounting this year.

Penny was wide-eyed as she leaned her hip into the high-backed booth. "So, what 'appened?"

Freckles wiped the foam off her upper lip with the back of her hand. "She cut him off almost as short as his willie."

"Noooo. Not the bloody leg. The dragon lady?"

"Oh... the rest of the day she was compliant as a village priest caught in flagrante delicto with the village strumpet."

The barmaid squealed with delight. "D'ya think it'll stick?"

The nurse morosely wagged her head. "I certainly hope

so. That woman has relentlessly tormented the poor doctor since she arrived at King's. It's gotten a wee bit better over the years, but going on five bleeding years is enough. She doesn't ride the men doctors like she does Jack. And the lord knows they could all use a dose of what she's capable of dishing out..."

The front door opened, and Penny jumped up. "Speaking of the Saint from Orleans..." As she passed Hannah, she nodded and quipped. "Evenin', Jack. Your pint straight away —and it's on the 'ouse this night."

Hannah unwound her scarf and shucked out of her overcoat. "Thank you, Penny. And we need a couple of trenchers, as well, unless Bert made stew."

The barmaid waved her hand over her head. The barman, upon hearing his name, looked up and waved. For them, it was just a regular night at the Pig and Duck. It began from uphill with the medicals and ended with everyone from downhill.

Hannah slid onto the bench seat, the bar's far end within her sight. Leaning in close to her friend. "Freckles, what have you been up to?"

The nurse batted her eyelashes. "Why, Miss Humphrey, I don' know nothing 'bout what you are asking on about."

The two laughed at the terrible attempt at a southern accent.

"You told her about Hemplewhite, didn't you?"

The freckles seemed to dance more about her face as she giggled even harder. Then, as she saw Hannah go silent, she froze. Hannah's attention was not anywhere near the conversation in the booth. Hannah's eyes watched the man with the curly hair enter and take his place at the end of the bar.

The two trenchers of fish and chips slid onto the table, followed by three mugs of beer. Penny leaned against the side of the booth closest to the room—blocking Hannah's view. "His name is Mickey. You two 'ay been moonin' afta each otha' for long these last years. I figured it was time you two met... seeing how you both speak that finger stuff together. So, he's coming ovah."

Hannah's eyes flew open. "No, Penny, you can't let him..."

The man in question had circled round and caught Hannah from behind. Slipping into the booth next to her, he smirked. "Don't let me what?" His accent was a light London, almost with no accent at all. It was what Hannah would expect of an American living in London.

Hannah slipped into her imitation of Hack. "Obviously naught wi' a cheeky bloke like you."

The man leaned his head into his left hand for support. He studied her silently for a moment. Hannah's eyes wandered over his dark curls laced around his fingers. His dancing green eyes, she tried to ignore—desperately tried to ignore.

Languidly, he raised his head and looked at the stunned, silent Freckles. "So, did that work for you, luv? Does this measure up for a Saturday night in SoHo?"

Freckles stammered and sputtered. He turned back to the doctor. "She won't answer, so I will. Mimicking a So Ho will only work if the Yank is falling-down drunk. You need to spend more time with Hack; maybe even buy him a pint or two. Although I'd best warn you, his drink is the evil black of Guinness. So, be prepared to pay dearly and listen to the Eddy squeal."

Freckles snorted. "You are the devil in one. Hank is the sweetest of men; an' he donna drink 'cept on Saint Crispin's Day."

The man laughed, turning back to Hannah. "You have a staunch friend here. She'll brace your back no matter what, even in the depths of hell and back out again." He stuck his hand out. "Michael—but everyone calls me Mickey, like your Mr. Disney's little mouse."

"Mouse?"

"The cartoon—Mickey Mouse?"

"I don't read the cartoons in the papers. I barely have time to read the headlines."

Mickey looked incredulous. "And you don't go to the movie theater either."

Hannah frowned. "How would you know that?"

He started to speak and then closed his mouth. His eyes searched her face for any duplicity or merriment. Finding none, he softened his tone. "You really don't."

"No time."

"Soo... for entertainment...?"

"This is it."

He scrutinized the open face, marked with freckles. She nodded in confirmation.

"Oh, Mickey, you are getting along famously. Eight

minutes and you still don't have either laughing or handing you their knickers."

They looked up at the laughing face of Penny, leaning against the dividing wall of the booth. With her right hand grasping her bar towel, she stuffed it into her upturned hip. "If 'e's botherin' ya, Jack, I can drag 'is mangy arse back ta the bar."

"It's fine, Penny. We're just still sniffing arses here. When you see him drop his trousers, then you know it's serious enough to come join in."

The barmaid snickered. "If 'e drops 'is drawers, I ain't joinin'—I'm selling raffles." She pushed off and headed for the bar, then turned back. "Oh, Mickey, your mate just telephoned. You're cut off, as of now." She picked up his barely touched beer. "You have a flight at dawn."

Hannah looked at the man. "Where are you going?"

He shrugged his shoulders and stood. "I don't know." He nodded. "It was nice meeting you, Jack, and Freckles. I hope we can meet again soon." He swiftly left before either woman could respond.

Freckles turned back and looked at Hannah. "Now that was queer."

"But fascinating..." Hannah smiled lustily.

Freckles peeled with giggles. "Oh, Hannah, you really are a nasty one."

The doctor leaned in with dramatic, wild eyes. "And who, pray tell, has been spreading nasty rumors about me? A certain uptown man of leisure, maybe?"

The two giggled and relaxed from their lengthy physical

and mental day. Cries of friendship broke the dark outside as the neighborhood gathered.

As they shrugged into their coats later, Hannah leaned in to be heard. "What is on your dance card for St. Crispin's Day?"

"Day or eve?"

"It falls on a Sunday this year." They locked their eyes with a knowing look. The nurse smiled lopsidedly and then nodded.

Hannah hugged her and whispered, "I'll let Hack know."

15

ST. CRISPIN'S DAY

HACK WATCHED the young men load boxes into the trunk of his large, black taxi. The man standing nearby nodded as they loaded the last. In the swirling night fog, the man stepped close and mumbled near Hack's ear. "Right, gov'ner, we'll see you this evening when you drop the ladies."

"Right as rain, Mick... and thank' again fer lookin' out fer the boxes and gettin' the extra from the ministry."

The man ran his fingers through his dark curls. "It was no problem, Hack. For years, you and they have been doing God's work... Helping was the least I could do." He gently pushed on the man's shoulder. "Now off with you before some copper comes along and thinks we're smugglers or thieves."

The older man laughed. "But Mick, we are."

"Yeah, regular medical Robin Hoods, we are."

Fog swirled around the two and then followed the retreating taxi. The man wearing a flight jacket turned to observe the shadow within the loading bay. The figure was silent, but nodded. He nodded, "Thanks, mum."

With a slight bow, the shadow turned and retreated into the building.

The fog filled the street with silence as the motorcycle disappeared into the night. Another dark shadow broke away from the rubble heap, filling much of the empty lot across from the loading bay. The heavily wrapped shadow shuffled off in the opposite way the motorcycle had gone. In the heavy wool, a muted voice wavered. "Well, I never..."

Many hours later, Hack leaned against the back of his taxi. The first wisps of evening fog curled along the circular driveway of the hospital. Spying the two women through the glass of the doors, he leaned forward and straightened. He opened the back door, quietly muttering. "'Ear we go, Gov'ner."

As the door opened, his face brightened. "An' a grand St. Crispin's Day to you two ladies..." His left hand waved through the open door. "Step lively, ladies. We have much night to be 'bout."

Freckles squealed as she stepped in and fell into Steven's arms. "You naughty boy... running on about going to nurse your sick aunt in Dorchester." She leaned back as Hannah climbed in and smiled, leaning over to kiss her friend on his cheek.

"Steven, it's good to see you. Riding with us—the entire trip or just a portion?"

"I'm in for the whole bob. I heard a rumor you need an

extra set of hands on the wet ward." His look was serious as he assessed his friend's reaction.

"Are you sure?"

"More than ever."

"You know the dangers."

"I'm only concerned about the rewards."

Hannah sat back as Hack eased out of the driveway. From me, you'll only get a hug and a kiss on the cheek. The tuther would be comin' from the freckles 'ere."

They both turned to where the nurse was sitting on the jump seat, leaning back with her arms crossed in her coat. "I'm not so sure about that. Cheeky bastard doesn't call, doesn't write, then just shows up when we're going for a fun time jaunt and thinks it's all just peaches and cream. A girl wants to think she has a chance at being an honest woman some year."

Steven gave her a hang-dog face, and then, looking forlorn at Hannah, he winked with the eye the redhead couldn't see. Reaching into the pocket of his overcoat, he fished out a small black box. Rolling forward onto one knee, he opened the box to expose the ring.

"Would this make things better?"

The young woman swallowed a gasp. Years of delivering unwelcome news had trained her deadpan face. "Looks ta be on the wee side." Looking up at the man she loved. "If we find a matching one for your nose, I believe we can resolve this."

Steven clutched at his chest as if mortally wounded as he looked at Hannah in shock. Then, he grabbed at his nose.

"Do you think your mum could set the ring so the swells on the Heath wouldn't notice?"

The three laughed as Hannah shook her head. Even Hack was laughing. He'd been in on the proposal from the start. "Let's get you through your first run on the wet ward, and I'll set the blighter myself."

Freckles snickered. "Core, she's been here too long. She's starting to sound like a southy."

Hack coughed from the front. "No bloody likely."

Steven weaved, kneeling on the floor, still unanswered.

Freckles snatched the box from him and showed it to Hannah, addressing her now-fiancé. "Of course, you silly toad—I'm tired of kissing so many princes." She leaned over and hugged him around the neck.

Minutes later, the black cab rattled away into the fog, leaving the three standing with the indomitable Father Joseph. In the dim light, the priest appropriately fawned over the blushing fiancés. "I don't suppose we will be having the wedding here..."

Freckles took hold of his arm as they walked down the alley driveway toward the back door to the basement. "Please, Joe, let's just get him used to calling at least once a week first. Weddings, we can plan any time after I get him trained up."

"I'm right here behind you, you know..."

Freckles leaned in toward the priest and looked around conspiratorially. "Did you hear something?"

The night ground through the usual paces in the church's basement. There were few breaks, and only when

Father Joseph begged the doctors to sit and have tea. Previously unnoticed, the stark walls now felt oppressive to Hannah.

"Hannah, is there something I can help you with?"

She turned on the stairs, which led to the outside, and weighed her answer. "It's alright, Joe. I just need some air."

"Would you like some company?"

She leaned against the wall—tired. "Father, it's your church and your alley."

"But it is you I'm concerned about." He started up the stairs and took her arm as he opened the door.

The door swung out and hit an obstruction halfway, then it swung open of its own volition. A smiling face stood in the alley's darkness. "Well, if I knew a door would beat me at the 'ands of a priest and Jack, I woulda stayed ta home."

Hannah squinted and then registered shock. "Mickey, what are you doing here?"

Joseph frowned at Hannah. "You know Mickey?"

"Well, I thought I did. Up at the Pig & Duck. He's a drunk at the end of the bar."

A frown creased the father's face as he almost laughed, then he turned toward the alley's dark figure. "Drunk...?"

Mickey smiled as he held a thumb and first finger up, separated by a tiny gap.

The priest nodded a knowing nod and turned to Hannah. "Mickey is the delivery for your supplies... among other helpful services." Turning back to the man. "It's only around three o'clock. What are you doing here?"

Mickey ran his fingers through his hair as he looked about the alley. "Umm... we need to talk."

"Mickey, what's happening? As for the good doctor, she's not someone to be afraid of."

"We just got word that Hitler moved troops and tanks into the Sudetenland last week."

Hannah frowned. "Where is this...?"

"Sudetenland—it is the mountain region of northern Czechoslovakia, along the Polish border." Joseph wrung a part of his skirt in his left hand. "How bad?"

"He's massing strength along the border and the passes. They probably won't take longer than next summer."

"And this is a problem?" Hannah was confused.

It was Mickey's turn to answer. "Joseph's and my mother came here from the same village just east of there. But beyond that, it means Hitler is not beyond invading other countries... or starting a war."

"But surely your Lord Chamberlain wouldn't let England be dragged into some kind of border skirmish?"

"Hitler's regime won't be content with any minor border conflicts. He has his sights set on the whole shooting match. And the water won't stop him. Yes, I foresee England's return to war, regardless of Chamberlain."

Father Joseph broke his pensive silence. "When are you leaving for Dover?"

"I'm leaving for Brighton now. I brought you the Christmas gifts now, just in case I'm not back in time."

Turning to the door, Joseph nodded. "I'll go round up a few blokes to help unload. Store them in the back shed temporarily; I'll move everything later. You know where the key is."

Hannah watched the men retreat silently, one disappearing into the basement, the other vanishing into the alley's fog; each held secrets. She hesitated, glanced about the alley, steeled herself, and then went back underground. For some reason, walking down stairs within a building to its basement wasn't the same as standing on a sidewalk looking down a set of stairs leading to the same basement. The dull thud of the door closing behind her made her heart skip a beat, and she took a sharp breath. She swore at herself in gutter Latin—correct tense or not.

16

'TWAS THE NIGHT
BEFORE THANKSGIVING

My dearest Mother,

This fall has remained a whirlwind of change in my life. I finally met the friendly chap at the end of the bar who signed with the French sign language. His name is Mickey Rose, and he signs the French version, as he has never come to America or known any deaf Yanks. I still don't know why he speaks sign language, with his perfect hearing, but speaks horrid French.

Before you get nosy, the answer is yes—he has been in my knickers. So there. Your daughter is just as naughty as her mother.

As nobody has flats or apartments large enough for parlors, entertaining is done in the public houses. (In America, we would call them bars or lounges.) I recently moved into larger quarters—the extra rent I augment from my salary. In the second bedroom, there is now a larger bed. Two individuals can sleep comfortably beside each other, rather than being stacked like I did with the young boy at Tulane. Which you three all found amusing.

Another benefit is that my dining table comfortably seats four people. Steven, Freckles, Mickey, and I occasionally dine together. We all enjoy the respite from the limited pub fare. Steven practices close to a superb butcher, and there is a greens market on his way. He has supplied the basis of food, while Mickey and I share the cooking duties. Mickey has a very grand flair for French cooking, but is extremely tight-lipped about why. He's like those funny black nuts from Brazil—hard to crack, but I trust the meat inside to be tasty and full.

I can't remember if I told you about Steven's moving taxi proposal to Freckles. Exceptionally sweet with unconventional romanticism, but unromantically. We were on our way down to So Ho on Saint Crispin's Eve. Steven planned a proper proposal for Freckles, waiting until she was rested and composed. But I'm not sure what faculties she had about her, as I had just permitted Steven to join me in dealing with wet leprosy.

But, back to my beau. Mickey's been secretly providing surgical supplies for our SoHo work. Where he has secured them from, I'm certain I don't want to know. Steven has been working to glean scarce medicines and financial/medical aid from wealthy doctors in the north. I do find it strange in a country that says medical treatment is open to all, yet cuts off the lower castes. As their system precisely mirrors a caste system. The South End is their third-rate citizens, and the leprosy caste is the untouchables.

Recently, I found a slight chuckle. There's a possibility I'm becoming a proper Londoner. I'm more apt to use my umbrella as a sunshade than a rain shield. Also, using the end to point, rather than the canopy for shade, is the tool's sole purpose.

My fear of being underground persists. Logically, I know it is a silly fear, as every day thousands of people use the underground trollies with total impunity. I have tried to overcome this fear, Mother, but it still grips me. Mickey's patience with me is appreciated. After staying late at dinner with friends last week, finding a taxi proved impossible. Finally, I gave it my all, as Walter would have called it, the college try. I let Mickey guide me down into the bowels of the underground. Unfortunately, the train we needed was on the second level down, and I became hysterical. Mickey carried me back up the stairs into the air. We then walked the four miles home. He never said a word about it. I wonder: Is he a prince, or just as broken as I am? Only time will tell.

You'll receive this as the theater season begins. Please share what you and Winnie have on your dance card for the season. Daisy is here in London for the next two weeks. We are planning to see nothing but all-women troupes. There's a troupe from France who will perform Falstaff, and I have secured a Saturday night booth. Unfortunately, Mickey's away on one of his secret business trips, but Steven and Freckles will round out the box. It should make for a jolly affair.

I miss you so much, and I would love to meet Winnie, all grown up. I'm so glad she found you, and the two of you have struck such a grand friendship. There's something about that house on St. Charles Street, which I believe creates fantastic friends who feel like family. I would call it magic, but I think it would be more of Leatha's deepest and most wonderful voodoo.

My bed is calling me now. In order to beat Nurse Hardnose to work, I have struck on the magic time of 4:25 as the fifty-six bus arrives at 4:28.

My deepest love and hugs

Cherie.

HANNAH SLIPPED the letter in the post slot as she walked the long hall. The extensive building was like a gigantic beast at rest. In the early morning, before others got to the surgical hall, the giant slept. Hannah fancied she could hear or feel the slow breathing of the heating steam system. The metallic groans, she imagined, like the churning of the digestive tract. She smiled her contented smile as she turned into the changing room—once more, a successful foray through the danger zone.

Her glee was short-lived. The form bent over in surgical scrubs was not her usual cohort. This form was larger, but no less familiar.

Unmoving, the voice remained frigid. "Nurse Murphy will join us late this morning, it seems." Hemplewhite turned as she rose from tying her shoes. "In her joy at seeing her betrothed last night, she forgot she had professional commitments this morning."

Hannah stood with her mouth open.

Hemplewhite straightened and shrugged with a wistful smile. "These things happen. Young and in love." Her eyebrow arched as she scowled at the chalkboard. "The gallbladder surgery scheduled second this morning, experienced complications overnight, and is now on its way down. I'll see you in scrub." She turned and pushed her way into the room next door.

Hannah blinked. "Well... I guess no tea or chatter this morning." She tugged the knit scarf from her neck as she glanced at the large clock on the wall. 4:28. As she undressed, she stared at the clock. *Traitor.*

Hannah glanced at the clock as the familiar nurse's form backed into the operating room with her hands held high and sterile. 6:58.

"So nice for you to join us, Nurse Murphy." The ice froze the young nurse mid-step. Her eyes cautiously tracked toward the figure standing where she knew she should have been two hours before.

As Nurse Hemplewhite dabbed at the blood in the open cavity where Hannah was working, she continued. "As you are unneeded here, please make yourself useful by retrieving and prepping number three. I believe you will find her waiting in the loan ward." She dabbed and then looked at the large clock. "We should close in the next ten minutes, and with sterile scrubs and a bit of morning tea for the good doctor and myself, we will meet you in room four at seven-forty." She looked for confirmation, and Hannah nodded but didn't look up.

As Freckles pushed the door with her now unneeded sterile hand, the voice changed. "Oh, and Nurse Murphy, please check the turntable in number four. I believe it is Vivaldi, which is extremely wrong for mucking about a woman's parts. See if you can find a nice flute concerto, or if you must, I think there is some lighter Mozart on the upper shelf. Thank you."

As Freckles walked down the hall toward the fourth operatory, she and Hannah were thinking the same thought: She said, "Thank you."

The hand movement almost slipped past Hannah's attention—she wasn't sure if it was the first signing or the second. She didn't look up, but ignored the blatant four words.

"We need to talk."

Two of the four words usually require both hands. Most signers are not ambidextrous, and even left-handed deaf individuals primarily use their right hand for signing. But Nurse Hemplewhite's right hand was busy holding a hemostat in place as Hannah sutured the surgical area where she had removed the large quad of tumors and the woman's womanly parts. Hannah thought as she sewed. It was a sad thing for this young woman, just starting her life in marriage, to have her productivity ripped from her belly. Hannah ignored the small interior growth; the young woman already faced enough challenges.

Finally, as she sutured the last bit of the belly, she muttered quietly. "What about?"

The right hand began finger spelling. At first, Hannah was unsure she had read the six letters correctly. She looked up into the eyes of her worst nightmare and nemesis. Both women's eyes were stone cold and noncommittal. Hannah blanched.

As the nurse verbally directed the other assisting nurse and the anesthesiologist, she signed the two critical words to Hannah. *"I know."*

Finally, in the evening, Hannah walked into the busy Pig & Duck. As Hannah stood looking around, Penny walked by with a pint of very dark beer in each hand. Hannah stepped in front of her, took the mug from her left hand, and quaffed the entire pint. As the surprised barmaid sidestepped around the surgeon, Hannah placed her free hand against the woman's upper chest, stopping her. As she finished draining the first pint, she held it out—exchanging for the full one.

Hannah looked Penny in the eye and drew in a full, deep breath. "I think we'll need a couple of rounds and full trenchers."

Penny studied the surgeon's eyes for any humor. Finding none, she nodded. "Straight away, Jack... Mickey's in the loo and here comes Freckles."

Hannah raised the pint of bitters and ale to her lips. Taking a full charge, she turned toward the door. The taste was not what she had expected, and she expelled the mouthful she finally tasted... luckily, little reached Freckles.

"Well, it's not the grandest greeting I've had—but it's still not the worst." She reached over and took the mug. Raising the nearly full glass to her nose, she sniffed. "Bitters and ale." She chuckled and took a strong sip as she noticed Penny telling Bert at the bar about what he had missed. The two had a good laugh as Freckles guided Hannah to their usual table.

"So, what are you going to do?"

Hannah slumped, torn between curiosity and apprehension. "I want to know... and yet, I'm afraid what it is."

"Cheese it—here he comes."

"Mum's the word."

Freckles drew her fingers and thumb across her lips in silence.

17

'TWAS THE KNIGHT
BEFORE CHRISTMAS

HANNAH WANTED to vent her spleen. Everything she had worked on that morning was spleen. Gall, spleen, uterus, spleen, and knife, and then there was the emergency which she was still wondering about. They transferred a man from Kent because there was a Yank surgeon who might have knowledge about gunshot wounds. A bullet, seemingly from a rifle, struck the man's left flank above the kidney. After rattling around, it had wound up next to the man's spleen.

In somewhat of a foul mood anyway, she was not enjoying the hard biscuit with orange preserves on it. She really wanted toast with peanut butter and strawberry jam. Also, she wanted her mother, or at least her letter. She spotted the letter through the glass of the post box door, yet time constraints prevented its retrieval. Her mother had taken to mailing her letters in a washed pink envelope. The pink had caught her eye as the wind had blown the door open with a tidal wave of bone-chilling December rain.

Her rush past the mail to reach the hospital by quarter

past the hour erased any humor she had felt at two minutes past four. She had smoother days when following her schedule.

In the quiet break room, she heard muffled voices in the hallway. The door, usually shut, stood open where the janitor had blocked it to mop the floors. A soft male voice sounded familiar, but wasn't one of the staff.

The door from the operating rooms swung open, and Freckles backed into the room, pulling a cart of surgical bundles, hot from the autoclaves. She stopped as she saw the scowl on Hannah's face. Then she listened to the voices. Her eyes flew open, and then she frowned. She mouthed, "Mickey?"

Hannah opened her eyes wide and shrugged slightly. Stepping to the open door, she leaned out slightly and looked down the hall. Freckle's head leaned out below her shoulder. They watched as Mickey embraced Nurse Hemple-white, kissed her cheek, then departed.

Hannah and Freckles backed into the room. Both stood in shock.

"What are we going to do?"

Hannah shook her head. Mickey had lied to her. He went to Calais yesterday. He planned two days in Calais, followed by a flight down the Norman coast to Le Havre for a passenger bound for the Isle of Wight. His duties wouldn't have him home until after Boxing Day. And here on Christmas Eve, she finds him kissing the evil one.

She glared at Freckles as she set her jaw. "We soldier

on." Her resolve felt like melted butter, but her voice held the steel she needed in her spine—and in her heart.

Hannah had gone from wanting to vent her spleen to killing something instead. Two surgeries remained; work was preferable. "Retrieve the face instead so that I can work on something meticulous and delicate. Inform the floor that the paperwork contained an error. Oh hell. I don't care what they think. Just tell them the face is next. Now scoot. I'll see to the operatory."

Three hours later, she pulled the latex glove from her left hand and shot it across the room at the trash bin. It hit the wall and fell into the bin. Turning, she leaned on reversed hands with her elbows dug into her sides. Her head hung as she muttered to Freckles, who was stripping beside her. "I don't suppose it would be good to start our Christmas work with a double pint of bitters, would it?"

"Probably not. But a shot of Bushmills afore the single pint sounds about right." She leaned over and embraced Hannah's shoulders. "There's got to be an explanation, Cherie. He's a good man, that one. You've just got to pin him to the corner and not let him out afore he tells you all—or you cut off his balls."

Hannah looked up with sad eyes. "You don't suppose they..."

"Eew, no! She's an old crone of, what, fifty, going on sixty?" The nurse shuddered in disgust. "Heavens no."

Freckles shucked out of her last bit of scrubs and started toward the showers. "Come along, girl, you ha' ta move. Hurry—and I'll scrub your backside." She pulled the water lever, and the gang showers thundered into their siren's song.

Hannah smiled reluctantly as she shucked out of her scrubs—she did like it when Freckles scrubbed her back. It reminded her of her mother or Leatha, and being a small girl.

18

CHRISTMAS GIFT

Hannah sat with the small girl and her mother. The child's eyes were large and wide with fear. Hannah wanted to hug her and tell her it would all be dandy by spring. But Hannah knew hugging the child would be dangerous for her, and then anyone she ever touched after she also contracted the wet version of leprosy.

Holding the small, dark-brown bottle of Moog oil, Hannah turned toward the mother. The proper name of the oil was Chaulmoogra oil. It had gained the nickname "Moog" or "Moogy" among people with leprosy. "You need to apply this to a clean rag on a stick. Then you rub it on her. But afterward, you must burn the rag and stick. Do you understand?"

The woman dipped her head silently. Hannah paused, taking in all the missing bits of an old face on a young woman. She knew the woman would continue to hug her child, touch her child, bathe her child, and be the same mother her child had known all her tortured life. It was the way of the world. It was the way of mothers and the way they would love their children to death.

Hannah knew certain actions would never change in the world. She even regretted having to wear the large, frightening black rubber gloves covering her arms to her shoulders. In her heart, Hannah recognized that it was only her soft, American Southern drawl and the mother's presence that was calming the little girl.

Rising, the surgeon could feel the toll of the forty straight hours of standing and performing the brutal manual work of surgery. She chuckled as she moved to the sterilizing room to change her scrubs for the ninth time that night. Father Joseph had a team of older, cautious women who boiled the surgical clothes Hannah wore on the wet side. The dry leprosy, while not contagious, received no less cautious treatment, and all were managed by longish poles with a red end and green end painted upon them.

"What is it you find funny in this purgatory?" The large nurse still had her mask and heavy protective scrubs in place.

Hannah bent to the routine of carefully removing her garments with the help of a barrier clothed assistant— usually a person with dry leprosy. "My father and mother used to joke about me when I was small—that I would become a doctor. My mother asked Walter once, *What if she doesn't become a doctor?* His reply was *In that case, I would become one of the meanest laborers on the earth—a surgeon.*" Hannah chuckled as she turned around, dressed only in her chemise, and stared into the eyes of Nurse Hemplewhite.

"You!" The word ricocheted off the stone wall. Hannah froze in rage and fear. "How dare you..."

"You would not talk to me in the hospital. I had no other recourse but to come here."

"But how did you know about...?"

"Here? Mickey."

Hannah was vibrating, and her rage overwhelmed the fear. "Your lover..."

The older nurse froze as if struck. Her breath caught somewhere between her large white brassiere and her throat. It was apparent her mind had stopped working. Then she scowled. Her shoulders jiggled, and then her upper torso began to bounce. She couldn't control herself and began to giggle, and then just laughed—her large breasts nearly jumping out of her brassiere.

Hannah flushed with rage, but also confusion. "You consider having an affair with a man twenty years younger than you to be funny?"

The woman worked hard to contain her excitement. Finally, she reached out and grasped Hannah's left shoulder. "Twenty-six love."

Hannah's voice was still strident. "What is twenty-six, love?"

"No, love—Mickey is twenty-six years younger than me. I was thirty when I married his father. He's my stepson. Well, that title is so cruel—he's my son." She smiled warmly, which almost scared Hannah. "You must have seen him at the hospital. He always hugs me, and then kisses me on the left cheek before he goes to fly. When he returns, he kisses me on the right and then hugs me. We have done it since he started first form as a wee lad."

"He's your son?" Hannah stood with her arms draped, taken aback and confused. "Why would he do that?"

Hemplewhite frowned. "Because I married his father. And I loved both men. Even though one still wore short pants."

Hannah had meant to ask why Mickey wouldn't have told her about the relationship... but kissing Hemplewhite's two cheeks interested her more.

"No. The kiss."

Hemplewhite touched her cheeks. "The kissing... The left side is the port side, and the right is the starboard side. It all started when I explained the term POSH to him. The swells book their preferred side of the ship as POSH or Port Out and Starboard Home."

To take control of herself, Hannah spoke. "So he kisses you port when he leaves, and..."

"Yes. And Starboard when he is home safe and sound."

"But why lie to me about where he is? Especially when he knows how important this mission is." She still vibrated with agitation.

The attendant stood holding the fresh scrubs. Her face remained a deadpan expression during the heated conversation. Finally, Hannah closed her eyes and drew a deep breath. And then, taking two more slow breaths, she opened her eyes and let the attendant dress her and Nurse Hemplewhite.

Seeing that the surgeon was calmer, Hemplewhite

continued. "The Nazis arrested the man that Mickey was to transport from Calais to Le Havre. Mickey rushed to take off as a Nazi car raced alongside his plane. They started shooting, so he pulled back on the stick and prayed. To aid in his escape, he eased the plane's wheels toward the open convertible. He thinks he hit the driver on the head. When he looked back, the car had smashed into a barn and burned."

Hannah stood, shocked. "He could have been killed."

The nurse shrugged and rolled her eyes. "He's been through worse. Anyway, he returned early, but had to leave again right away. He only stopped to tell me where the supplies he had gathered were, and what I needed to... well, shall we say... borrow."

"So where is he?"

"Back in Calais, I suppose, but a different field. The French resistance attacked the convoy carrying the spy, and they needed Mickey to fly him away."

"To this Haver?"

"Le Havre—no, there too has become dangerous. He's bringing the man back, but to Ireland."

"So Mickey is a spy."

Hemplewhite stopped and frowned at Hannah. "No... wait—you really don't know what Mickey does when he flies?"

"He flies rich people where they want to go."

The woman calmed and closed her eyes. She stood still and slowly breathed. Finally, she opened her eyes. "Things started that way, but he's one of the best pilots in small planes and make-do fields. He flies people into very dicey places."

"So he is a smuggler? Like the pirates or free traders of the Caribbean."

The nurse thought as she scrubbed her hands. She turned and smiled. "You know… I never thought of Mickey in such light. But in a way, he's sort of like your Douglas Fairbanks—only he does it quietly and without the sword."

Hannah and Hemplewhite giggled as Hannah observed. "He has the hair."

The next surgery flew past, as did the following four. The flow between the older nurse and the surgeon was seamless. Hannah hadn't realized just how effortless it had all been. She didn't need to explain the unusual and some-times archaic procedures, as she did with Freckles. Hannah stood suturing the last incision. As she turned to give instruction, she found Hemplewhite already painting the legs with the soothing oil.

Hannah watched the nurse apply the ointment. Noticing her, Hemplewhite shyly looked up, embarrassed to be working without the doctor's instructions. Her shoulders relaxed, and she stood straighter—not with her usual bris-tle, but still with her ubiquitous iron spine. "What? You thought I wouldn't know about Moogy?"

Hannah smiled, but would not be caught surprised. "No, everything's peaches—I usually start at the top of the legs and work toward the feet. It seems to be more calming for the nerves. But I'm sure after a few minutes, it all becomes calming, anyway." She nodded her head to the other nurse, who sat watching the breathing, having removed the gas mask and ether cup. "And he won't be with us living for at least a bit longer. But his legs will feel much better when he regains consciousness."

Later, the two women reclined in the pair of wing-backed smoking chairs secured from a long-defunct men's club. Across the large room, Freckles and Steven sat at one of the tables. Skeptically, they observed the new warming of the ice queen and their friend.

"So you know about Mickey and me. You know about our..." She gazed around as she waved her hand with the palm up, "Skulduggery."

Hannah scrutinized the older woman, who sat relaxed but attentive. Hannah was exhausted and scrubbed the heel of her palm across her eyes. The time was taking its toll. Her hand fell back as she blew out her breath with a sigh. "So, what else do you know about me?"

The woman pinched pensively at her lower lip—weighing the question. "Let's suffice it to say that anything I know about you, private or secret, I hold in the highest regard and confidence."

"So Mickey and you talk..."

"About you? Never. Well, other than you two had become an item, which was..." She glanced at Freckles and Steven, "Well, not quite as... um... substantial, but has possi-bilities."

"Then what would you know...?"

The woman rolled forward so only Hannah could hear. "From the first day I saw you walk down the hall, I have known you are not fully Caucasian." She sat back as she studied Hannah's face.

Hannah's heart froze. Her hearing turned to fuzzy cotton with the buzzing of the cicadas in the summer heat. She had not thought about her being of negro blood and passing for white since the fall day in Black Water while she watched the colored girl across the main street.

The woman rolled forward again. "Yes, I see I'm right. I don't know what you are, nor do I care. What I do know is that you are the best surgeon who has ever walked the halls of King's College. I also saw that on the first day—your potential."

She eased back. "I know you thought I was your worst enemy. I have ridden you hard. But you were mistaken. Your worst enemy was whatever drove you to become the surgeon you are—was no longer in place once you left America. I feared you would assume the level of perfor-mance exhibited by most of the others."

She looked back over at Steven. "He's another one. But as a woman, and a nurse, I would have no place riding him like I could you. For his sake, I hope he doesn't become one of the sloppy messes usually gracing the north end—even the swells don't deserve that."

Hannah was catching her breath. The conversation had passed her and her greatest fear.

"Look, love, just lie there and breathe. When you are up to it, we can chat. But for right now, excuse me. I need to close my eyes and rest a bit. I'm not young like you and them." She closed her eyes, and Hannah could see by the third deep breath that she was asleep.

"Hannah? Hannah? Oh Cherie… little miss loverly…" Freckles bent close to Hannah's ear. "It's Christmas Day… and time to open your present, love."

Steven snickered as he looked at the other man. "Or at least undress him… as it were."

Hannah's eyes fluttered, and a face full of freckles filled her vision. "Freckles?"

"Yes, dearie. It's Christmas morning, and you need to wake up. They are tossing us out on our ears and arses. The holy rollers need the room, and they don't want to mingle with the likes of us or our friends."

Nurse Hemplewhite rushed out of the south hallway. "Come along, little one. We let you sleep as long as we could. But we really must be off before someone calls the coppers and we end up having gruel in the nick instead of plum pudding after Yorkshire pudding and roast beast."

The woman stopped and signed: *Besides, your ride is here.*

Hannah frowned and signed a question mark.

A right hand and a large white mitten of gauze wrapping slid by both sides of her head as the right hand signed the word *now*.

Hannah's eyes flew open as she grabbed the flight jacket, encased arms, and pulled Mickey to her back and neck. The other four laughed at her squeal.

Mickey whispered in her ear. "We really must hasten. Hack is waiting, and people are already arriving upstairs.

Besides, I brought you back a little lacey thing from France. I want to see you in soon."

Hannah rocked back and forth with her eyes closed and her head buried against Mickey's head. "I don't want to wake up. I know this is just a dream."

Freckles grabbed one hand, and Steven caught the other. "No, it's really time to scoot. To stay would mean Joe having to answer questions we never want asked."

The five rushed and secreted into the early morning. The large black car started as they came out the back door. Hannah leaned into the window and kissed Hack on the cheek. "Merry Christmas, Hack."

The elder man blushed and shied. "And to you, love."

Chugging from the alley, the cab cut off a couple dragging their children by the hand. The couple noted the big car, filled with laughing, obviously drunk revelers, as it burbled down the lane. The woman strengthened her resolve never to let her husband stop at the pub on his way home.

My dearest Mother,

I have received the most amazing Christmas gifts I could ever have imagined.

The nurse I have written to you about for years, who has always been a thorn in my buttocks, has turned out to be just the opposite. In fact, I think we are going to become wonderfully close indeed.

As I mentioned before, on holidays, a few of us medical professionals sneak into the basement of a church and minister to those in need. Especially for me, people with leprosy. A society that rejects people born with a disease destined to cause a lifetime of pain, suffering, and premature death is incomprehensible to me. Therefore, we strive to alleviate their suffering and demonstrate to them that they are cared for.

This weekend, I had a mystery nurse in the wet surgery. Something about her was familiar, but I knew she was new to the wet leprosy surgery. When she removed her mask, it was none other than Nurse Hemplewhite herself.

I must admit I was mad. I was angry that she was there, and I was even angrier that she had discovered our little illicit endeavor. Even angrier when she told me Mickey had betrayed me, whom I accused of being her lover.

Upon my accusing her of having an affair with my gentleman, and him being twenty years her younger... mother, she laughed. I'm sure my face was a sight to see, as my anger must have filled my facial capillaries into a lovely shade of purple red. I would have been a hit at Mardi Gras.

Finally, she explained Mickey was her son. Truly, her stepson, but she was the only real mum he had known since he was a wee lad. I was stunned. All this time—and Mickey never told me.

Mother, Christmas could have stopped there, but a few minutes later, Mickey showed up out of the blue. He was supposed to be flying across the channel. But something went wrong, and his left hand was in a large bandage. He can't use the fingers for now, so I'll take a few days off to minister to him. And if he doesn't tell me what happened, I might be away from work for a longer time as I serve a sentence in what they call the "nick" (prison) for killing my lover.

I miss you horribly, and I miss the theater season and our going dressed to the nines. Give my love to my sister and make sure she rubs your feet every night. I will catch the postman in the morning, and hopefully, you get this before that horrible man Hitler does anything worse than what he has been up to as of late.

With all my love,
Hannah

19
WAR

My dearest Mother,

I pray this letter reaches New Orleans, which is where my heart and thoughts are. I need to distract myself. Mickey is flying his deliveries, and the household is at sixes and nines—in quite a frenzy.

As we have been rationing, it made no sense for Freckles, Mickey, Hemplewhite, and me to live in three separate locations. We have pooled our resources and rented the small flat next door to Hemplewhite and Mickey. A crafty workman has built a common door, so the two flats are one. We believe that we can conserve in many ways. Cooking mostly involves breakfast. We spend our shares at the Pig and Duck for dinners when we can find time.

Over the summer, Hitler, the awful little man, has become more audacious, leading to non-stop air raids. We have been lucky. Those targeted factories are located a mile or more away. But we do get their injured, on top of our usual load of surgery. Hemplewhite has been invaluable. She was a field nurse in France during the Great War. (Why it didn't end all war is beyond me.) When the ambulances stream in with wounded stacked like cordwood, her cool and calm at triage is worth four nurses.

As you know, since that fateful Christmas in the church's cellar, Hemplewhite has joined our little circle of skullduggery. Poor Penny, and Pig & Duck, took some time to come around, but they are now fast friends and even exchange hugs.

I remember us reading the gripping German novel, All Quiet on the Western Front, the summer before I started residency. It always made me wonder if man could truly visit such inhumanity on others just because they wore a different uniform. Uniforms and armed men are not required for recipients of hatred. The bombing appears to be at least somewhat targeted at factories. This I understand. But there is much that falls on the rows of flats. Casualties span the entire lifespan.

Steven volunteered with the ministry for the duration and negotiated a billet near the factories. He visited the office once; the following day, it vanished. Hitler's bombers arranged for him to be transferred up the hill to the hospital. We contemplated a thank-you note; however, the ministry might disapprove. Mickey suggested we just write it on a bomb and have one of our boys drop it off.

This past week, I was called in to triage to be an interpreter. I couldn't think of what language I might be called upon to translate. A young woman, spirited and quick, possessed a mass of red hair. Her smile was warm, but she was dreadfully pale from loss of blood. Her partner and copilot was holding her hand. Mother, they were from Santa Monica, California. Hemplewhite thought I would want to talk to her before I met her, already under anesthesia on my table.

The two of them are part of an air group called the WASPs, the Women Airforce Service Pilots. These young girls left college to learn how to fly bombers. Officially, they fly them from the United States to England. Emerald and Connie discovered the planes are fully loaded, and the route is less than direct. They refueled in Ireland; afterward, their route took them over a German city in the north. Emerald received some bad shrapnel in her side, along with a bullet the size of your thumb, I found resting just under her skin at the base of her neck.

While we were in surgery, the rest of the crew showed up. Mother, it is a full bomber crew of girls who look no older than those in high school. Hemplewhite ordered medication and sent the prescription to the Pig and Duck, where we typically obtain such medicines. Three days later, they headed somewhere to return to the States. They promised they would check in from time to time and bring any letters I needed to send. So at least I now know I can count on one avenue of communication.

Mother, as the bombing continues, I will descend to the basement, and have occasionally even taken refuge in the steam tunnels. But I still find myself in a panic when I stand at the top of the stairs going down into the earth and the underground. I would rather take my chances walking in the middle of the street during a bombing than my fear of being under-ground. One day, someone may force me, and I know I will just pass away as I stand. I know it is irrational, but it is a paralyzing fear gripping my very soul. If only I had an understanding of Leatha's charms, I would surely wear anything that would help me overcome this. I know there are people in the underground, during the bombings, in need of medical attention. I'm just not the one to provide it. You three raised me to understand that there is a person for every place and need, but Mother... it eats away at my soul like a festering boil. I just wish someone would drop the right bomb on Mr. Hitler and put an end to all this suffering.

I will put this aside for now. It is past the hour when all the lights must be turned off.

I love and miss you, Mother. Hug my sister for me.
With all my love,
Cherie

THE YOUNG NURSE jumped as the solid concrete and linoleum floor jolted from the bombs less than a mile away. Her eyes were wide over her surgical mask.

"Sponge."

Hannah looked up at the nurse. The young woman's clothing trembled slightly with every bomb blast. "Those factories across the road and down the hill. The disgusting Mister Hitler hasn't deemed to kill us who are repairing his offenses. So, you can either run down into the rabbit holes closer to the real bombing, or you can mop up the actual blood in this man's abdomen." She stood solid as the rock she didn't feel, but she was the lead she knew they all looked to in these times. The reckless American who prefers surgery to hiding underground. "Which is it going to be? Get it sorted. In a few moments, this man will wake up, and I don't want him to see a scared little girl in my operatory."

The nurse jerked and grabbed a swab. "Yes, mum."

The hand barely flinched as she mopped at the open wound. The bombing worsened as they listened to the German Messerschmitt airplanes, mixed with the high whine of the Merlin-powered Hurricanes. Occasionally, there were the new, heavier roars of the Spitfires.

The RAF officer on loan as an anesthesiologist, administering Pentothal, looked up as the sound of a larger, closer bomb exploded. "It sounds like Hitler is trying to find me again."

Hannah smiled under her mask. She had cut off his leg the year before, so instead of trying to learn to fly with one leg, he volunteered to become one of the new cadre of anesthesiologists. "Not to worry, Captain Pleasance, we won't let him take your other leg."

He nodded as he looked at the rate of the dripping medication. "I'd appreciate that. My new bride could easily scold me for being late, and I wouldn't have a leg to stand on."

The laughter was barely more than a fluffing of the new softer cotton masks.

Hannah focused harder on the man's bowel. Somewhere, there was a leak from shrapnel. It wasn't large, but the concentration helped her take her mind off the airplanes. And more importantly, the even smaller, delicate one she knew was flying onto a field in Normandy.

She completed the stitching, then retreated. She pushed her fists into the small of her back. "Gwendolyn, please plaster if you can. I need to run a fast trip to the loo and then, hopefully, Nurse Hemplewhite has some bites to sustain us before the next one gets trotted up the hill."

"Certainly, mum."

"WELL, at least Hitler's hellions have cleared off." The captain adjusted the pipette's drip.

Hannah hummed in thought. When the bombing stopped and the planes moved off, that was when they found the wounded. She glanced at the youngest nurse. Only fingertips from her right hand grazed the tray's rim. The scared, jumpy rabbit of earlier had settled into a focused calm. "Murphy?" The young woman started. Her hand jumped to the middle of the tray.

"Mum?"

"We're almost done here. Please ask Nurse Hemplewhite what's next on the board? If anything is coming, she'll have a sixth sense about it."

"Yes, mum." The new, crisper, white surgical gown vaporized into thin air.

"How's the breathing, captain?"

The anesthesiologist looked at his notes. "Fifty-six about five minutes ago."

Hannah looked at him out of the corner of her eye. "How about now, sir?"

The man watched the clock as he counted breaths. "Fifty-two."

Hannah hummed as she leaned into her stitching in the cavity. Intact gallbladder notwithstanding, the intense pain he felt must have severely impacted his life. She eyed the appendix on the young man. Being the size of her index finger wouldn't go the distance if the man grew old.

She watched Nurse Murphy disappear through the door. She reached over and took up the next scalpel. Calmly, she reached in and excised the worn-out appendix and dropped it in the bowl with the gallbladder. Two stitches and she returned to her other row of stitching.

"Mum?"

Hannah didn't even raise her eyes. "What is it, Murphy?"

"Mum?"

"Out with it, girl. This man is waking up, and I'm still twenty stitches to heaven."

The voice was much deeper. "Mum, we need you to come away right now."

Hannah glanced over her shoulder at the grizzled man standing in the door. The man's Civil Defense uniform was a patchwork of dirt, filth, and what appeared to be blood.

Hannah looked back at her stitches. "Nurse Murphy,

please explain to this man why cleanliness is essential in the operatory, perhaps with tea and biscuits. I'll be with him in ten or fifteen minutes."

The man's arm rose to reach out and grab the surgeon. "Mum, a man's life hangs in the balance."

"Murphy!"

"Yes, mum. Sir, you need to come out of here."

"But a man's life..."

"Yes, sir. And the man's life on the table rests in her hands right now. Now, please, come with me."

The door snicked as it closed.

"Four more stitches, Captain. Slow count to twenty, then you can stop the Pentothal. Blood pressure and respiration, if you please."

NURSE MURPHY STOOD in the doorway. The Civil Defense man sat at the small table. Untouched tea sat beside a biscuit plate, bare except for crumbs.

Hannah stopped a foot from the nurse.

"Murphy?"

"You need to grab your bag and hurry along, mum."

Hannah blinked once.

"We have three in the ward, vying for my dance card. If the man needs a surgeon, they can bring him here. Why is this concept so difficult for people to grasp? We are a hospital, I am a surgeon, and we have an operatory."

Nurse Hemplewhite stepped up behind her. Leaning

close to her ear, she whispered, "It's not as simple as that. The man was caught in a bomb blast. He has a length of steel through his chest. If they pull it, he dies. If they cut the rod and try to move him, he still bleeds out and dies."

Hannah slowly ground around to look at Hemplewhite with her coat on. She noticed the man behind her.

20

DEATH, BURIED, AND LIFE

THE MORNING HAD SEEN the building awaken. Flats filled with multiple generations, getting by. Those with jobs scurried to their stations. Everyone helped in the war effort. The neighborhood was at the bottom of the hill, and therefore, it was at the bottom of the economic caste system the uppers deemed did not exist.

Dust and smoke still hung in the air, which had been formally filled with three levels of living. The rubble was the only evidence left. Small fires spotted the bricks, wood, and plaster. Hannah knew this was what preceded the bodies on her operating table, but the nose-searing stench of half-cooked bodies and building was nonetheless arresting—even for a surgeon.

Hemplewhite gently touched her arm. Hannah turned from the horror. Hemplewhite nodded toward the former street, now a jumble of rubble and scrap metal. The battered black box looked like any other taxi in London. But Hannah's eyes were drawn to the green dot painted on the right rear bumper just below where the rear light would glow. The yellow numbers she knew by heart. Her head snapped back around in fear. The taxi was unquestionably Hack's.

The older, more experienced nurse took over. "He would have rushed to help others take shelter."

The white helmet ascended the stairs. The circle and bar sign, denoting the subway entrance, lay beaten to one side. "This way, mum." He waved urgently.

Hannah froze.

Her usual strength and calm drained. Her face, unmoving, as her hands rose along each other's arms—rubbing like curling wisps of the smoke in the rubble. As her hands reached her upper arms, they gripped until the knuckles blanched.

Hemplewhite stepped to her side. Her voice was soft. "Hannah?" She noted the dilated eyes. She turned to the shattered entrance to the underground. "Hannah, you've been down there before."

A slight, slow shake denied it.

"Cherie. It's only a basement."

Hemplewhite could feel the vibration in Hannah's elbow. It was now or never.

Hemplewhite layered her voice with the starch in her white uniform. "It's Hack down there. A man faces life-or-death. Only you can tip the scale for him living another day."

She pulled Hannah around to face her. Childhood fear, not the steel of a surgeon, shone in the deep brown eyes. Her tone softened. "Hannah, Cherie... I'll hold your hand the whole way. But only you can do the surgery. Only you can save this man. Not Steven, not another doctor. Only you. He needs your hands and the guidance of your Leatha. But I will never leave your side. I promise."

A torn newspaper, blown into the railing above the stairs, gripped Hannah's eyes. The slow waving of the light-blown paper beckoned her like the hand of death. The roar of blood in her ears completed the horror of the only hell she understood. Calling, beckoning, enticing her to the cold of the earth.

Hemplewhite stepped in front of her. Breaking the spell. "If it is Hack down there. And he dies... You can never live with it. You need to sort yourself out—but do it later. Some poor soul is in need and only you—"

Hannah stepped around her. "I know."

As she reached for the railing, she could feel her hand shaking. Hannah watched the crowds moving unconcernedly up and down the stairs amidst the rubble.

"Here, mum. I have a torch."

She turned to find the Civil Defense officer drawing a flashlight from his belt. "It will make it easier for you to see, mum."

His age exceeded hers by at least ten years. She bristled as her indignation hardened her resolve. "I'm not your mother, and I'm almost young enough to be your niece. I'm Hannah or Jack, but you may call me *miss*." She locked eyes with the man.

He cleared his throat. "Yes, miss." He held his hand out. "This way, miss."

Hannah quietly reached her right hand back, grasping at air until Hemplewhite's hand gripped it and gave a comforting squeeze.

As they reached the bottom of the stairs, large dark lumps in the darker tunnel took shape as people. There were tiny bits of light here and there.

Hemplewhite explained from just behind Hannah. "They are living here now. Some out of fear. Mostly those who have no other home left. The bombings..." As they walked into the camp on the underground platform, she observed. "Many of these work in the factories."

"Jack?"

Hannah froze at the voice. "Hack?"

"As clear as the sky on St. Crispin's Day. We're on the left, past the tracks. Never mind the electric. It stopped cackling two days ago."

The Civil Defense took her elbow. "This way, mu... err... Miss."

She stopped, and he turned. "I don't even know your name."

"Smythe, miss. Danial Smythe, miss." He pulled at her elbow with urgency.

The halo of light led her feet across and down the tracks. It was easier to concentrate on the spot of light than on where they were.

The voice was low. "Up here, Jack."

Danial swung the light up. The wall's side showed a

tumbled mass of rubble and metal. The man lay battered in the ruins. A bent metal pipe, thick as his thumb, sticking from his chest.

"Have you tried to move him?" She studied the frightened man's expression. He seemed in shock, not particularly pained.

"No, m... miss. The pipe is one of the hydraulic tubes to move the switches." He looked at her, pleading. "We think..."

Hannah took the flashlight and swept it over the injured man's chest. Only a hand-sized blot darkened his coat. She grabbed the end of the pipe and wiggled it some. The man moaned, but the pipe moved. She returned the flashlight to Danial. "We need to cut the pipe. It's not hydraulics, it's an old lead pipe for water." Her eyes rolled. "It's probably something the Romans left."

"But mum..."

Hannah glared at him. Turning, she searched for help. "Hack?"

Hemplewhite stepped over the rubble and scrambled up to Hannah. "He's bandaging down the tunnel. What can I do?"

Hannah turned to the impaled man. "I need to see his back. Help me turn him, but be careful. We need to see what's on the other end of this old pipe."

As they began to roll the man, Hannah noticed the pipe suck back into his chest. "Stop." Hannah used the flashlight, moving rubble to look beneath the man. She dug deeper, finding no end to the pipe.

She rolled and sat. "The pipe is loose... but buried in the debris. We just need to cut it." She looked at Danial.

The man shook with the realization of his cue. "Right. I'll just go sort it out."

Hannah watched the man hurry away. She turned to Hemplewhite. "You didn't think to bring some morphine in that handy bag of yours—did you?"

The nurse nodded. "There should be six fresh ampoules and a couple of syringes. A dozen packets of sulfa and a liter of alcohol."

"Bushmills or scotch?"

The wiser nurse smirked. "Bottom of the bag. The flat flagon with the skull and crossed bones. I believe it's a young, blended scotch." Her smile pulled back on one side. "For him or us?"

Hannah rolled her eyes as she felt for the flat bottle. Pulling it out, she weighed its fullness. She peered down the tunnel, then swiftly returned her gaze to the man. "I'm twenty of your meters under the street. I think we'd best share."

She aided him in drinking, then drank deeply herself, finally handing it to Hemplewhite.

His voice: gentle, yet distinct. "Thank ye. I've been needing that since the sirens started."

His lack of a cough confirmed Hannah's suspicion. The pipe had missed the lung.

"What's your name?"

"Rupert, mum. Rupert Blacksmith, mum."

She stuck her hand out behind her. Not feeling the

bottle, she snapped her fingers. The cool of the glass slapped into her hand as securely as a scalpel. She brought the bottle round to the man's lips. And then hers. She rested the bottle in her lap. "Where were you when the bomb hit?"

"I'm an electrician. I was below ground level in the apartment building. They've been having a bugger of a time with their electrical. I was sorting it out when the gods started playing rugby with me. Next I know, I'm looking at a grizzled face and a voice that sounds like me da gargling."

Hannah smiled. "That would be my friend, Hack. He's the best cabbie... Well, he was the best cabbie in London. I saw the aftermath of his cab as we were on our way to see you.

"Miss?"

Hannah saw three men at the rubble pile's base. One held a pipe saw. Hannah waved him up.

Moving to one side, she shone the flashlight under Rupert's body. The light only exposed a few inches of the dull silver pipe. "I need you to cut as near to his coat as you can. We'll want to carry him out on a stretcher on his back. But first, I need to numb him."

"Ya neigh the toop too?"

Rupert smiled at her blank face. "He wanted to know if you want him to cut the top piece as well."

Hannah closed her eyes and thought. One country, yet with so many languages within it. She looked at the man. "Yes, yes, please. But let me give him a shot first."

Rupert smiled and bobbed his eyes at the bottle in her hand. She gave him another sip. And took another for her.

She traded Hemplewhite the bottle of whiskey for a syringe full of morphine and an open packet of sulfa.

Carefully, she injected the morphine where it would do the most good. Passing it back behind her, she felt the syringe taken from her hand. She dusted the sulfa around the pipe where she could see. Remembering Leatha's talent with people, she gently patted his chest, avoiding the pipe. She watched his eyes. Her eyes turned glassy and rolled up as she backed out, nodding to the man with the saw.

Minutes later, the other men scrambled up the rubble and carefully transferred Rupert to the stretcher. Hannah stopped them at the bottom of the pile. "I'll be along shortly, but the nurses will start prepping him for surgery." Realizing how short she sounded, she rested her hand on Rupert's arm. "Thank you, gentlemen, for doing this. There is a special place waiting in heaven for your kindness."

While crossing the tracks, Hannah peered down the tunnel, into the black. Small camps designated households. The tunnel was their new neighborhood. She recognized the form of the large, lumbering bear of a man. She pointed at the small encampments. "How permanent are these camps, Hack?"

He glanced back over his shoulder. "It's probably going to be as long as the duration, miss." His smile furled into a set of rolls as his eyebrows arched. "Ya thinking about trading the basement for these? If you are, know that there are more people in need here than those who come to the basement."

She looked longingly at the dull light filtering down the

stairs from above. "I guess we'll need to work on that." She held up the small flask of a bottle. "And you need a new cab."

He took the bottle and pulled a small sip. "So I've been told." His second sip resulted in a few bubbles gurgling back up the bottle.

Hannah patted him on the chest. "Keep it, Hack. I must go play Jack. If there's a *later*, I'm buying dinner at the Pig."

21

LIFE ABOVE AND BELOW

My dearest Nana,

If I need to convince Hemplewhite or Hack to write you a letter to confirm this, I will.

This last week, I was called to save a man's life. He is an electrician who was working in a residential building near the factories. As the bomb dropped into the building, the floors collapsed, causing him to be impaled on a rusty pipe in the underground tunnels where the trollies run. He was stuck with the pipe, running him through and through. But the pipe was still connected. Had the rescuers pulled him off the pipe, he would have bled out and died before ever seeing the light of day. So they came and got me.

I can hear Walter mussing about bringing the mountain to Mohamid. But it was more of dragging Hannah into the cave of being buried alive. When we left the hospital, I did not know where the man was. But at the stairs to descend into the subways, I froze. I am forever grateful for Hemplewhite, for she was my guiding light.

In the street stood a crushed taxi. I knew the numbers by heart. It was Hack's cab. Whether he was the injured man or just assisting in the bowels of the earth, as he usually is, remained unknown to us.

The Civil Defense man carried a hand torch, and Hemplewhite held my hand the entire way. Mother, there were hundreds of people now living in the tunnels, as they are afraid to come above ground because of the bombing. Someone needs to bomb that horrid little man, Hitler. There are many injured individuals who have been injured and require medical attention. Others simply need the general medical care they haven't received over the years of war.

Regarding the man with the pipe through his chest. We had morphine and sulfa. Equally crucial, Hemplewhite's bag held a small flask, a potential lifesaver. I might have drunk as much whiskey as he did. We dulled his senses to the pain and surroundings as some workmen cut the pipe. They carefully carried him back to the hospital while Hemplewhite and I applied the rest of what she had in her magic bag of medical tricks.

Mother, we have been back every night with medical supplies, and it's never enough. Each night, we drag ourselves into the flat, dead tired, after midnight. Surgeries that used to start at six sharp now start after seven. I don't know how long we can keep this up. But I don't think I can stop. If I do, I'll think about it and never bring myself to go back down.

I don't know if I'm cured, but I'll be damned if I'll let that little bastard in Berlin beat me.

I'll not post this letter, as Mickey should be back by the weekend. So I'll let him read it before I seal my love with a kiss.

The two pilots, Emerald and Connie, are due back on Monday. I'm not supposed to be privy to the war movements, but the commander of the airfield needed his appendix shown the dustbin, and he feels he owes me a wee bit of leniency. The Messenger Service, which usually transports our live blood, can also deliver this letter for the girls to bring back to the States.

I need to trim the wick. We have an officer being delivered from Dover in five hours. I'm not clear on what is wrong with his leg, but I'm not looking forward to another amputation this week. Four is the limit of my heart. Some of these boys don't even have a whisker on their chins yet.

I miss you with all my heart. Hug my sister.

Cherie

MICKEY LAY BACK against the few pillows stacked against the wall. He had read the letter three times as Hannah lay snuggled on his right arm and chest. His left hand and the letter lowered pensively to his hip as he thought.

The window was dark as most of the expansive city restricted its light. A lone candle glowed from the nightstand, providing him with light to read. The steady flame rimmed in reflection in his searching eyes as they looked about the small bedroom and narrow armoire. He smiled at the hooks Hannah had fastened to the outside ends to hang his clothes.

"Well?" The small voice vibrated on his chest.

"Interesting." He held up the letter to glance at it. "Your description of your earthly descent resembles my account of a turbulent La Havre departure. Neither dart hits the target."

Gently, Hannah raised his left hand from her naked breast and inspected the scars on the back and palm. "How is Mister Mitten doing these days?" He had worn the large white bandage for a couple of weeks as a reminder not to use his dominant hand. The nickname had stuck.

He slowly spread his hand and then made a fist a few times. Then he returned it to its former warm station. His thumb and forefinger gently pinched and rolled the nipple. A soft shutter and moan rewarded the movement. "I believe he does quite well for himself. Do you concur?"

She snuggled in tighter and pulled the blanket up over her shoulder. "Aces."

He snickered. "Oh. You're spending too much time with those flying girls from across the pond. Speaking of which, I heard a rumor they're bringing in more of those new bombers to Heston. The twenty-fours."

Hannah rubbed her head against his chest. "Connie and Emerald both said they were training on them, but they weren't sure they would like them. The higher wing made it feel more like strolling with the family cat rather than the usual family dog.

"Hmm." He glanced at the candle. Licking his thumb and finger, he reached out. Pinching the wick, the room fell into darkness. "After they have finished their business, I have seen them turn almost as tight as my Lysander. But I can imagine what kind of flying pig they must be with a couple of lorries' worth of cheese in their belly." He rolled into her. "But enough about flying."

She knew better. "When do you fly out tomorrow?"

"After dark." He nuzzled his nose into her hair. "Speaking of the dark. It's time to sleep. You have surgery in a few hours."

Her hum was more sleep than acknowledgment.

DENSE FOG FILLED the back mews; three figures moved to the road's center. Their habit of walking in the middle of the street, they had come to call the *war walk*. In the dark, it was the most likely walkway to avoid encountering a stray brick or part of a fallen wall.

Freckles looked at the gray blob in her hand as they walked. "Gah. I can't believe you wheedled Clancy into a whole dozen. I haven't had a second egg in years. Maybe I should save this one for later. I'm nearly full."

Hemplewhite crossed her arm in front of Hannah and snapped her fingers. "Hand it over. I'll suffer the consequences."

Freckles laughed as she swung it away protectively. "Core. I'm working on it. I didn't say it wouldn't fit. You had your two."

They made the corner in lockstep as Hannah snickered. "Children. Children. Don't make me get the quiet chair."

Freckles laughed. "Yes. We heard the quiet chair last evening."

Hemplewhite harrumphed. "Has she always been this nasty?"

Hannah smirked as they turned into the curved approach to the hospital. "Only when Steven hasn't graced her nickers in a week." They nodded at the darker shadow near the front door. "Morning, Sergeant Salford."

"Top of the day to you three. The marine reports heavy storms along the channel. We might have a quiet day."

Freckles muttered under her breath. "Just means they won't fly. Which means they'll just send their god-awful rockets instead. Let them find a field to plow instead of babies."

Hannah pulled the scarf from her neck as they walked in a brace toward surgery. "We'll muddle through whatever the world grants us."

Freckles put her fist to her mouth. "Oh. My." Her freckles blended in a flush.

The other two looked at her. Hemplewhite fanned her hand in the air before her face. "Did you just pass gas?"

The young nurse turned on her heel. "Certainly not. That would be Sergeant Smither's job." She continued deeper into the surgery ward.

Hannah called after her. "See that the sergeant receives his tea." She eyed the chalkboard. "Someone added more surgeries last night." She glared at Hemplewhite.

The woman held up her hands. "I'll sort it all out. Get scrubbed. First up this morning, you have a gall bladder gone bad. The rest of these ducks I'll gather and sort."

THE AIRFIELD always seemed to be on the edge of an emergency. Jeeps going here, lorries going there, and a motorcycle or two stitching the hither and yon. Mickey disregarded it. It was irrelevant. He turned the polished brass doorknob on the blank door into a nondescript building on the edge of the real airfield. The war department deceptively painted buildings to mimic age and decay. The interior of the Quonset hut said otherwise.

Mickey stepped to the wall of maps. A recent paint smell still hung in the air.

The colonel stepped out of the inner office. His pink scalp shone through his thinning hair. Several had poked fun at the man's prodigious mustache, saying that there was more hair below his nose than over his head. "Good morning, Stork." He pointed at a red-topped pin on the map of Belgium.

"Morning, sir."

The colonel set the papers down on the desk and sat on the edge. "The shop tells me they laid on more silk and glue patching your plane. This officially makes it more patches than original skin."

"Yes, sir. Dusty will ensure I stay in the air as long as the Jerries only shoot at the fabric."

The man hummed. "Yes. I saw the last ventilation. It must have been a cold ride home."

Mickey rocked his head from side to side. "It keeps me awake on those long flights. Personally, I'd rather not be making those flights down into the Bourdeaux region, unless I can bring back a few bottles."

The man stood. "Well, hopefully that Yank Patton can move out of Italy soon and open a doorway from the south. Then we won't need you to make those long flights. Just the short hops like tonight." The man raised one eyebrow. "Just make sure you're all in one piece, coming back with some chocolate." His finger wavered over Wales. "There's a package the Yanks need delivered. There seems to be some kind of big push on, and they need their man on the ground."

"Where?"

His hand moved to the northeast of Spain. Three hundred kilometers beyond Bourdeaux. "Sorry, old chap. But the Yanks were most insistent. Besides, you will also come back to Limerick instead."

Mickey tips his head. "Why Ireland?"

The colonel stepped to the desk and found the thin folder. He handed it to Mickey. As the pilot opened the cover, he explained. "She's been behind enemy lines since thirty-nine. They want her out. I gather, from Limerick, she will catch a ferry back to the States, along with their crews bringing over the bombers."

Mickey nodded. "Hann... um. Yes, I had heard a rumor there would be a new raft of bombers being flown in, in the next few days."

The colonel took the folder back. "Yes, the cousins have been holding it tight to the vest since Saint Crispin's Day, but they have been building up everything. Whitehall figures there are three times as many Yanks in England than this time in forty-three."

Mickey pointed at the folder. "Can you find me another winter flight suit? I think hat and arctic gloves would be prudent as well."

"I'll see what I can requisition. And... um... err on a taller size. More like your size. Some of the Yanks are tall. Even the women."

Mickey smirked. "Make sure it fits loosely in the crotch. Some of those Yank women have a prodigious pair."

The colonel studied the pilot, who landed in small fields on moonless nights. "It sounds like you've had some experience."

Mickey groaned and turned for the hanger. "I'll go check the new skin patches. I don't want her to feel a draft."

22

NEW LIFE, SAME OLD EAGLE

A SOFT SCUFFING noise of a shoe came from the other room. Hannah rolled her head to look at Freckles. The hard biscuit slanted, and Hannah felt the first dribble of the orange marmalade drop onto her chest where the narrow lace of her chemise formed a valley. "Core." She wiped her finger up the drop and stuck it in her mouth. The biscuit and jam followed. "Who is in the ready room?"

Freckles frowned, but rolled forward to look, as she was the only one still dressed in her bloodied scrubs. "Hemple-white is out at the desk..."

The door swung softly to reveal a tall American with tan hair and a trimmed rusty mustache. "Oh. Hello. I thought everyone was in the operatory."

Hannah studied the man in doctor's surgical clothes. Only his polished boots were for a different profession. "Can we help you?"

"Um, yes. Captain Adams, with the 64th Medical Group. John Adams. I'm supposed to report to the Chief of Surgery.

A Jack Murphy, I believe?" The red at his collar was a soft glow.

Hannah's hand reached out and stopped Freckles. "And what, pray tell, wouldst thou do with yon, Jack?"

"I've been attached to this hospital to help with the war effort?"

Hannah frowned at Freckles and her deadpan face. Turning back to the now blushing youngish doctor, she narrowed her eyes as she also realized her lack of attire. "Dost thou converse in the tongue of English? I perceive thy murmurings, yet they resemble the discordant cries of creatures from the dustbin dwelling amidst the ruins."

Confusion twisted the man's face. "Excuse me?"

Hannah's head rolled to one side as she watched him. "Sprichst ze Deutsch?" Speak German? "Peut-être en français?" Maybe, French? Hannah sensed Freckles twitching.

Freckles turned and signed. "He's not responding. Maybe he is deaf? But he did ask to be excused. Maybe he farted or just needs you to excuse him."

Hannah signed back. "How long do you think he will survive?"

The wall of starched white filled the doorway behind the American doctor. "Oh, good. You've met your relief. Doctor Jefferson, I believe." Nurse Hemplewhite signed low as she stepped around the blushing statue in scrubs. *You two are horrible. However, the SoHo accent is improving.*

"Adams. John Adams."

Hemplewhite dismissed him with a wave of her hand

through the air. "Oh, yes. I knew it was one of those colonial upstarts." She stood with one eyebrow raised at Hannah, clad only in her chemise.

Hannah didn't move. "My scrubs got soaked with blood. It's hot in here. And we were grabbing a bit of tea before we dove back into the next ten hours of surgery. Are the three amputations ready?"

She noted the blood drain from the Yank's face at the reference of ten more hours of surgery. She wondered if medical schools had changed since her days of standing for days in surgery as a resident.

Hemplewhite sighed. "The arm passed away last hour. We have two left. Both are legs. One below the knee and the other..."

"Freckles and I'll take the below-the-knee. Throw the sacrificial lamb into the deep end. But we don't have a spare gas passer, so he's on his own."

The captain's face, already pale, now appeared cadaverous.

Hannah recognized the tiniest smile pulling at the older nurse's mouth. She glanced back at the young doctor. "You are a trained surgeon, are you not?"

"George Washington Medical School. Last year, ma'am."

The three females groaned.

The blush returned as he stammered. "Third in my class."

"Grand. You can take the lead, and Jack will assist." Hemplewhite leaned into his face. "If you muck this up, we'll have a hole waiting for you down the hill. Survive, and you can try again tomorrow. And so you know, we start here at a quarter past four in the morning. Sharp. We terminate at half after four, in time for tea."

His voice turned slightly eager to be rid of the females. "So, Jack is here?"

Hemplewhite turned sideways to slip past the young man. She pointed back at Hannah. "Your lord and mistress. The term Jack is short for Jack the Ripper. England's notorious surgeon... until Miss Humphry. It's single, not plural. At least we are hoping it's not plural. This world is only big enough for one of them." She looked back at Hannah. "The leg is here."

Hannah stood. "Operatory two, if you please, Nurse Hemplewhite. Vagner, I think. *Flight of the Valkyries* is most appropriate."

"Certainly, miss."

The leg lay shot away about the knee. The air base flight medics performed admirably, with their limited capabilities. At a certain point, only a hospital, with its surgical team, provides the solution.

The American stood staring at the ground meat of what used to be the critical right knee of a copilot. His voice was less than self-assured. "What do you think happened?"

Hannah peered at Freckles over the white mask. Neither one was going to respond. Hannah looked at the gas passer, who rolled his eyes and then nodded. "How many amputations have you performed, Mr. Adams?"

"I assisted with an arm in my third year. We didn't get many amputations at George Washington. People in Washington, D.C., are more prone to getting paper cuts than anything substantial."

"Well, when the time runs out, this man dies. How do we decide where to cut?"

"Where the strong muscle mass ends."

"How do we determine such?"

"Palpitation?"

Hannah glared at him. "You're down to fifty-eight minutes. Are you asking me or telling me? In ten seconds, Nurse Freckles is going to hand you a scalpel."

The man grabbed the leg and began to feel the muscle. "Just above the knee. He won't have—"

Nurse Freckles grabbed his hand and slapped a scalpel into it as Hannah raised the leg and secured the tourniquet.

John's eyes grew wide as he looked at the scalpel in his hand and then looked at the nurse. Her left hand was already touching the bone saw. He glanced at the large, white, ticking clock and cut.

At the front desk, Nurse Hemplewhite glanced at the small watch hanging from the alabaster silhouette of the rod and a single snake—The Rod of Asclepius. The lending of a surgeon by the Americans to help in the war effort could be a blessing, or just a yoke of burden to bear. If the former, she was hesitantly grateful. If the young man proved the latter, she wouldn't suffer his presence past the end of the week. Hannah didn't have time to teach. The sick from the usual places, plus those from the bombings down the hill, were now combined with severely injured airmen being sent from the airbases.

The maiden arranged the fresh surgical gown on Hannah. "What's in the hall, Freckles?"

"The kidney from last week. His back is hot to the touch."

Hannah braced her lips in hard rolls as she looked at where the wall met the floor, and at nothing. "Let's get him open. John?"

The voice was from the other room. "Yes, Jack?"

"How many kidneys have you removed?"

"More than a dozen kidneys and pieces of livers. Politics tends to be abusive to both."

Freckles leaned over. "Thank Saint Crispen for some experience beyond carbuncles and knee plasters."

Hannah growled, "Yes, but let's hold judgment until after we stop at the Pig & Duck on our way down to the hole in the ground. He'll think his day is over. But he'll soon learn this isn't the eight-to-six he thought hospitals ran on."

Freckles feigned shock. "Yank surgeons only work half the day?"

"Easy girl. Let's let him down softly. The hole will harden his metal, or have him running back to the Yank base in Somerset."

Five surgeries later, Hannah and Freckles stripped from their blood-splattered surgical gowns. The maiden jammed a hard biscuit layered with orange marmalade into their mouths. Cups of warm tea sat on the sideboard. The two sipped and ate another biscuit each as they stood in their chemises.

The knock on the door was soft. Hannah rolled her eyes

closed and sighed. "It's open, John. We're adults. And you'll need the biscuit and jam for the next act."

Nurse Hemplewhite stood in the open door. "He thought his day was done." She held up her hand. "Not to worry. I stopped him. What supplies do we require for the hole tonight?"

Hannah sighed and looked at Freckles. "They didn't bomb today, so mostly lots of plasters and alcohol. Sulfa, morphine, and iodine as well. If anything requires surgery, we can send them up or call them in the morning. But send John in. He'll need some sweets and biscuits. He earned it this afternoon. It will give us time to get dressed."

"Very good, miss." She pointed at Hannah's chemise. "Go get dressed. I'll wait a moment before sending the child into the lioness's den."

The Pig & Duck was just getting started and only half full. Freckles whistled at the barman and held up all four fingers. The barman waved and called back to the kitchen. Four shouldered their way into the back room.

As they stripped their coats and sat, Hannah explained to the confused young captain. "In your daily routine, this would be what you Yanks call lunch. It splits your morning work from your later work."

He squinted his eyes as he cocked his head away from her. "What later work?"

Nurse Hemplewhite unceremoniously pegged her elbows on the table as she leaned her head onto the ball of her two hands. "Your day's work is in a clean operatory with refined tools and surgery. Your night work is the one which pays you dearer to the heart, but takes its toll on your soul."

Freckles leaned her chest across her crossed arms on the table. "It's not your fault, but you blighters came late to the dance. Now, you dance with what's left. Or who is left, as matters be. The bombing started"—she pointed at the gold bars on his collar—"about the time you were thinking about which fine hospital you wanted for your residency. Where we are going tonight, the people have been living ever since. Their houses and flats became rubble with some of the first bombings. They live where they used to take the under-ground train to work. Now, there is no train. So they bring water for themselves and others. They make small fires to cook whatever they can scrounge that day, and they make do as they share with their neighbors."

Hannah brought it home. "If you have any fleeting thought of them being beggars, leave it up here in the gutter. These are the same proud people who once lived in the buildings that are now reduced to rubble, which we will pass on our way. Most of them now get up in the morning, look after their neighbors, and then go to work. They work in the hospital, the factories still being bombed, and about the city. At the gate to hell remains a mangled black mess of a taxi. It belongs to a very dear friend. Someday, I will buy him a new one. Because he's that dear of a friend."

Penny backed through the door, holding the four pints in one hand, and the trenchers stacked up her other arm. She placed the beers and distributed the trenchers. "Jack, I swear. If'n you make one more friend, we're done. I kin only carry so much."

John stared large-eyed at the pint of dark liquid and the trencher of fish and chips.

The three ladies grabbed their beers and clinked the glasses. "To blood and bones." The glasses hit the table half full. As the women sprinkled vinegar on their food, Hannah looked at the stunned captain. "Don't think this is one of your leisurely spent meals along the Potomac. In five minutes, you're going to be left here. The barmaid will look to you for her due. Eat, drink, and keep up. We have a fuller evening than our lazy day was."

His eyes grew wider, but he grabbed his beer.

23
FINDING SPINE UNDER GROUND

HANNAH WATCHED AS THEY WALKED, carrying bags, satchels, and boxes of supplies. The rubble of buildings, homes, and shops didn't escape the Yank's notice. A banty of a man stood at the top of the stairs. "I was worrying. The light left twenty minutes ago. We can't have you out here waving a torch at the Germans."

Hannah kissed the man on his cheek. "Not to worry, Owen. The round of Bushmills was to celebrate bringing an extra set of hands. Being a Yank, we have low expectations, but any help is welcome."

The man wobbled his white helmet. "In wartime, we make do with what the good lord provides."

Freckles and Hemplewhite nodded as they passed with their boxes. "Aye, we do. Saints or sinners all."

Hannah stopped. "Are you coming down, Owen?"

"Shortly, miss. The Trapper boys are bringing supplies. They were supposed to be here by eight, so I'm a wee worried."

She patted him on the arm with her elbow. "It's comforting to know you worry about them. We'll be down if you need help shifting boxes when they arrive."

"Aye. Now off with ya. The women have your duties lined up."

The soft whistle blew just before midnight. Hemplewhite finished sorting the boxes and supplies that the Trapper brothers had finally arrived with. Hannah and Freckles finished the last plaster on a small boy.

"You are a stalwart young man." Hannah looked up at the mother. "Does he ever cry?"

"He was only four months when the bombs dropped. He cried until the second round shook the front of the flats off. Then he stopped. Not a peep since. He's never shown fear, but also never broached a word. He's not a dummy. His second-level books lie around here. And his penmanship's better than me own."

The boy watched Hannah. Hannah smiled. "There are other ways of talking. Her fingers and hands moved before the large, round eyes. This is how the deaf communicate. This is how they speak in America." Her hands moved. "And this is the same signs in English... and then in French."

The mother frowned. "But they look the same."

"To the deaf, they know which you are speaking. My beau speaks the French way, which is like the Americans."

"Is he deaf?"

Hannah laughed. "Hardly. He can hear what the two flies are whispering in the next flat." Freckles blushed. "No.

He learned sign language from his mother." Hannah pointed at Hemplewhite. "And I can tell by the tilt of her ears that she is listening to us talk. If you're here when we are, we can teach you how to sign." She looked up at the mother. "Both of you. And we'll start with the alphabet. You can spell while you learn the signs."

"That's most kind..."

Hannah smiled and took the boy's right hand. "Make a fist. Now hold it up, and think of it as a puppet who is nodding." She moved the fist. "That is yes. For no, you can make the two fingers, and your thumb snap shut like a bird's mouth. Or just shake your head. Either works for now." She smiled as he looked at his hand. "Do you want to learn sign language?"

The boy smiled shyly and nodded his hand.

"See, you now have your first sign."

Freckles stopped and held out Hannah's coat. Her thumb and little finger extended as she dropped the hand like an open hammer.

Hannah chuckled and pointed at the hand. "She's telling me the word now. It means we need to leave, but we'll be back tomorrow." She passed her open hand past the side of her face in a forward move.

The boy mirrored the movement.

"Yes. Tomorrow."

As they stepped to the street level, John sighed. "It's still here."

Hemplewhite softly nudged her elbow into his. "We

were lucky. No bombers tonight. Which means we must be down in the hole before dark tomorrow."

"They bomb at night? Why? How do they see?"

Hannah placed her hand on John's elbow. She pointed down the street. "Do you see the dog sniffing at the rubble in the next block?"

"The white one? Yes. But he's white and the starlight..." He glanced over at the wagging heads. "What am I missing?"

Hemplewhite stepped behind him, grabbing his shoulders. She lined him up and then laid her arm on his shoulder. Her finger extended—pointing. "Beside the white dog, it is on the left. The heap of deep brown."

Suddenly, the heap backed up, and the dog turned to see what the white was doing.

"Oh."

Hannah and Freckles continued walking. "When the entire city is burning, you will notice the fire brigades working feverishly to extinguish every fire until it stops smoking. In the moonlight, the smoke is the white dog. Yet, they are aware of the brown one, along with the black and brown setter, being there too. So they bomb the Hades out of the entire neighborhood."

Hemplewhite swung her arm to the left. "Only a few blocks over this way was the machining factory. They produced engine parts for farming tractors and such. With the war, they switched to crafting parts for the Merlin airplanes."

"Now, what do they do?"

Hannah stopped. "The tunnel we were in tonight continues under the old factory. They moved the factory's remnants underground three years ago. You re-wrapped a man's left leg tonight. Two weeks ago, I pulled a small shard of an engine's crankshaft out of his leg. They brought him to me at the hospital. He and his wife live next stop down the tunnel. Bessy is a grand cook and makes soup out of everything the boys can bring her. Her pride and joy is her large pot. You could cook shrimp gumbo for half of Mardi Gras. It's all she has left of their flat."

He frowned. "For three years, they've endured such squalor?"

Freckles nodded as Hannah and Hemplewhite glared. "Your squalor is another man's home. Where are you sleeping tonight?"

The man stopped. His eyes grew round. "I don't know. I thought I was catching a taxi back to the base, but then someone shanghaied me, got me drunk, and then hauled me into the underworld."

Hemplewhite rocked stoically with her acknowledgment. "You have two options before it all starts again in four hours." She waved back down the street toward the underground entrance. "You can go back, and hope Bessy finds you a delightful spot on the platform to sleep. Or you can sleep in the hospital's morgue on a table. Your choice. Squalor, or with the dead." She continued to walk.

Hannah passed the stunned man. "It's a lot to take in on

your first day. But now you can try to understand how those people felt the day their world was torn apart. Only because they lived close to a white dog in the night."

❧

HANNAH SLAPPED the switch—one she'd never used during her career in the surgical ward. The lights were always on.

Freckles bumped into her back and looked over her shoulder.

"Hey, respect for the dead. Turn the light off."

Hemplewhite braced on the other side. "Do all Yanks look that dead when they're dead?"

Hannah shrugged. "I don't know. Our cadavers never looked this bad. And before college, Leatha cooked the remains after the lessons."

"When did you start surgeries?"

Hannah smiled at the older woman. "I think I was eight or ten when we started on suckling pigs. Usually kidneys, livers, spleens, or hearts. It all ended up in the kidney pies. But the roast pig was Sunday's dinner."

Hemplewhite slid past Hannah and started undressing. "Why Sunday? Why not Wednesday?"

"The middle of the week, it would have been rare for my father to entertain a gentleman caller. But on Sunday, the theater didn't have shows, so we took in the scenery instead. Usually, it was all understudies."

Freckles kicked the polished boot as she walked past.

"Tell us more, my dear Portia, about these gentleman callers."

"I will not bow to your titillation, now or on the eve of midsummer. Your direction doth lean toward nothing but nasty. And dallies from the mean labor at hand."

The cadaver groaned. "Your pentameter bounces horridly. Time for more bowels and guts?" The zombie rolled forward. "I need coffee and I'll be right as rain."

Hannah pushed his head. "First up is only an inflamed appendix. We don't get to your specialty until the second round. The tainted water awaits in the other room."

The three watched him focus on each step as he stumbled through the door.

Freckles snickered. "You're evil, Cherie. It will take him at least ten minutes to realize he's in the hall."

Hannah smiled. "Where Nurse Hemplewhite can have her way with him."

The older matron rolled her eyes as she walked past them. "He's going to learn, or retreat to America. Either way, he will be a better man for his brief time here."

Hannah sighed. "Be gentle. Show him the coffee and some toast. I want his strong back for the leg. The young man isn't going home with both, I'm afraid."

The day flew by, and with only seven surgeries, it came to an early end.

Nurse Hemplewhite pushed open the door to the changing room. "Captain Adams? Do you know a sergeant by the name of Magpie?"

The surgeon smiled, slapped his hands together, and rubbed them vigorously. "Excellent. Where is he?"

"At my station. He doesn't look the sort I would trust back here."

He stopped beside Nurse Hemplewhite and raised his eyebrows. "But he is exactly the man you can trust in the hole tonight." John stepped through the door. "Magpie. Glad you could find me. Show me what you have."

The three stood in the surgery doorway, watching the two Yanks walking hip and hip. The officer's arm lay draped over the sergeant's shoulder like a younger brother.

Ten minutes later, the officer returned. "Who's ready for a quick beer and trencher of fish and chips?"

Hannah pointed toward the front door.

John waved his hand in dismissal. "He's a Mormon. He doesn't drink, and his dinner will wait back at the base. Just as soon as he unloads the truck at the hole."

Hannah's eyebrow rose. "And just what's he putting in the hole?"

"A few things we need. A few others are nice to have, and a few more for those who probably didn't get a visit from Santa last Christmas. What is it you Brits typically remark about Americans? That we're oversexed, overpaid, and over here?"

Hannah hummed in agreement.

"I have been faithful to my high school sweetheart for twenty-three years and will remain so. I married the daughter of the town's richest man. Which isn't really saying much, but it's enough. I'm an Army captain. My salary's mine to manage. And, well, I'm over here. So, dinner is on me."

Freckles patted his chest as she squeezed by. "So right you are."

The captain paired off with Hannah as they cleared the front portico. "Now, about those gentleman callers of your father's…"

24

OVER HERE

My dearest Mother,

The countryside's flooding of American soldiers is now explained. If the Picayune mirrors the London Times, its coverage of the Normandy invasion dominates the first eight pages.

Our on-loan surgeon, John Adams, has proven to be a skilled surgeon. It's a pity. As he also has an affable bedside manner with the children living underground, he will someday make a respectable father. His sign language is coming along. Where, at first, he sought to talk to the mute boy, he tuned into the language of all the underground children. I hope one day the boy's acceptance spurs him to overcome his trauma and, once again, make noises. Until such a day, we will continue to help those trying to survive this war, one day at a time.

Mickey continues to stretch his luck and skill as a pilot. He brought me a photograph of him standing next to his Lysander. I now understand why he calls it the Garden House.

The entire cockpit, including the walls and roof, is made of glass, allowing him to see everything. I don't know if his ability to see everything is reassuring, or if the glass scares me more. I only know I sleep better when he is home. And I wish someone would hurry and deliver a private bomb to the ugly little man in Berlin.

Meanwhile, the hospital is overflowing with voices sounding much like home. Many nights, I am asked to spend a moment interpreting the American Southern drawl into English. At first, I thought the nurses were pulling my leg. Yet, there was a soldier in the ward I had worked on just two days prior. I'm afraid that when he returns to his family's shrimp boat in Shreveport, they will have to find a job he can do from a wheelchair. I ended up spending half the evening with him. Mama, he is only nineteen. This war is breaking my heart. In surgery, we only see them as the surgery or the body part. But in the ward, I can hear the bayou noises, and the Spanish moss hangs from his every word.

Normandy's beaches made up the solitary action of war for many young men in the wards today. Several brave young women from the underground climbed the hill. They have taken pen in hand and written home for the boys who cannot. Some just need someone to sit and listen to them talk about home. Others still, we just see them sitting quietly, holding a hand. As Daddy would have noted, it is the proximity of care that is the superior anesthesia. Pain suppression or not, it calms them to feel another hand on theirs. And the healing flows both ways. We see some of the young ladies returning and bringing their friends with them. I believe these broken boys will offer much-needed healing for the tunnels, in addi-tion to our medical efforts.

Well, I just heard a Civil Defense blackout warden's whis-tle. So I must trim my wick for now. We are expecting another invasion from France in the morning. They will have brought them across tonight in the dark.

Give my sister a big hug, and look after each other.

With all my love,

Cherie.

As Freckles mopped the surgery area, she leaned closer to Hannah. "We missed Easter."

Hannah peeked at the nurse, then shifted her gaze to the American physician. "Ham was unavailable at the market. And the Americans have become very stingy with their canned pork. Alternatively, we could dress up some potatoes as a ham substitute for the celebration."

"You're being obstinate."

John leaned closer over the exposed guts of the young flyer. His voice was low and studied. "I believe she's refer-ring to a weekend of skulduggery in the under bowels of a certain church in So Ho?"

Hannah's hand and scalpel froze.

The man looked up. "Oh, please. You thought Hack could keep a secret, and that you wouldn't invite me to join the fun? Supplies might be scarce around here. But with a word to the right person, and a quick invite to share some fun—I bet I know someone who'll happily fill a truck heading south. This orderly isn't gentle, but he's physically strong."

Hannah leaned forward and pointed to an area she needed to be mopped. Freckles' hand followed the pointing finger as it returned to cutting away the shredded abdominal wall. "Can he keep a secret?" She peered into the man's eyes. "And I do mean better than Hack. If the authorities found out, they would send us all packing."

"Which authorities? Ours or yours?"

Hannah held his gaze. "Yes."

John thought. "The man's nickname is Magpie. He... um... collects things that are needed. And evidently, no one has caught him yet. His plan for after the war is to retire. He's been in the Army since 1927. The enterprising sergeant is still young enough to make use of the occasional jeeps and trucks he drove home on leave." His eyes rose and twinkled over his mask. "But he consistently used the city bus for his return trip."

"Clamp." Hannah pulled up the curved needle and cotton thread.

"Cotton instead of the silk?"

Hannah glanced up with a smile hiding behind her mask. "Oui, Papa. The cotton will be more forgiving as his digestion returns to normal. A larger meal won't bind him up. We want him comfortable, so he eventually returns to the air where he belongs."

The American nodded. "Good call."

"I've been making the right call about guts since my

practice surgeries at age ten. But then, we usually enjoyed a meal of roast pig or jambalaya, leaving no evidence."

John's head snapped up from his stitching. "Do English people eat jambalaya?"

Hannah sighed. "I wish. I have tasted none such heaven on earth like these last fifteen years."

"But you're English... Where did you grow up?"

"Aside from a few years spent in Black Water, Louisiana, mostly in the Garden District of New Orleans. My older mother was a Voodoo Queen and cooked anything Cajun. Gator tail to beef, shrimp to the hind quarter of a hog. Thankfully, she drew her line at hooves and brains." Her eyes crinkled over the top of her mask at his stretched mask that she knew hid a gaping mouth of a question. "You just never asked before, Yank."

"Touché. And about the coming weekend?"

"I'll draw up a list of supplies."

His eyes twinkled in the light. "Or you can simply review the list Nurse Hemplewhite was so kind to draw up last week."

Hannah and Freckles both chuckled. "Well met, D'Artagnan."

The Pig and Duck's noise forced them into the back room. Freckles whistled. With her four fingers held high, she indicated the order and the backroom. She didn't wait for the man to nod. The telling of the tale was something she didn't want to miss any bit of.

"New Orleans?"

Freckles and Hemplewhite laughed. "Cheeky bastard.

She doesn't even have time to take the first sip of her beer before he's making demands of her."

Hannah turned, snickering. "You should try dating one. It's not a handshake or peck on the lips they be wanting on the front stoop."

John recoiled with a shocked expression. "I never. I was always a perfect gentleman. Besides, that's what the Model A is for on the third date."

Hannah leaned back as Mac and Penny set down the trenchers and beers. "The prosecution rests." Grabbing her mug, she lifted. "Here's to skulduggery by the light of a gibbous moon."

John put down his mug, wiped his lip, and closed his eyes. "All that I have to say is my lantern be the moon. I be the man in the moon, this thornbush, is my thornbush, and the dog doth be my dog."

Hannah smiled. "Close enough, my dear Puck. School play?"

"High School... which would be your second form, I believe."

Hannah shook her head as she pointed at Hemplewhite and Freckles. "Their second form. My first true classes were at Tulane. On my entrance exams, I scored high enough to start as a second-year student. But quickly found I could have taught both my Latin and German classes. I began reading my father's medical textbooks when I was eight or ten. For my fourteenth birthday, we went shopping for more. But Tulane was helpful. They supplied the list of required medical texts and readings for my studies. My father bought every book on the list and had more book-shelves built."

John rolled his head to look at Hemplewhite. "Which you had finished reading by the time you were eighteen. And ready to sit their entrance exams."

"Seventeen. And yes, I was restless to get on with it all."

He continued to look at Hemplewhite. "And you bought all of this…"

The nurse glared at him out of the side of her eyes. Her head shook gently. "No. This is all news to us. We heard nothing about her growing up with two mothers and a father—the voodoo priestess, a theater waif, or her rogue doctor father." Her hands were signing to Hannah. *Are they all this slow?*

John's head flopped back forward and bobbed. "Yes. And who preferred the company of men." His hands responded. *Yes. Slow. I'm a…* He squinted at Hannah.

Hannah laced her fingers together and made a small circle with her two hands. "It's the split-rail fence of Lincoln."

"Ah. That explains it. He was the Prairie State. I'm a Buckeye. It might even explain why I became a surgeon."

Hannah's mouth pulled back as she remembered learning about each state. "Because they consider the state to be the heart of it all. But now I believe the center of the country has moved west some."

John chuckled with a nod as he picked up more chips. "After all this." He waved the chips about in the air. "Have you thought about going back?"

The other women watched Hannah, both with their own concerns. "Maybe to visit. However, there will always be a requirement for certain doctors here. She glanced at Hemplewhite. Besides that, Mickey and I discussed a small cottage near the ocean, either Cardiff or Bristol. Probably raise a couple of wild hooligans of our own."

Hemplewhite frowned and tilted her head. "But..."

Hannah placed her left hand atop the woman's. "Yes. And I have known for years that I can't either." She turned back to John. "So, whatever we do, it will be through adoption. Finding two or three won't be difficult. Many have perished in this war, irrespective of their origin."

He started to sign, but gave up. "Well, if you get to shop for what you want, you can always opt for the quieter of the crowd." He made the sign for deaf and mute. "I wrote my Midge about the mute boy in the tunnels, and about the signing. She reminded me about the Christmas pageant we attended upstate. The actors were from a deaf college in Washington, D.C."

Hannah tipped her head as she took a bite of the fish. "Gallaudet?"

John poked his nose as he chewed.

Hannah smiled. "One of the greatest things President Lincoln ever did. He signed the charter for the original funding. What was the performance?"

He held up two fingers as he swallowed. "The first was the poem *Twas the Night Before Christmas*. But the actors were children from a deaf orphanage there in Toledo. The chorus was composed of deaf students from Gallaudet. The speakers... Well, if they hadn't introduced them at the end, we would have never known they were deaf."

Freckles wiped her hands of the grease from the food. "What was the other performance?"

The man smiled. "None other than the best from your Dickens. *A Christmas Carol.*"

Hannah smiled. "Oh, yes. Much better than Macbeth or killing Caesar."

Hemplewhite raised the last swig of her beer. "Hear, hear. And we're off," as she nodded toward Penny standing in the doorway.

25
SANCTUARY

Magpie tilted up the hand truck with the six boxes. Swiping the hat from his piebald head, he turned to the priest in the black cassock. "This is the last of them, Father. Is the truck good parked in the alley, or do I need to stash it somewhere else?"

Joe noted the man's genuine concern. "Years back, at the outset, I would've expected police scrutiny of a strange truck in the mews. But now, if it's not bombed out or burned, it must be working. I think they will probably ask upstairs if they have any actual concerns. But you're staying?"

The balding man smirked as he licked his lips with the tip of his tongue. "Judging by your setup, an extra pair of hands is something you need. I have a truck, so procuring necessities won't be a problem. Now, where should I start?"

Hannah grabbed onto the man's shoulder as she walked past. "Bring your items here; we'll combine them with existing supplies. You're going to be the dispensary. The women will know what they need. They will come to you.

Can you keep track of what you dispense and what we have left? Then we'll know our future requirements."

He smiled and tapped his head. "I already know what everything is. Once we finish, I will have everything written down for you so we can review the hospital-related details. I saw the three autoclaves. One of them needs some serious work. You have a bad electrical cord. If you can do without it, don't use it. I'll take it back to the base and get it rebuilt. Perhaps it will attract some of its siblings to follow when I return."

"I think the good father would say the man upstairs sent you. Me? I'm just thankful you and John are friends. Do you have a real name? We use nicknames, but it is also good to know who we are sharing our bread or burden with."

He smiled. "The men mostly call me Mag. The ladies call me Pie. Only my mother called me Sweetness. And as for any other name, it's probably best we stick to the names we know. Eh, Cherie? Or was it, Jack?"

"Jack works just fine. Now, if you'll excuse me, I'll see you in a couple of days." She slid past him.

"Aren't you staying?"

She pointed up the hallway. "We will be up this hall. No one may enter. For your own well-being, don't even set foot beyond the archway. We'll see you Sunday night."

Hemplewhite turned, and they walked down the other hallway together.

John held the young man's jaw as he injected the novocaine. "This will take a few minutes to numb the jaw, but when your lower lip feels like rubber and you can't talk right, you won't feel him pull your tooth."

The young man smiled. "Eh. I see ya already nicked some of your own medicine."

John shook his head. "Nah. I've been talking like this since the family cow kicked me in the head."

The young dentist, they called Nod, stopped at John's shoulder. "I could have saved you the shot. 'E's losing five teeth today." He held up the cup holding the chloroform.

"Hmm. I thought I smelled something familiar. Why not something like Pentobarbital?"

"Hard to get right now. This is cheap, easy to get, and they don't walk out of here with a hangover. I got it from the veterinarian down the block. A liter will last us well past Saint Crispen's Day." He pointed at the other room. "I think Steven was asking about you. I think he's got a patient holding a light."

The Yank nodded. "I'll leave you to the teeth."

Father Joseph set the tray of food and coffee on the box in the middle of the hall's archway. The woman, wearing white cotton mittens, bowed gently and, picking up the tray, stepped into the room. Crossing the hall, she stepped into another room. "Father Joseph has brought your meal."

Hemplewhite nodded as she continued to blot the skin around where Hannah was cutting away the dead flesh. They knew that by Saint Crispen's Day, the woman would likely have to have her last two fingers removed. It wasn't a battle, and it wasn't a war. It was a long, slow slog as the person's whole being disappeared. Wet Leprosy was the saddest of all medical conditions, and was practiced by the fewest practitioners.

The trio of Wynken, Blynken, and Nod fell into the three chairs like falling dominoes: plop, plop, and a deep sigh. Winkum studied the sandwich in his hand. "I never thought I would say that working in practice for ten hours would ever feel like a holiday at the beach somewhere."

"Or that a sandwich made from questionable canned meat could taste like heaven."

Magpie leaned over the young Nod. "Shoulder and ham. They process the larger meats on uglier pigs that nobody would buy at a butcher shop. My brother sells his old sows who have stopped throwing litters, and the piglets who don't put on hearty weight. At six months of age, everything goes to market to make room for the next batch of money ready to drop."

Blynken bobbed his head as he pointed at the older, balding man. "Me pops said the same. He wound up mixed in with a Yank company during the Great War. The Wadies wouldn't touch it because it was a pig. So only the Yanks and pops ate the canned meat."

Freckles and Steven frowned. "Wadies?"

Blynken pecked his head as he chewed. Swallowing, he cleared his mouth with tea. "He was in Persia with the French Foreign Legion until his platoon, or whatever they called them, got blown up. He got attached to a Yank group that was fighting alongside the Arab Revolt against the Ottomans. They called them Wadies, same as the gullies in the desert. Them and their camels could smell water from a two-day ride. If it stood well, it was an oasis. At worst, it was the leftovers of a rainstorm. But it was water."

Chewing and sipping greeted his revelation. The silence took hold as the tableau ate in silence. They all knew the next round of surgeries would follow this brief rest.

In the early lifting of the morning's gray, Hannah heard the distinct double click of the door from Hemplewhite's flat to hers. It only took Mickey seconds to become naked, but to Hannah, it felt more like hours. "The alarm rings in twenty minutes."

Mickey slid into bed. "I turned it off. I have it from the highest authority that the first surgery won't happen prior to ten... or when Mother decides to go to the hospital. So go back to sleep."

Hannah rolled over, and Mickey snuggled behind her. It wasn't like she was much smaller, but the two spoons fit on the bed better. The two sighs turned to muted breathing as the first starling left the eaves in search of morning tea.

A soft tap sounded at the connecting door.

"Yes?"

"Freckles just gave notice. Tea in ten minutes."

"Thank you, mum."

"Good to have you home."

Mickey found the soft part of the neck just behind the ear.

The voice muffled through the pillow. "I heard. Go ahead. I'll wait until the water is warm."

He snickered into her shoulder. "You're still dreaming of

your mother's home in New Orleans. There's a war on, so even the king's flat in Buckingham is a cold-water flat."

Hannah sighed and threw the covers back off them both. "And you Brits call yourselves the superior culture. Even the Romans in three twenty-four had hot-water baths." She straddled his legs and rushed to the bathroom.

He watched the retreating legs and buttocks. "Well, at least we have our own plumbing and don't have to run down the hall anymore." He listened for the first *hoot* as she stepped into the spray. It wasn't a true cold-water flat, but it also wasn't a hot-water flat, either.

"I expected your return last night."

Mickey, having given in to her freer ways about human anatomy and works, sat on the toilet while he waited for his turn in the tiny, curtained stall. "I didn't go to Normandy. At the risk of giving away secrets, I flew into an area just south of Denmark."

The curtain bent back. The white cloth framed Hannah's scowl. "Were you flying a bomber?"

He hung his head. "Those will come soon enough. The reception sounded more like Russian or Polish."

"Are they that close?"

"I only fly where they tell me. But the Americans are pushing across France. I suspect they intend to liberate Paris this summer."

She turned the water off. Mickey stood holding the towel for her. "Well, we're aware the little bastard is facing a shortage of pilots and bombers. I would say thankfully, but those buzz bombs he's shooting at us now are scary and worse. Though swift, the Hurricanes cannot shoot down those rockets. Our boys need to adjust their bombing and find his rat hole."

Mickey kissed her forehead as he stepped into the tub and then pulled the curtain. "Like most cowards, he's hiding in the residential neighborhoods. Our Churchill, known for his bulldog-like toughness, refuses to bomb innocent women and children, despite years of ours being bombed by them."

The tap squealed as Mickey turned on the water. "Oh, bloody hell."

Hannah smiled and nodded as she hung the towel and stepped into the bedroom.

26

END OF SUMMER IS NO
RELIEF

Dearest Mother,

Summer seems to have battered its last warmth here in London. Muggy as Black Water was, it was better than London, with those buzz bomb messages from the ogre in Berlin. Watching the sky always looms over thoughts of a leisure picnic on the sunny grasslands of the Heath.

Although we look forward to the rain, it is only to wash the stone dust from the streets and buildings. The black creosote from the burning of the bombed buildings turns the dust into a plaster-like substance that sticks to even the smallest trees or flowers. The owner of our building used to wash the Cornwall stone front step. He has given up, and we now call the dingy gray Berlin granite.

The other night, Mickey took us on a brief journey. He was quite mysterious, as he wouldn't tell us where we were going. We spied a young couple standing quietly on the sidewalk. As we approached, we saw what they had spotted. A small rose bush sprouted from a cracked wall, a remnant of a former garden. The sunset illuminated the peace rose, its yellow, pink, and white hues glowing as if from an inner light. No words were needed as we all wiped away tears, standing and admiring this magical growth.

Departing, the neighbor, with the window open, reported that they had been continuously gawking at the magical flower since Thursday. If Mickey had dragged us to the upper reaches of Hampton Heath, it would have seemed no less remarkable. We slept soundly that night.

Our Yank surgeon, John, mentioned an orphanage in Toledo, Ohio, for deaf children last summer. They put on plays each year with the students from Gallaudet College in Washington, D.C. The orphans act in the play, while the college students vocalize as a chorus. The idea has lingered in my thoughts. Once this nasty war ends, I want to take a train trip to see the troupe. John and his wife had seen A Christmas Carol in the winter, but they also performed Midsummer Night's Dream—our favorite of Willie's plays.

Tomorrow will be an auspicious day if I'm quoting Leatha correctly. It will be thirteen years since I graduated from medical school. This Christmas, I will cook a pig, of whatever sort I can find, to celebrate my eviction from my childhood home—Father's decision set in motion my hardest endeavors, but with the most rewards. The best reward will come when this war is finally over. Mickey and I aren't superstitious, but we both will feel more comfortable getting married when our lives are done with dodging flak and bombs. We're still talking about a small village in the south of Cornwall. Sufficiently large to require a surgeon, a convenient airport for Mickey, and London theater easily accessible by train. Mickey believes Hemplewhite's Bristol home is too small to house the three of us. But he does entertain the idea of another cottage nearby for us.

Surgery is in six hours. I will post this in the morning.

With all my love,

Cherie

My Love Cherie,

I received your letter just before supper. Your sister sends her love. I read it over our Thanksgiving meal to acquaint our new doctor with the other woman in our family. We decided a woman would nicely round out the household, as our medical duties primarily involve women's health issues these days. Her name couldn't be any more afield from the pursuits and humors of our household. Our third-floor resident is none other than Miss Chastity Feelgood, MD, from Loving, New Mexico.

She may have struggled to secure a scholarship to a small Christian college for women, but she won support from donors to grant her a scholarship to continue her studies in medicine. Your father would have approved, as she knew her benefactors believed she would pursue the womanly art of nursing. But she studied hard and prevailed on their hearts to support her in her pursuit of becoming a female doctor at Tulane. There, she heard tales of heroism leading her to investigate the renowned Dr. Humphrey. So here she is.

She had also heard quiet talk about Leatha's voodoo, and was sad she was too late. I've introduced her to some shops near the French Quarter; they'll further her training. It appears that one of her grandmothers is a Navajo medicine woman who taught her the traditional American Indian ways of healing with plants and stones. We face a new language learning challenge beyond Navajo; Plains Indians use a unique sign language. Additionally, she hasn't attended a play before, but is eager to join us as the season begins.

All our love,

Mother

"So she's a Navajo Indian?"

Hanna glanced into the sparkling green eyes of her nurse, friend, and confidant. "From mother's letter, I am led to believe her grandmother was. However, she made no mention of her grandfather's lineage or her parents. So, if my math is correct, she could be anywhere from one-eighth Navajo to full-blooded. Is that a problem?"

Freckles mopped at the incision as Hannah held the retractor and clamp back to one side. "Problem? Certainly not. You have a mother who chases young men for pleasure. She grew up... um, shall we say, less than a puritan. Your sister, who is from the other side of the street, and is of a darker persuasion..."

"Because she practices voodoo?"

Freckles frowned. "I thought your mother did that. Wait. Who takes care of the front door?"

Hannah peeked at the top of the man's cap at the head of the table. "Andy?"

The anesthesiologist glanced up. "His respiration is seventy-two." His eyes and brow rose as he understood what was being asked of him. "You'll have to excuse me. I'm rather new to all this other talk. I've only been here since Hitler bombed my other hospital with the second wave of bombings in forty. So I might be lost as well. But I've been under the assumption that the front door was for your white folk, and your father ministered to them as well as your mother. But I can't remember if she's a doctor, a nurse, or just your mother. Then there is a sister. And if I remember right, she received a nursing degree from somewhere other than Twin Lanes. But now there's a new doctor who sounds like she's a puritan. So, I'm assuming she's also taking care of the front door while there is a colored person in the kitchen stirring up the voodoo soup. But I don't remember who that exactly is."

Hannah's eyes twinkled back at Freckles. "He only pays attention to half of our discussions and hasn't read the letters at all. And he has it mostly right." She glanced at the anesthesiologist. "But the college is called Tulane. Not... oh, never mind. Two more stitches here, and you can begin to let him come back to us." Her hands worked the needle and gut.

Hannah glanced up at the door opening. Hemplewhite's face and hand peeked from behind the second swinging door. "Hannah?"

"Just in time, Nurse Hemplewhite. I have eight external

stitches left, and this appendix is finished. His time in the gray world of gas is coming to an end. Is the gallbladder down and prepped?" Her hand drew the last internal knot closed and snipped the gut.

"Hannah?"

She looked up. The face hadn't changed. Yet, the hand clutching the door's edge shook ever so slightly, despite the tight grip on the wood, causing white knuckles.

"Hemplewhite?"

"We need to see you. Please. I need you."

Hannah glanced at Freckles, who was already tossing her head toward the door. "I'll finish the stitching and plaster here. You go along now."

As Hannah pulled the bloody smock from her body, she felt a wave of weariness wash over her. She knew she needed to hurry, but something held her back. Dropping the smock by the door, she paused for a moment, wiping the mask and cap from her head with a conflicted sigh before letting them fall onto the smock. Pushing through the door, she couldn't shake the feeling she was leaving something vital behind.

The slender man, holding his hat, stood silent with Hemplewhite. She had seen him before, but she had never met him. Only a few times had she seen him talk to Mickey at the Pig and Duck.

"Hannah, this is Max Chasewell. He was Mickey's... they were comrades in arms."

He swung his hand forward with an open palm. "I was

his Special Operations officer with MI6, military intelligence abroad."

Hannah ignored the hand and glared at Hemplewhite, who stood biting into her lower lip with a sharp intensity. Hannah's fiery eyes locked back onto the man. "You speak as if he's gone. Yet, you stand here before me."

Hemplewhite reached out and placed her hand on Hannah's shoulder. "Hannah..."

The man's voice was quiet. "Yes, mum. Mickey was returning from the treacherous northern border of Germany and Denmark, charting a course he'd never flown before. Instead of safely entering our northern airspace, he headed directly toward London. We can only assume he was running low on fuel. Skimming perilously low over the water, he was maneuvering past the Maunsell Sea Forts before aiming for the mouth of the Thames."

Hannah's hands flew to her mouth, half-open in shock. "Did they shoot him?"

"No, ma'am. Those forts only have massive cannons to repel ships. But a squadron of Hurricanes shields them. The pilot must have mistakenly believed he was launching an assault on the fortifications."

Her voice was a mere whisper, heavy with disbelief. "He was in a fucking glass cage with delicate wings, for God's sake. How could he threaten anything more than a seagull?"

Hemplewhite wrapped herself tightly around Hannah's shoulders, her voice a gentle balm. "This man isn't to blame. No one is. The fighter pilot probably realized his mistake the instant his finger squeezed the trigger."

Hannah's head swung in horror, her voice escalating into a piercing wail. "He was your son, for God's sake. How can you..."

Hemplewhite's voice snapped back with meat. "Because I have no choice." She calmed. "Mickey and I talked about this possibility many times over the years..." She embraced Hannah more fully as they both trembled and wept, their grief entwined.

The spy master stood helpless, a void opening within him. He had lost a friend, but no arms reached out to console him. His dried tongue dragged along his dry lips as he turned away. Placing his fedora back on his head, he lurched down the hallway toward the hospital's front, each step heavy with the weight of solitude.

27

BRISTOL

My dearest Mother, sister, and Doctor,

These days, I feel estranged from my own life. Without Hemplewhite, Freckles, and Steven, I doubt I'd have reached Easter. During surgery, there were moments when a sense of ennui would overcome me, especially with young flyers. My light for surgery, medicine, or even continuing of any kind seemed senseless. I could stitch the young man back together. He would rehabilitate for what? For what purpose should he re-board his aircraft? Just to be another target? Another fiery ball in the sky, plunging to earth, to cause even more death and destruction? Where was the use? What happened to the idea of repairing people so they can go forth and live long and fruitful lives? Ubi est medium aureum? I needed to know I was striking, at least near some kind of balance. The only time I felt assured that the recipient of my care wouldn't return to the circus was during an amputation or when I couldn't save them.

The tremors began sometime around February. We were

laboring on the wet leprosy when Hemplewhite first noticed my hands. I had to take the last two fingers of a woman I had previously treated. I knew she would be entirely at the mercy of her daughter's care. The child was only recently reaching her maturity and had already lost her left foot. I'm sure her right foot won't survive the year.

Freckles first noticed my tremor in March. It wasn't right for her to finish the removal of the man's kidney, but she would have made Father proud. The three of us talked long into the night. All in English, but the sword of Damocles was no less present. Even Hemplewhite confessed to her failings: that to avoid the operatory, she buried herself in the department's paperwork. The war's duration weakened all of us; Mickey's death was just the ultimate blow.

As Steven lived most nights in our collective, he eventually returned home. He gave up his northern affectations and small, shared apartment. He will be a better man for it all.

That Thursday, there was a long discussion over less than a pint of beer about them putting off their nuptials. To avoid the wedding seeming like a men's club party. Penny and Mac included Father Joseph and several female patrons in the bouquet toss——all in memory of Mickey. That Friday night, on our way to SoHo, they became a duo. Hemplewhite and I fittingly also ended our SoHo run that last weekend. It seemed fitting.

Over the years, we worked to train several in the leper community to care for their own. They best understand the inherent risks. And other than a crazy Yank, the system wasn't coming to their aid before the paupers' field. And sadly, for the wet lepers, even that field is off limits. I hear they cremate many of them in backyards or industrial furnaces while they make steel for the war effort.

As a going-away present, the Yank surgeon, John, and his friend Magpie borrowed a truck from the air base to move us down to Bristol. We had little, but Father Joseph donated two of the leather smoking chairs we used to sleep in between surgeries in SoHo. As Hemplewhite already had a Queen Anne chair that she has always been sweet on, she calls the leather pair Mickey's and my chairs. I think the worn, soft leather reminds us both of his flight jacket. And I find comfort between them.

If you are looking at a map of Bristol, think of the island of England as the mirror image of the state of Louisiana. We took that Pierce Arrow out to a place called Grand Isle for my sixteenth birthday. Although England doesn't have the bayous, it abounds with beautiful blue waters, as well as coastal gardens and farms.

Near our cottage, the city let locals use part of Perret's Park for victory gardens. Mother, the victory garden is larger than the entire French Quarter. Many tack their ration cards to boards around the city because they have little need for the items they trade vegetables for. As we provide a wee bit of medical help to the community, we find a most embarrassing amount of food sitting on our stoop when we return. I think they never bring the stores to our hands, because they know we would kindly refuse. Occasionally, it's challenging to find someone in need nearby, so we have pinpointed a few locations that could benefit. Heaven help us as the summer takes hold, and the harvests of summer foods begin. I have learned to love cabbage soup, baked cabbage, sauerkraut, fried cabbage, and bangers, as well as cabbage with cabbage.

Here, war news is scarce; sometimes days elapse without considering the world's suffering. However, newspapers arrive occasionally, and these remind us of the world's situation beyond Bristol. From the BBC and last week's London Times, Paris is secure, and the Yanks have finally broken through the hard winter in the Ardennes Forest. Hopefully, the boys can make up for lost time and push their efforts to crush the little cockroach in Berlin this summer.

John, the Yank surgeon, telephoned us the other day. We couldn't talk much, but he hinted that the Russians are rushing across Poland to put pressure on the eastern front. If we were faithful, we would pray for them to make it true. As it is, we toast them with every pint of beer. The local pub isn't the same as the boisterous Pig and Duck, but it suits our quieter nature these days.

Love and hugs to all,

Cherie

My Dearest,

The Christmas news of Mickey's death shattered us. I hid in the third-floor garret for weeks. Chastity brought me soup and stew, which I know your sister had laced with some of the voodoo they had found in the city. The Otis acquired a small shelf in one corner, which they had conspired to glue to the walls. We have since engaged the company to add a few more, as we deemed necessary. The remedy of the day sits on the lower shelves, but the top shelf is the home of the happy voodoo doll that cajoled me to quit my solitude.

I have taken over the top floor, as I enjoy afternoon naps in my senior years. And don't you dare tell Winnie, your sister, my true age. My hair is silvering nicely if I do say so myself. Even younger gentlemen give up their seats on the trolley. However, I miss them giving up some time as well. My time has become bits and pieces of filling sheets of paper with poetry. Not to worry, I haven't even let the girls read any of my chicken scratches. These are just for me. Mostly thoughts of the past, but also upon bits and pieces of my day-to-day, I see on the trolley or around the city.

Your letter arrived with the morning delivery of the Picayune, screaming about the Russians standing at the eastern gates of Berlin. I genuinely hope this is the end of it all. And hopefully, the emperor across the other water reads the handwriting on the wall and joins in. Every mother can tell you that every country needs rest. I require several non-olive drab, non-black dresses; dying fabric with lamp black and octopus ink is unacceptable.

Bristol sounds wonderful. To get fresh summer fruits and vegetables again. It has been a long and harsh winter.

I look forward to cucumbers and sweet melons. The man at the market keeps squeezing lemon juice on his slices of cabbage and telling me the sweet lettuce and paw-paw fruit are right around the corner. And I know that corner's far down a long block.

If it wasn't for my deathly fear of the water, if the war really ends, I might be persuaded to take an ocean cruise to a magical seaside town of Bristol. However, I'm not holding out any hope that such an event will ever happen. And with that thought, I will seal this missive with all my heart and post it tomorrow. We don't have Civil Defense wardens to warn us, but I can read the clock that is telling me it is already morning.

 Love,
  Mother

Dear Cherie,

 I couldn't catch the postman to add this in the last letter. The Picayune headline screamed BERLIN FALLS at the top of its front page. The desired news emerged only at week's end. To avoid trial and hanging, the ugly little man and his companion committed suicide.

 To celebrate, I bought a watermelon at the store. They are growing them in Mississippi, across the river from Black Water. Leave it to your sister, Edwina, to know these things. It tasted like summer.

 All our warmest love,
  Winnie, Chastity, and Mother

THE LATE-SUMMER SUN drew out the crowds to the harvest market. Vegetable bounty enhanced the summer's peace. A warm, late-summer sun caused even the staunchest of the stiff Bristolian upper lips to smile. Soft, kind greetings met the two spinsters, known for lending their medical knowledge to the well-being of the small community. Soft braided baskets, woven from rags and worn-out clothing, hung from their arms. A squash purchased here, checking the condition of a plaster there, and always the calm, joyful conversations among friends.

"Oey. Doctor Hannah. I've got some of that marmalade you love so much. Fresh in on my brother's boat from fishing off the west of Spain, he was."

Hannah leaned into the man, holding the two jars of preserves. A conspiratorial smile played on their lips. "And was he smuggling cod to the natives?"

"Aye. The poor sods know nothing about grand tasting fish. But he did bring back a grand load of sardines and some hack." He pointed down the alley. "He's the one on the end. With the bandage on his head. Some husband caught him in the pub last night."

Hannah smiled as she took the jars of preserves. "I'll let Nurse Hemplewhite examine his head whilst I find our dinner. We haven't had a pleasing bake of sardine since last Christmas." She drew back to look over his onions and Jerusalem artichokes. "These chokes are rather grand, Hubert. What have you been feeding them?"

"Now that the vicar is running the sheep on the church grounds again, I've been cleaning the night bedding ground.

It pays to age it a bit, first. But the results are grand. However, if you're baking them, don't peel them; instead, scrub them gently with a soft-bristled brush and slice them up. The missus makes a grand ratatouille from 'em. Thems will go well with the squash you've got."

Hemplewhite laughed softly. "Hubert, everything out of these gardens has been grand this year. Our larder and even under our beds overflow with this year's preserves. We'll require additional Yanks personnel to consume everything."

"No, mum. We want no more Yanks. If they are here, it means we're back at war. And I think we've all had enough of that to last a dozen lifetimes."

Hannah tilted her head. "I lack only delicious melons. Watermelons in particular. The first sweet bite of the red... That is how you start summer."

The man licked the tip of his tongue along his lips. "I'll tell my brother. Maybe he can find something down in Spain. It would probably be a casaba, but it's melon."

Hannah stroked the man's cheek. "You would be a dear for any kind of melon your brother can find. Even if they are horrid, we must just soldier on and eat them to hide the evidence."

28

COME TO VISIT

Dearest Cherie and Hemplewhite,

The 1949 season will soon be upon us. I have confirmed four seats for Midsummer Night's Dream. Performed by the Tyson Orphanage and students from Gallaudet University. I've bought the tickets and reserved the train car, so we'll only accept confirmation that you are on your way.

The Queen Mary has returned to standard trans-Atlantic passenger service, and the proper sums have been deposited with the White Line against your reservations. I have included the receipt for you to make reservations.

Winnie and Chastity have decked out their lodgings in the basement. I don't know why the workmen seemed to work late into the night, and yet were already here at work by the time I rose in the morning. The girls, like I once was, are young. They remind me of Leatha and Walter; with the time they spend in silent communica-tion. Who couldn't have known you would choose one of the next members of our unique family when you were just a school child in Black Water? It seems like a lifetime ago.

So many memories. It will have been forty years since we took you to your first play. You probably already know that playbill's hiding place on the bookshelves. Crucially, which other playbills hide within that same book? Oh, Cherie, the mere thought of you coming home soon gives me vapors, and we'll be off to another play.

I can hear Jonathan downstairs. He has brought us some vegetables from the market. You would remember his father, the vegetable seller, with the pushcart. His son didn't follow in his father's footsteps, but followed his love for our trolley cars. He is a morning driver along St. Charles Street, but occasion- ally brings us a box of produce. I think he might be sweet on Miss Chastity. So I must run along and chaperone.

Love from all of us.

HEMPLEWHITE AND HANNAH stood in the doorway to the tiny cabin. The narrow bed lay along one wall. A short stool braced the small dressing bureau. The bureau lacked legroom for applying makeup. Obviously, no one thought nurses had such concerns. Hannah laid her hand on Hemplewhite's shoulder. "It's only for you. I'm here, across the hall. And it's only for the seven days of the crossing."

Hemplewhite glowered at Hannah. "It lacks a porthole."

Hannah chuckled softly. "To watch the fish swim by? Honey, we're below the waterline. Just because we are fancy medical staff doesn't mean we are above steerage. Here is where the crew lives. If I can go underground to treat people, you can live with being underwater for the week. It's not like we're following in the footsteps of the Titanic. This captain made crossings every week through the war. I think if he knew how to avoid those nasty U-boats, I trust he can avoid something the size of an iceberg."

"But I thought the letter said upper-class accommodations. Or did I misread it?"

"Your reading is accurate; the return trip involves a suite upgrade. Currently, a small stipend compensates us for our usual unpaid underground work. Perhaps medical staff wear stylish uniforms, similar to the purser's."

Hemplewhite tilted her head and glared at the doctor. "I doubt they have a nice-looking uniform in my size. And if they do, it probably matches that horrid greenish uniform dress I had to wear when you first arrived in London."

Hannah batted her eyes at the nurse. "Oh. Do you think they have any of those snappy paper hats you wore?"

"If they do, I'm spending the crossing in the sick ward."

Hannah laughed. "Yes, dear. Right next to me. Now come on, where's my spirit leader?"

"She's looking for a pint of ale at first chance."

Hannah's eyes grew wild, and she leaned her head to touch Hemplewhite's forehead. The whisper was pure skulduggery. "Do you think they have a pub on board?"

"It's a British ship."

Initially, the women's white slacks and officer coats surprised many. Hannah nodded at the first matron with a gaping mouth and muttered in a conspiratorial whisper. "We're still on war rationing. I'm sure they will sort it all out by 1950, and we'll dress in snappy dresses. But for now, this is what we've grown accustomed to. Spit and polish, you see."

The woman leaned back. "Well, I think the White Line made a most avant-garde fashion decision. There are days I wish we women could wear slacks instead of the same old dress." She glanced down. "Do those slacks have pockets?"

She showed her hand in her pants pocket. "Just like Katheryn Hepburn." Hannah thought about the convenience of pockets. "You know, a clever seamstress could secret some pockets in the folds of a dress. They would prove quite handy. Don't you think?"

The woman swayed back slightly. "You know, I like how you think. It's almost wicked, and I'll have to speak to my seamstress just as soon as we get home." She glanced at the others in the foyer. "You're the doctor and nurse, and sitting at the captain's table, are you not?"

"I believe we are."

"Well then, you're to sit next to me. Where are you from? You sound like London."

"I only spent the war years in London. We live in Bristol now. But we're visiting my family in New Orleans, where I grew up. And you?"

"Ohio. My Clarence owns a factory in Akron. He made tires for the war effort. We were just in England to open a new factory in Leeds. This world is growing, and we will all need lots of tires."

"Leeds, you say. I thought that's where the steel plants are." She glanced at Hemplewhite, who shrugged.

"I think you're maybe thinking of Liverpool or Black-pool." She searched for her husband among the crowd waiting to be seated for dinner, then waved her hand in the air. "Oh, never mind. We can ask Clarence at dinner."

The yards of white tablecloths and exquisitely polished silverware reflected in the crystal stemware. The crystal chandeliers cast tiny points of miniature rainbows. And along one wall, the ensemble played softly as the excited patrons found their seats and took their places. The purser guided Hannah and Hemplewhite to the head table, with Ethel and Clarence in tow.

As the captain finished his modest portion of a salad, he laid his fork at the five o'clock and dabbed at his mouth with the yard of white cloth. "So, Doctor Humphry, my purser says you're originally from New Orleans. Is this a visit, or are you returning home?"

"Just a visit, I think. It's been years since I've enjoyed the theater, so we'll be going for the season. In fact, we plan to travel up to near Ethel and Clarence in Ohio this summer to take in a unique play in the Toledo area." She looked at her dinner companion. "It is near Akron, is it not?"

Ethel, caught with a small bite of salad in her mouth, brought her napkin up to cover her quick recovery and swal-low. "Well, it's closer than London. But no, it's a couple of hundred miles from us. But what is the play?"

Hemplewhite smiled from across the table. Her hands wove in the air. "A Midsummer Night's Dream."

The woman's frown mirrored the captain's. "But what

could be unique about one of William Shakespeare's most performed plays?"

Hannah wove her hands in sign language in the air as she explained. "The play's young actors, though silent, communicate via sign language. Students from Gallaudet University, in Washington, D.C., a university for the deaf, vocalize the play as a chorus. All the performers are deaf. So we've been told."

The woman's eyes sparkled with her fascination as she watched Hannah and Hemplewhite's hands. The captain's one eyebrow raised as he waved his hand back and forth. "Please. Continue. Who are the children? Another school for the deaf?"

Hannah shrugged. "School? We're not sure. We only know their origin: a Toledo orphanage. I thought we should stop on our way to New Orleans and scout out the lay of the land, as it were." Her hands never slowed from interpreting in sign language.

Hemplewhite continued in both vocal and sign language. The railway schedule shows a one-day trip from New York to Toledo. We have flexible plans that will let us explore Toledo beyond the orphanage.

Ethel looked at her husband. "Clarence, I want to go. Who do we know in Toledo? Or is there a pleasing hotel there?"

"I lack hotel specifics. However, we were told to consider the Niagara. The American surgeon who told us about the play told us the Niagara is where he stayed with his wife. So we're sure it's safe, if not pleasing."

Hannah suspected Ethel's husband lacked influence beyond his factory, as Ethel's gesture suggested. "Then we'll stay there as well."

The captain cleared his throat. "I can see that you are both quite comfortable with the language. Is this akin to French-to-English interpretation—hearing one language spoken and speaking a different language?"

Hannah hummed as she smiled at Hemplewhite. "Similar, but more like listening to a French Cajun doctor teach in German, and you must interpret it into Latin. Until you get used to it."

"Those are some extremely specific parameters. I'm assuming you have experience in this case?"

Hannah blushed slightly. "You mentioned New Orleans, and so it sparked a memory of growing up in my household. My birth mother brought French and sign language to the house. Because my father was a doctor, he trained in German, as did all scientists. But in medicine, he was also fluent in Latin."

The captain gently put down his butter knife along with the morsel of a dinner roll. "But you also were specific about a French Cajun doctor. Your father?"

"Not at all. He came from plantation stock up the Mississippi, closer to Natchez. My second mother was closer to Cajun and studied to be a doctor of the voodoo persuasion."

"They have doctors?" Ethel's forehead wrinkled in deep concern. She began, "I thought they were..." then paused, considering her words.

Hannah chuckled as she patted the woman's hand. "It's

alright. The doctor part's most accurate. The mistake lies within the witch's role, confusing many. If my mother mixed turmeric, cinnamon, and curry, most people would think she was cooking a dinner dish more common in the subcontinent of India. But if she stirred the spices into a poultice of bees' wax and lard, then applied the plaster to a sprained muscle, is she a cook, witch, or healer?"

The captain's eyebrow raised. "My question would be more of: does it work?"

Hemplewhite nodded. "Ten years ago, I would have said quack. But since Cherie's coming to the hospital, and having to make do during the war, I can tell you wholeheartedly it does. The wax and lard only serve as a carrier; you can replace them with a bandage wrap. However, curry and cinnamon provide a chemical heat that relaxes the muscles, while turmeric is a natural anti-inflammatory. If you didn't know Doctor Humphrey, you would bathe in a tub of hot water and take two aspirins." She shrugged. "Hot baths, a century ago, were met with disbelief. Aspirin's effect would have appeared magical. It's all perspective. I, for one, look forward to learning about more remedies I can grow in our tiny garden."

29

A NEW WORLD

A DOZEN large elm trees adorned the front lawn of the orphanage. The building resembled a large, old stone manor house near London, guarded by two lions. Hemplewhite giggled at the two cats. "Do you want to pet those cute cats?"

Hannah smiled softly, looking at her long-time friend. "I think in my dotage, I would like a large lap cat to keep me sitting and quiet. One, I can read wicked mysteries to."

The front walk leading to the entry splits the large park-like frontage. The two strolled to the middle. A streetlamp and a water fountain sat in the middle of the wide walkway.

Hannah bent and sucked in the chilly water, bubbling freely. The muted slurping remained childish, not womanly. She pursed her lips as she straightened. The blush was slight at the sight of Hemplewhite's raised eyebrow. Hannah patted her lips with the back of her forefinger. "I always wanted to do that."

"Slurp like a horse or drink from a public fountain?"

Hannah narrowed her eyes as she watched the woman on the side as she walked past. "Maybe both."

Hemplewhite snickered once through her nose. "Mickey would have joined you."

Hannah pointed at her. "And then made you join in."

The older woman laughed. "Point." And then she reached out. Stopping Hannah.

"What?"

Hemplewhite nodded toward three children in the shade of a tree. They watched. The two girls were acting parts and speaking in sign language. The boy voiced the play, simultaneously directing it using a script.

Her voice was a mutter. "Which play do you think they are working on?"

Hannah smiled and responded in sign language. "*Midsummer Night's Dream.*"

"*Of course. Do you think the smaller blonde is Puck?*"

"*Maybe if we get closer I'll know by her script.*" Hannah held her palm out.

Hemplewhite stepped onto the grass cautiously. The lawn was dry, but it supported her, so she continued with more grace. Hannah took Hemplewhite's hand in the crook of her arm as they listened to the boy's voice. She wasn't sure if the boy was hearing or simply hard-of-hearing. His voice lacked the flat, pitched tone most deaf people spoke in to feel the resonance on the roof of their mouth.

The boy stopped talking as he spied the two women approaching. "Can I help you?"

Hannah smiled and signed. "*Act one, scene two, I believe?*"

He and the girls smiled. With a sweep of their right arms, they bowed. "You know the play."

"We will be coming back and bringing my family later this summer for the play with the university students."

The smallest girl tilted her head and only signed. *"But then you'll spoil the show by sneaking a peek now."*

Hannah laughed and signed. *"Since I was about your age, I have seen the play every year. Different ensembles performed some years. But this summer, I will finally experience my favorite play performed in my two most favorite languages."*

The girl stepped forward. *"What is the second language?"*

"English."

"But sign language is English."

Hannah shook her head softly. *"You sign in American sign language."*

"Yes."

"American sign language comes from the French sign language, not English. But they verbalize or speak the chorus in English. Two languages together." Hannah slowly finger spelled n'est-ce pas?

The girl drew a question mark in the air as she frowned.

Hannah pursed her lips in a smile and signed. *"It is French for, isn't it so. Signing in French and speaking in English like this boy, it is a beautiful joining."*

The girl collected her two left fingers in her right hand.

The boy cleared his throat. "Brother."

Hannah frowned and, making the sign of an L, she touched her right thumb to her forehead and then dropped it onto the L sign of her left hand. "Isn't this the sign for brother?" She still didn't know if the boy was deaf or hearing.

"That's the correct sign; however, she's only six, still learning." He collected his three left fingers in the grip of his right hand. "We are a family and deaf. Therefore, no one will ever adopt us."

Hannah's shoulders shrank slightly. "My name is Hannah, and this is my mother-in-law, Hemplewhite. Marie." She touched the first two fingers, making the H sign to her two shoulders. She stuck her hand out.

"Robert. Little Bet and our sister Alanna." They shook.

Hannah looked at the smallest. "Well, Bet, have you memorized all your lines? Puck is a vital role to play."

She stuck her left fist into her hip as she signed. *"I knew all my lines last year. But they cast Tommy as Puck because he got adopted the week before."* Her hand shot multiple Hs into the air as she silently laughed with her body. Hannah recalled Puck's distinctive, squealing laughter from years past.

Robert nodded. "We have all learned several parts. I also know Macbeth."

Hemplewhite looked at the older girl with raised eyebrows and signed. *"And you?"*

The girl's voice was crystal clear. "I know both Helena and Hermia. Also, I have studied the witches in Macbeth, but I love Sophocles' Electra if I'm not performing Shakespeare."

Hannah glanced at Hemplewhite. "A family of thespians, and appreciators of the arts."

Hemplewhite nodded and signed. *"We'll leave you children to practice. Even though, parting is such sweet sorrow."*

Robert bowed slightly. "We bid you fair ladies adieu until later this summer." As he flapped his hand in the B and Y signs.

The tall windows of the director's office looked out into the thick, dark green of the elm trees. Most of the expansive lawn lay hidden underneath. Even at this early date, Hannah could tell that, other than the many fat, gray pigeons, most sought the shade during the summer heat.

The waffle-obscured glass of the door rippled darkly before the man opened it. Hannah and Hemplewhite faced the balding gentleman in the tan, coatless three-piece suit. The pencil-line mustache was a gray line below his nose.

He held his hand out toward the two seats as he stood behind the large, officious walnut desk. "Please." As they sat, he flipped open the thumbed folder. "You were asking about the Yoder children." He spoke as flatly as a shopkeeper asked about pricey goods nobody could afford.

Hannah glanced at Hemplewhite, who quietly turn-keyed her finger and thumb in her lap. Hannah pulled at the close edge of her helmet-like hat. "They appear to be exceptionally bright. How are they about their studies?"

The man opened a pair of gold, wire-rimmed glasses and wrestled them onto his ears. He blinked several times as he adjusted the glass on his nose. He thumbed through the file. "It would appear the older girl has a disciplinary problem, but it only occurs with her math teacher. So that may be an outlier. Other than math, her marks are above average.

Her English and literature are marked as exceptional. Even her Latin and German are well above her grade level."

Hemplewhite's voice was soft and almost grandmotherly. "And the boy, Robert?"

"Ah, yes, Robert." The man gently removed his glasses with both hands. "I can personally attest to his academic prowess. I moved him to the next grade level in his coursework two years ago. He is fluent in French, German, and comfortable conversing in Latin. He is at the top of his class... well. He was at the top of his class in calculus. My other students lack that level of mathematical proficiency." He leaned back in his chair.

Hannah adjusted on her chair. "And the tiny elephant on the front lawn?"

"Hmm, yes." He closed the file and folded his hands on top of it. "By age, she would start school this fall."

Hannah twisted her head. "But she started when?"

"She was reading before she was three—"

Hemplewhite cut in. "The Oxford primer?"

He looked at her and finally recognized the soft accent. "No. But close. I noticed her when she was already reciting parts from Midsummer Night's Dream. It wasn't hard to find a script, as we—"

Hannah dove in. "Yes, we already have plans or tickets for this summer's performance."

The man's face expanded. "Oh, I sincerely hope you didn't buy any sort of tickets. We don't sell any. The performance takes place on the lawn. We provided roughly one thousand seats; however, some prefer a picnic blanket on the perimeter. The actors move through the crowd as they act out their roles. Elevated, the university chorus ensures optimal sightlines and sound projection. But the performance is free."

"But you accept donations, of course."

"We have a small trust, but yes. We live and breathe by the munificence of our patrons. Some have been regular attendees at our performance for years."

Hemplewhite's finger bobbed and danced in the air. "And back to little Bet. Where is she in schooling at age six?"

"Six? Oh no..." He fingered open the file. His index passed down a form and stopped. "Yes. Born in August 1945. Which makes her—"

"Five." Hemplewhite looked hard at Hannah. Her voice was softer than in the wet side of a SoHo surgery. "You'd have your hands full with that one."

Hannah looked at Hemplewhite. Her mouth never moved. "Any of them. But taken together..."

"You would require a nanny possessing Freckles' resilience."

Hannah burped a quick chuckle. "You haven't met my mother yet." Turning back to the man, she adjusted her gloves on her lap. "What is the process for adoption?"

"Normally, it is straightforward. But it's not like choosing a new puppy at the pet store. Adoption isn't something you do on a whim..." He studied the two women. Statues of marble or granite could be more giving of information than these two.

"What makes it abnormal at this time?"

He winced. "I'm retiring. My wife's health is failing, and the doctors have strongly suggested we move to Arizona for the dry heat. The foundation has been searching for a new director, but I doubt we will complete any adoptions until they find one."

Hannah turned her hand over in her lap—palm up. "But you can start the process." Her hands finished her query. *"Or do we need to talk to someone else?"*

His left eye and eyebrow rose. "The children…"

"Needn't be told at this time. Hope is a fragile commodity."

THE WOODEN TROLLEY moved with a gentle rumble down the historic St. Charles Avenue, its wheels clattering a soft rhythm against the tracks. The air whispered with the soft rustling of leaves from the towering live oaks, their branches stretching out to form a delicate, lacy canopy overhead. On the lush grass beneath, a squirrel froze, its eyes wide and alert, as a pampered fluffy yellow dog trotted down the sun-dappled sidewalk. The dog's paws padded and nails clicked softly against the concrete as it passed by a pristine white picket fence, each post gleaming in the sunlight. Now released, the taxi with its quiet engine purring, motored away, disappearing into the distance.

"He wasn't Hack, but then, nobody ever will be." They turned toward the stately white home and the three steps leading to the back stoop.

The older woman reached out her lace-gloved hand and stopped the younger one. She gazed up the stairs to the door; its upper half featured plain glass. "Are you sure this is the proper door for us to use? Isn't this intended for tradesmen or something?"

"Proper? After all these years, now is when we worry about what is proper. Were you concerned with propriety when we were surrounded by people with wet leprosy in SoHo? Was it proper to steal supplies from the hospital?"

"That wasn't stealing. That was an alternative reallocation of needed supplies. Stealing would have been the butter we needed for the Boxing Day breakfast."

"I thought Steven brought that from Paddington."

"Nay, he brought the ham that I'm sure he nicked from one of his swell's larder."

Hannah feigned shock. "Steven? Steal? From a swell? How could he sleep at night?"

They both turned at the soft squeak of the door opening. The black woman, wearing a multicolored head wrap, stood in the doorway. Her dressing gown was a full-length, diamond-upholstered, red velvet smoking jacket. Her fist was buried in her hip, matching her scowl.

"Are you two hooligans going to lollygag out there all day? Or are you coming in to help with the biscuits?"

Hannah rushed up the three steps and then paused. She studied the woman's face. "You're younger than I remember."

The woman fluttered her lips. "If you was expecting Leatha, she done finished her adventures of these earthly delights and is now among the stars." She reached out her arms and gathered Hannah in. "What took you so long to come home?" Hannah could still smell her father in the plush of the dressing gown. Winnie sighed. "Finally, we ain't separated by no nasty street in Black Water no more. Sweet Jesus, here it just be home." They hung on each other like long-lost souls.

Finally turning, Hannah looked at the understanding form of her constant companion, savior, and so much more. And the five suitcases.

"Winnie, this is my... um..." She smirked at Hemplewhite. "My mother-in-law? Hemplewhite."

Hemplewhite mounted the stairs, hand outstretched. "It's Marie or, properly, Morgana. But Hemplewhite has a special meaning for me, as it was my husband's name. I miss my men, but Nana works as well as Mum. What kind of biscuits are we making, Winnie?"

Winnie took in the fine lacing of red spiderweb under the pale English skin. "Square-cut buttermilk, but I think we'll be needing some lavender and cardamom, so I might as well add cinnamon and raisins."

The soft smile tugged at Hemplewhite's cheek. "Only if we make a powdered sugar glaze to top them with. After that, we'll have to roll the dough before cutting it into square rounds."

Winnie's eyes grew large as she looked at Hannah. "Oh, she be a wicked temptress." She held the back of her wrist to her forehead. "I just as like to swoon out here on the stoop as I'm under her spell."

Hannah cleared her throat with a growl. "I think

propriety would call more for taking your swooning back into the kitchen, away from the prying eyes of your neighbors."

"Ain't nobody awake at this hour. It be Sunday. But please fetch the bags in. This is a proper neighborhood, and we don't allow vagabonds to camp on our sidewalks." She turned. "Come, Hemplewhite, you have secrets to divulge before the mistress of the house awakens."

HANNAH'S MEMORY of the dining room's opulence and gentrification failed her. Walter and Leatha commanded attention from two smaller walls wainscoted in the dark paneling bracketing the great wall of the library. Ornate antebellum frames housed the stately portraits of the founding patriarch and matriarch. Two gleaming candlesticks reflected on the polished black walnut table. The single leaf extension added to its imposing presence, yet only filled half the room's capacity. The room vibrated with the powerful presence of the original figures. Hannah felt their spirits hung lingering in every corner and crevice.

The knitted cozy lay cold beside the now-empty teapot. As did the wrap on the coffee carafe. Chastity's long, slender finger and thumb picked at the small bits of frosting lining the long empty service tray.

Hannah signed to her mother. *"The little one is still starving."*

"I am not." Snapped Chastity's hand, but it returned to

her lap instead of the remains of the cinnamon rolls. Maintaining her demure appearance, she returned to a previous part of the conversation. "But Mickey was your stepson?"

"Yes. But Hannah didn't know that at the time. She didn't even know his proper last name. She only knew he had taken a flight and should have been in Calise."

Hannah stepped in. "Back then, he was still secretive, as he wasn't sure what he could even tell his mother—much less *un nouvel amant*. For you, the war was seven thousand miles away. But for us..." Her finger whipped back and forth between Hemplewhite and herself. "We only had to step outside our door each morning. Every day, a short flight reminded us of the war. Both for Mickey's overnight flights and Hitler's horrid pilots in their bombers. And if that wasn't enough, he started shooting rockets at us. Buzz Bombs, they called them. Bombs large enough to flatten blocks of flats, a factory, or worse: a hospital or school. They couldn't guide them to the eventual target, so they aimed the rockets in London's direction and let them fly."

Winnie worried her finger under her head wrap. "Did you know what he did or just had your suspicions?"

"Not really. I knew he flew a small airplane. I suspected he was taking swells here and there, but I never suspected spies. But I also didn't know what a Lysander even looked like, or how small. It was later when he showed me a photograph taken of him standing next to his new plane. And later still, when he divulged, they retired the older plane because it had so many patches on its skin that it was falling apart. However, the cockpit was spacious and entirely made of glass. They called it the Greenhouse. It was all glass so that he could see all around him. An important feature if you're flying mostly by the light of the moon."

Winnie adjusted her turban and mussed. "Flying at night. It sounds like owls, bats, or ghosts."

Hannah's smile pulled softly as she looked at the turban and the matching turban in the painting behind her sister. "Is that a new hair wrap, or one of Leatha's?"

Her mother sagged. "Leath's." She looked over. "After she passed, I didn't have the strength to go through everything, much less throw anything out. Winnie found everything in Leatha's house closet downstairs."

Hemplewhite frowned. "House closet?"

Hannah rolled her head. "Hmm. Head wraps and house coats, for the most part. House-only clothing. Slippers or bare feet came and went with the seasons. Her clientele expected exotic or eccentric, and she didn't disappoint." She pointed at the painting. "The gold lamé dress was her favorite to wear to the plays and operas. Willie had it made for her the Christmas we moved back from Black River."

"When were the portraits painted?"

"After we sent you off to England. I believe they both knew it wouldn't be long, which was one reason they sent you packing. Leatha was already sleeping most days away. And Walter seemed to tire with little effort. Walter was born just before the War Between the States. His father had shipped his mother and him off to Texas. When he was four, his mother hired or bought the thirteen-year-old Leatha to be the child's wet nurse. So by 1932, he was already near seventy, and she... well, was timeless. The Christmas play with Hannah was the last. I reason both slept through much of it." She looked at Hannah for confirmation.

Hannah nodded with a slow blink of her eyes. "They did." She waved her hand at the two portraits. "But how did they stay awake long enough to be painted?"

Betsy snorted softly. "They didn't. We had a photographer take their pictures, then the painter painted a good part from the photographs, and we only woke them up for color and tone. The light in the study was better, but Walter wanted a softer light. Well, a back light to show off his mustache."

Hannah giggled. "As a little girl, I thought his mustache would cause him to fall over if he ever bent to tie his shoes. But did it truly grow to such a considerable size?"

"You were three when Mark Twain performed at the new Civic. It's unlikely you remember. Due to our standing in the theater community, we were granted backstage access to meet the man. Your father told Mr. Clemens that his mustache was a respectable start. Those last years, he set his mind to prove his statement."

Hemplewhite smiled and then covered her mouth with her napkin to sham shock. "Oh, my."

All five laughed as Chastity stood to clear the table. Winnie waved her down. "Oh no, dear. The maid will look after this."

The woman snapped a sharp, "Hah. And do you think I'm going to let you get to the sweet potato pie first? You wouldn't leave anything for us."

Hannah stood and grabbed several dishes. "Sweet potato pie for a breakfast dessert. This maid is fresh home from the land that knows nothing about fine pies. She'll clear this table."

Betsy poked at Hemplewhite. "Quick, Nana, grab some dishes. I think this just turned into a mad dash for dessert in the kitchen."

Hemplewhite rolled her eyes as she stood giggling. "Breakfast has a dessert? This is a household of children." And then calling out loudly, "I'm the oldest. I'll cut the pie."

As Hemplewhite and Hannah rode the trolley just to view the neighborhood and recover from breakfast with dessert. They talked of what had changed and what had never changed.

"What about your alma mater? Would they have listings of open positions?"

Hannah turned her face to Hemplewhite but continued to study the flooring. "Nothing would be open today..."

"When did we start rushing so much? There is always tomorrow. This isn't picking butter squash over summer squash for dinner. This concerns your American career. And I still don't understand why you're so set against living in New Orleans."

Hannah smiled. "Ask me again in a month. Or after the next hurricane. By the end of next month, most days are expected to be 36 or 37 degrees Celsius. The humidity you will bathe off, dry, and feel the same as if you had just stepped out of the bath. It never stops. In August, you can wring out your blouse any time of the day."

Hemplewhite shrugged her face as she adjusted her soft cloche hat. "So, northern areas, such as Toledo and Ethel's origin, are similar."

"Cleveland? No. I've had enough hurricanes, and I never want to play Dorthy and Toto. No, I was thinking more about the cities on the West Coast. But not a congested one like San Francisco. I've seen pictures, and it would seem like living in Piccadilly Circus."

"But not Bristol."

"No. Too remote in America to warrant a hospital needing a surgeon."

Hemplewhite patted Hannah's arm. "Well, there is no disgrace in being just a fine family doctor. And I'm sure there will always be a need."

"Oh, my lord. Treating patients' sniffles, boils, fevers, and coughs. At the early age of eight, I was already diagnosing fellow riders here on the trolley. I'd rather be a librarian in a convent. Or join the men on a fire truck. Rushing into burning buildings to save the poor damsel in distress."

The older nurse held Hannah's chin in her cupped hand. "We had a war worth of that. You conquered your fear of the underground. We risked our lives every night in SoHo. You've had enough of that. My three grandchildren require consideration. So, what's a family-friendly place that's cooler, yet less urban? Without tornadoes, hurricanes, and dropped bombs."

Hannah slumped. "I do not know."

"Are libraries in America open on Sundays?"

Hannah's smile grew from memories of years gone by. "I know of one that would be."

Hemplewhite frowned, and then her face cleared into a knowing smile. "A college."

Hannah held up her forefinger. "Not just any college."

31

MIDSUMMER DREAM

To MAKE their journey more comfortable, Betsy had rented a pair of luxurious Pullman sleeper cars built during the opulent Gilded Age. These elegant cars boasted six sleeping rooms, leaving them with an entire room dedicated solely to their luggage storage. As they neared Toledo, a plan was devised to sideline the cars and use them as accommodations if the need arose. The attentive dining car staff graciously offered to serve their meals in one of the Pullmans, allowing the other to be left as a cozy lounging space.

Hemplewhite and Hannah stood on the narrow balcony at the end of the train, where the landscape unfolded before them like a moving tapestry. The fields of cane gently transitioned into golden expanses of sorghum, which then gave way to vast stretches of corn, their stalks swaying in the breeze. They both relished the sensation of the cool, invigorating wind as it caressed their faces and rolled around their heads and necks.

"It's the closest to a Bristol breeze since the second day

of the crossing." Hemplewhite tilted her head and closed one eye with reference to the gale-force storm as they had entered the North Atlantic. And this train is most definitely not the London to Bristol sleeper."

Hannah hummed as she watched the magnificent swath of corn pass. "I slept soundly from the train's rocking and the rhythmic sound of its wheels. I didn't wake until I heard Winnie talking to the staff in the hall. Should you proceed to the standard carriages, you'll find them comparable to those in England. Except here, the separation between blacks and whites is total. Winnie would be forced to sit in a standard seat the entire way. I'm not even sure what kind of food accommodations they have. These two cars are a treat from my mother spoiling us. Don't look now, but I think she is secretly happy I'm home and talking about returning to America."

"Have you told her about the children?"

Hannah wagged her head and snuck a peek at her friend. "Not yet. And I certainly haven't broached the subject of where I prefer to live. I'm sure she thinks I will stay in the basement or move in next to her on the third floor."

"But with children..."

"Absolutely undoable. We all made the double flat work because of the war. But I'm sure Steven and Freckles were relieved when we decamped to Bristol. But what about you? Will you stay in Bristol all alone?"

The woman snorted. "Alone? Between the gardening club, the knitters, and maybe getting a cat... I'm hardly alone. However, forgoing feline companionship could enable travel to say... Seattle. To visit my grandchildren?"

Hannah held out her forefinger toward Hemplewhite. "In Thursday's morning post, I received a letter from a hospital in Seattle."

"Yes. I noticed the return address, but I wasn't going to pry."

Hannah swallowed a chuckle. "You don't have the freckles for it. And Steven snooped as well. It's one of the major hospitals downtown. Upon returning from our family adventure, they inquired about my availability to fly over for a job interview. I think the glowing recommendation from London has their interest most piqued."

"Fly?"

Hannah understood the trepidation, and she reached out her hand. "Mickey didn't die because he was flying. He suffered at the hands of a nervous young pilot. Hundreds of planes fly around the world these days. And besides, it's on their dole. And if you can guide me through stepping into the hole, Mickey's spirit can lift me to the heavens. And I'll finally understand the fascination it held for him."

They turned at the door opening into the Pullman. Winnie appeared majestically in her iridescent green, purple, and red with gold flecks, turban, and red smoking gown. Oozing to lean against the doorframe, she mimicked a silent film diva's swoon. "That handsome young man has delivered a luncheon sent from heaven."

Hannah laughed. "Sent from heaven. Are you talking about the food or the server?"

The Nubian princess hummed. "If these beds were only larger."

Hannah glared at Hemplewhite. "I have a naughty-minded sister."

"I hear it runs in the family."

True to Winnie's words, the meal was delicate, tasty, and well arranged, from the tossed Caesar salad to the sweet bowls of two kinds of melon to finish. Seltzer water sweetened with honey and tinted with Campari refreshed the afternoon.

Frances, the tall black steward in a six-button vest, knocked at the end of the hall. Betsy tittered at his formal nature and waved her fingers for him to enter. "Frances, dear. You're almost like family. No need to be so formal. What is it, dear?"

"We will arrive after dinner, ma'am. We can offer either Chicken Cordon Bleu or a Beef Wellington. Either will start with the last of our Gulf Shrimp Scampi, ma'am."

Betsy turned her head to Hemplewhite. "You are our English expert and guest. Which would you recommend?"

Hemplewhite smiled with Hannah. "I'm sure they can do a lot better than our miserable attempt, so I would vote for finally tasting a Wellington done with honor. Hannah?"

Hannah widened her eyes. "Oh, agreed. I never want to be reminded of that St. Crispen's Eve again."

Frances nodded. "Beef it is—an excellent choice. And the sous chef is working on making pineapple sorbet for dessert. Where do you plan to stay in Toledo?"

Betsy looked at Hannah for confirmation. "Hannah?"

"The Niagara."

He froze, his gaze sweeping the five seated.

Betsy's voice dropped deeper to a register that even Hemplewhite's deep chest couldn't assume. "Frances. As I mentioned earlier, you are like family to us in this room. Speak up, son. What is the problem?"

"The Niagara..."

Hannah narrowed one eye. "What about it?"

He cleared his throat. "It is... um... selective, ma'am."

Hannah slumped only slightly. "This establishment only serves white patrons. Yes?"

"Yes, ma'am." He nodded toward Winnie.

Chastity finished dabbing at her mouth and laid the napkin on the gleaming white tablecloth. "Winnifred is my nurse. She is a highly skilled and trained registered surgical nurse in the state of Louisiana, United States of America. And here we are in the northern states, seventy-some-odd years after we fought a horrific war to settle the separation of all the people. And you are saying I can stay, but my nurse cannot—only because of the color of her skin?"

Hannah growled. "Chastity, it's not his doing. He's only the messenger." She turned toward Frances. "Can the staff accommodate us here on the train cars for the four days?"

"Certainly, ma'am. And we can arrange for a car service to take you wherever you'll be going."

Hannah looked around, holding her palms up in presentation. "We have wonderful beds to rest our heads, exquisite food to nourish our bodies, and the best of cheer to sustain our spirits, so I can't think of a better place to stay." She held her palms out toward the man. "And with family. As my sister told me upon my return from two decades of war, this be home. Thank you, Frances. Extend our gratitude and good wishes to the staff."

He bowed slightly. "Very good, ma'am. We'll make all the arrangements."

SINCE THE PLAY was during dinnertime, Betsy suggested a lawn picnic. She winked at Frances as she laid out her plan for them to enjoy the entertainment as well. Those with food expertise were necessary, as well as those handling the host's transportation. Which meant—the railcars emptied. Hannah would leave nobody behind. The rail yard could provide the guard for the prestigious Gilded Age cars.

They secured an excellent view of the performance by arriving early and laying out their blankets. Their off-to-one-side location acknowledged the possibility of offense from the party mix, but could be misinterpreted as a way to accommodate the service staff.

Frances set out bottom-weighted glasses on saucers. The crushed sprigs of mint swizzle refreshed the sweet teas. Hannah whispered as the man set down her tea. "Frances, please provide refreshments for all the staff. We won't need dinner for a while, and they have all worked hard. They would enjoy a bit of a rest to enjoy the shade and air."

"Very good, ma'am." Mirthfully, his dark eyes twinkled at the arrangement's subterfuge.

Winnie leaned their way. "Missy Hannah, is Frances bothering you?" And her voice lowered in volume and took on a husky quality. "A cause, iffen he ain't, he can come this a' way and bother me anytime."

The man straightened and tugged once at the hem of his morning vest. The darkening of his throat threatened to wash higher than his chin as he strained not to smile at the flirting. "I'll just see to the staff, ma'am."

Betsy pawed the air at the nurse, who had French braids. "Hush there, Winnie. Leave the poor man alone. He has work to think about." She leaned closer and hissed. "Besides, I saw him first."

The young man's step took a soft jump at the jolt, causing the women to giggle softly.

Hemplewhite glared with her best charge nurse stare. "You children are behaving wickedly, and should be turned over someone's knee and spanked."

Chastity snootily stuck her nose in the air as she pretended to study the nature of the trees. "Don't make idle threats unless you have a specific master in mind to administer the punishment." Her head slowly wound down to turn into a hard look at the matron. "Nez pas?"

Hannah growled a soft mew of appreciation at the response. Turning to Hemplewhite, she laughed. "Now she would get along famously at the Pig and Duck. Don't you think?"

"She'd give Freckles a run for her money, but I'm thinking Penny might be more of the contender."

Freckles was a common topic, as was the Pig and Duck,

but the unknown factor raised the young doctor's eyebrow. "And who, pray tell, is Penny?"

Hannah and Hemplewhite mirrored each other's pursed lips as they echoed. "The barmaid."

Hannah smiled as she noted the other's pupils dilated at the title. "It's amazing to consider the years spent in the pub without our dear Porchia."

Hemplewhite rested her hand on Hannah's. "We always had Penny's care, so we never really struggled."

Hannah raised her glass of sweet tea. "It's not the strong black arm of a pint of stout, but here is to the heart and soul of the good woman, Penny. The grandest serving wench in all of London."

The cadre of women, as well as the service staff, raised their glasses in salute. "Hear, hear. To the good wench, Penny."

Frances stood and turned to the cook staff. "Supper?"

All about the picnickers spread around the expansive lawn, the soft sounds of eating mingled with light conversations. Hannah looked at the canopy of the massive shade trees as she patted the last of the Shoo Fly pie from her lips. Her hand and napkin fell to her lap. "I've missed shade trees." She turned toward her mother. "Bristol has some grand trees, but they are coastal trees."

Hemplewhite nodded. "Nice to look at, but to sit in their shade, one must keep moving your chair. The sun keeps chasing your feet, and then your legs." She giggled to Hannah. "Remember that horrid burn?"

Hannah hid her laugh behind her hand and napkin. "She

fell asleep. And I'm afraid I wasn't much help. I was completely exhausted from weeding around the fence. I only meant to sit down for a minute and enjoy my cup of tea..."

Hemplewhite dismissively glanced at the other. "We awoke at the sound of the four o'clock postman."

Chastity's eyes grew large as she stared at the milk white calf under the sheer stockings. "Did you get any blisters?"

Hannah, napkin still at her mouth, raised two fingers. Hemplewhite burbled a chuckle. "My legs had turned into two blisters by the next morning."

A child's high-pitched staccato laugh caromed off the trees. A bouncing movement of a curly head of something caught Hannah's eye. The little lamb in its woolly helmet danced among the people and trees, captivating her. The others followed, watching as Hannah watched, the child winding its way, dancing, twirling, and skipping through the dappled shade.

Suddenly, the forest sprite stopped in front of the group. She paused as she scratched her fingers in the curly wool cap between the two small, curled horns. The pensive smile grew from amused to delighted. Her first two fingers of both hands formed the letter *H*, as they drew the shape for a temple or church ending with the right hand spreading like a spider on her chest and pulling away as if drawing a string —the sign for white. She beamed as Hemplewhite recognized the sign for her name and clapped.

She stood, left foot down, right foot raised, poised for a race. Her head rolled over in a smile as she bounced the right hand *H* from her left chest to the right. Hannah smiled and clapped as the young Puck laughed in the shrill giggle, shooting the air with the finger sign, and racing off.

Betsy frowned and put out her hand. "Wait. That child knows you two?"

Hannah raised a conspiratorial eyebrow at Hemplewhite and then her mother. "A child should always recognize their mother and English grandmother, should they not? After all, it is Shakespeare, be it not?"

3²

GOING HOME

"No, miss, not one; all."

The sky was on the verge of becoming a real summer as the clouds, no longer sources of rain, had become targets of creative imaginations. Ducks followed elephants—to become a larger teddy bear—as wisps of Indian smoke drove through it all, making a field of cotton ball clouds scattered across a pale blue sky. Hanna surveyed the muted grounds of the deaf children's home.

Her hands purposefully clutched at the beige gloves. It was too warm for gloves, but it gave her hands something to do. As a surgeon, her hands always remained calm. Even when performing surgery on the family's dinner at age ten. But now, she was in uncharted territory, and the lifelong commitment had her folding the gloves and refolding them lengthwise. She wasn't sure which was correct, but she funneled the butterflies from her stomach and into her fingers.

"I have brought clothes for the girls and boy and would

like them to wear them for travel." She stared at the window. Her lip started the queer little buzzing quiver she so hated since she was a small child in Mississippi. Long before today, long before the doctor's degree, and even longer to the days of riding the trolley on St. Charles Avenue.

"That would be fine, Mrs. Humphry." The director eyed the woman doctor from New Orleans. "Will Mister Humphry be joining us today?" Puzzled by her extensive journey to adopt three strangers, whom she had only previously seen performing.

"No," she snapped. Her head almost jerking around, but locked like an iron trap on the rusted child's tricycle in the play yard. Regaining her calm in the desperation of her focused endeavor, she turned.

"No, he won't. He was called back to New Orleans when we arrived in Toledo. Something to do with the upcoming elections." Hannah's voice took on an edge as her concern grew about an issue or, worse, a delay in securing the children and her own life. "The former director led me to believe that all the paperwork was done, and our arrival was just a final formality."

A tiny panic fluttered to her heart, but then calmed to a mere resting butterfly. "And, of course, the civil thing to do."

She turned to the window once again, leaving the young director to muddle through her social misstep of asking questions that may or may not be her business or concern.

Hannah's right hand absent-mindedly pulled at her hat as an imaginary curl errantly broke loose. The hat hid her hair, which she permed monthly to achieve a wavy style.

"I see a tricycle in the yard." Hannah turned to the director, shuffling the last of the paperwork. "I have a new Brownie camera. Could a staff member photograph the children and myself? In the yard." Her hand waved at the yard past the window. "On the tricycle. Not me, of course, the children." The flutter of the butterfly beat softly in her chest.

The director noted the slight hint of panic then as it washed away. Not her concern, but she wonders at the devils that drove this quirky woman doctor from New Orleans. "I can do it." She offered. But the woman stood once again, looking through the glass. She appeared lost in a distant memory.

"Do what?" Hannah turned as her hands refolded the gloves. She focused on the gloves, then looked up at the young blonde woman sitting behind the desk in her crisp, starched white blouse and skirt. Hannah's mind slipped back to a not-too-distant time in another country. Nurses' uniforms had changed, and now even the director took on the affectation."

"Take the photograph. I have an Argus camera. How different can they be?" The director sensed she was no longer the focus of this woman's attention, but that it had turned inward as she wrestled with her thoughts or demons. Quietly, she stood and walked toward the office door, "I'll just see to the children."

A disassociated hand waved in dismissal in her general direction, a muted sniffle masked by the snapping shut of the woman's purse.

Hannah leaned against the window frame. "Oh, Father.

What would you think of me now?" Three white children, and an imaginary husband and father, slain at the prime of his life. All would dispel any doubts about color in their new residence, as well as her new job at a prominent hospital in the tranquil town of Seattle, Washington.

"Mrs. Humphrey?"

"Yes?" She turned from her past and the window, and toward her new life. "Are they ready?"

"Almost. They'll meet us in the yard." The director offered her hand in guidance as they walked down the hall. She paused, then turned to face the woman. In a muted, confidant voice, "You can tell me it's none of my business, but these are... were our children. Can I ask you why?"

She reacted as though struck. "How dare..."

"I don't mean to pry." She rushed on. "It's just that it's rare for even one deaf child to be adopted, but angels are waiting for you to take all three. And I just wondered where you find the grace to shoulder such a yoke. I mean, your heart must be either huge or hurting, to take on so much." After blushing from crossing a particularly fine line, she averted her gaze briefly before locking eyes with the woman once more.

The woman, only slightly older, remained stiff and emotionless. Hannah saw understanding in the young nurse director's soulful gaze. Then she warmed. All the fear and worry from the lies washed away as she understood and owned in her heart—a truth. A truth that was not only universal, but also about her personality. One she had learned but not recognized from her father and the other mother. She gently rested her hand on the other woman's shoulder and squeezed just ever so slightly, a motherly squeeze.

"Every child needs a home, someone to love, and someone to love them."

They stepped out the side door of the building. In the yard, the children stood in their travel clothes with the four women. Young Puck held the hand of Hemplewhite. The boy's arm pressed against his older sister's.

"It slipped my mind you were visiting a relative here in Toledo."

Hannah smiled wanly. "No, my husband's mother came all the way from England. However, my mother, her doctor, and nurse also live in New Orleans. We all came up for the play. And it was the last test of the puzzle..." She looked at the director. "To see if my mother would be as captivated by the three as I was."

"Well, it appears someone has captured young Betsy's heart."

Hannah smiled. "That is the job of a virtuous grand-mother." She handed the new camera to the director. "Is it not?"

33
SEATTLE MORNING

THEIR MEAL HAD GONE on long past the time of picking at bits and pieces of the roast leg of goat. The baby carrots and cherry tomatoes from the garden were few. The four were on the second or third cup of coffee with its wistful scent of Amaretto. They gently folded the cloth napkins on the table and eventually tossed them into the wash as the story unfolded.

They sat on the enclosed deck, watching the twinkling lights of Seattle rolling out from Saint Anne's Hill to the black water and sky beyond. From the glass door, the reporter observed the massive fireplace dominating the living room. The single large Ming Dynasty vase stood with what looked like a simple, large cork stopper in the mouth. Looking back at Walt, he asked. "So, were all four of them cremated?" Walter dipped his head, his right fist pumping up and down to confirm. "I noticed the large porcelain vase on the mantle...." The man nodded his fist again. "All four of them?"

Walt pursed his lips and nodded as he looked at his two sisters: the family secret. "This isn't material suitable for an article, let alone a book."

"I understand." The reporter closed his notebook and laid it in his lap.

"It was her last request. So when we got her ashes back, we mixed her in with her family."

The reporter thumbed back over his shoulder. "And so there they are. All together again."

"Some is left." He looked at his older sister, Leatha, who nodded in response. Betsy also nodded in agreement as she made the small turnkey sign for *"go-ahead."* Walt turned back, took a sip of his coffee, and finished the story as the dark sky softened with the approaching day. "They loved the theater and music. Yet only one of them had the chance to see some of the grand houses around the world.

"The year I finished high school, my sister, Leatha, graduated from the University of Washington, in Letters. As a gift to the whole family, mother took us to Europe. We spent time in London, and then down to Bristol, but by then, everyone was gone. We were mostly visiting graves and the hospital. It was a time of closure for our mother—a time to lay it all to rest.

"In France, we went to visit Mickey's grave. It was an opportunity for us to meet our beloved, yet unknown, childhood hero finally." He looked at his sisters as Betsy blew her nose. The three were facing a tough moment in the narrative of their lives.

"We went to Vienna and to an opera. When we were

sitting in a box on the second tier, Mother never watched the opera. She only listened as she looked at the grandeur of the building. At the end of the performance, we stood across the street, looking at the beautiful building. And that was when she told us her thoughts. And her request.

"She pointed at the building and then signed, so only we were privy to her idea. She told us she would love to be buried there. And then they took us around to the side we had originally approached. There, staged along the one wall, was equipment for repairing the mortar between the stones. They were repointing the stones.

"She described witnessing this event in London following the war, and again here in Seattle. Wherever there were old buildings made from stone, eventually, they needed to be repaired. And those repairs usually required mortar to be mixed and troweled in between the stones."

Betsy chimed in, "If you didn't know, mortar is nothing more than cement and sand, with water. And with some special buildings, some ashes."

The reporter smirked in understanding.

"Over the last decades, our careers have required us to travel around the world. We have taken a small gold bottle containing a couple of ounces of ashes. For us three, raised by one of the greatest magicians, adding a bit of ash to the mortar is nothing. The workmen never noticed the ashes, and it doesn't compromise the mortar. The four now grace renowned performance halls and museums around the world."

The reporter found the ashes' audacious final resting

place amusing. But he finally grasped the depth of this family, including its three children. He nodded with his understanding and sipped on his coffee as they moved back inside.

"How long did you live in New Orleans?"

Leatha stopped and smiled. "Just for the rest of that initial summer. We call it our summer of grandmothers. For that summer, we had both grandmothers." The trio laughed, sharing a look.

Lost, the reporter frowned and placed his index finger in the middle of his left palm. The three frowned as he didn't move. He finally resorted to talking. "What?"

Leatha chuckled. "Move your finger to ask the question." She drew her finger across her left palm. "It was a summer of intense joy, fear, fun, and education. At first, we feared our new home would magically disappear in a puff of smoke. But as our grandmothers taught us about our family, we also learned about the house, its secrets, and our key place in everything."

Walter assumed the mantle. "It was important that we learn our parts in the critical play of our mother's life. Our father's background and death in war mattered. Hemplewhite quizzed us at the oddest times."

Betsy laughed, shooting her two fingers into the air to form the sign for *H*. And then she made the sign for 'dead' and 'small buildings.' Finally, her praying hands lay against her head, as if she were asleep. The other two laughed as Leatha blushed.

Walter rolled his finger in the air. "We were wandering

through the famous cemetery in New Orleans. The one where the Voodoo Queen Marie Laveau is buried. All the tombs were above ground, and the afternoon heat was putting us to sleep. Leatha lay down on one and fell asleep. Hemplewhite woke her up by asking about what drove our father to fly to other countries." He pointed at Leatha. "She said to buy our mother dainty lace underwear. Grandma's laugh, followed by a blush, ended the lesson. We later confirmed through our other grandmother that he had indeed done just that."

The reporter glanced at his notes. "So you have lived here in Seattle since."

The long, slender fingers and thumb snapped together. "No."

Walter wobbled his head back and forth. "Yes, and"—he pointed at his sister—"no. In the summers, we children lived in New Orleans for several years. In the summer of 1962, we all decamped to Bristol. That was when we discovered that we could buy seating behind orchestras on a stage —otherwise, it was the pit for plays or ballets. Bare feet on the wooden floorboards make an outstanding sounding board to hear the music. And with our mother interpreting the plays, we got more than anyone else in the theaters. Someone always invited us backstage after every performance. The actors and musicians were more fascinated by us children than they worried about keeping any patrons at bay. The summer lingered into the fall season, but there were so many plays to experience. But the highlight was our performing for the actors at the Globe Theatre."

The reporter laughed. "Shakespeare's Midsummer Night's Dream?" The three bowed.

Leatha continued. "That magical summer of 1962 turned out to be Hemplewhite's swan song. She said she would join us the following summer in New Orleans, but she was laid to rest in the spring there in Bristol. Mother took one of the first polar flights to London to settle her affairs."

The conversation had drifted from the formal dinner table, with its two gold candlesticks, to the screened-in large porch overlooking Seattle to the south, and was now migrating back to the smaller kitchen table. The first blush of morning began to wash the darkness from the eastern sky over the Snoqualmie's peaks and ridges.

They settled around the round oak table in the kitchen.

"Okay, so I understand why she hid the fact she was black—it was the only way she could get ahead as a doctor. But I don't understand adopting you three." He fumbled to articulate his confusion delicately. "Each of you three succeeded remarkably, but why three of you? Even more important, I just can't get my head around why three deaf children? It wasn't like she was deaf, herself. She could have adopted hearing kids."

Betsy had a silent conversation with her brother, who watched, smiled, and then nodded in response. She stepped back to the stove and lifted the coffee carafe. "Everything is about perception." Her diction and quality of voice reminded the reporter that she was a celebrated English professor at the University of Washington.

She started pouring coffee into the coffee mug he had

been drinking from all night. Picking it up, she placed it in the sink and reached into the cupboard above, bringing back a glass mug. Behind the reporter, whom they knew was a trained observer, her brother bustled about gathering other items from the cupboards and refrigerator. Betsy poured the glass mug full of coffee with slow deliberation. "Are you paying attention?"

The reporter nodded as Walter placed a large butcher knife, a small cumquat, a potato, and an orange on a cutting board in the middle of the table. Carefully, he arranged the still life and withdrew, pulling another glass mug from the cupboard.

"You must watch everything at once. You must miss nothing." Betsy coached as she placed the coffee mug on one side of the reporter's left hand. Turning, she topped off her own mug and then put the carafe back on the stove.

She reached out and gently took an apron from the hook on the wall, placing the loop over her knotted gray hair. Adjusting the collar to lie on her shoulders, she then tied the strings as she approached the table. "As I said, perception is everything. But people's perception aligns with their belief. In reality, they see only what they want things to be." Her open hand stabbed at each fruit as she named what they each represented. "Our wants, beliefs, desires, needs, and even our prejudices shape how we see everything." She slightly shifted the large knife.

Leaning forward with her hands on the table. "We may not like blacks because we don't know any. Then, we have the chance to work with one or two, and they turn out to be nice people. Eventually, we spend time with them and some others. Perhaps we will even attend church with them. And then we find we're even comfortable with them, and they are with us. But one day, we find ourselves wondering about those dirty backward Muslims or the Mexicans or whoever. But it is just about perception. If you grow up with black people, then there is nothing wrong with them. However, there is always another person who makes you uncomfortable.

"Last night, you admitted you had never spoken to a deaf person before. And yet, here you sit at my sister's table with three deaf people. And by the way you are sitting, you seem relaxed." She took a sip of coffee, as did her siblings.

The reporter thought and nodded in acknowledgment of the truth of her point. He took up his steaming glass mug and also sipped.

"So, perception isn't always about what we believe, but is more often about what we are watching, and just focused on. So, are you watching or just listening?"

"I'm watching."

"I'm sorry, I didn't hear you..."

The reporter sat up and said louder, "I'm..." He then noticed the small smile creeping across her mouth. He laughed at being caught. "Right, I had forgotten you were deaf."

"Exactly. But you are not at fault. It's your perception that is faulty. All night, we three have been talking, but only you have been hearing. We always knew you could hear, but you were lulled into forgetting our inability to hear.

"So, I'm going to show you something. But I need you to pay remarkably close attention to everything. Can you do that?"

"Sure."

"Okay." She nodded and began by placing both hands on the edges of the large cutting board where the fruit and butcher knife lay. "The secret of a talented magician is not about him doing real magic, but that he can talk you into paying attention to what he wants you to pay attention to while something else is happening."

The reporter nodded at this statement of given knowledge. "Yes, misdirection."

Betsy smiled and ignored his words. "You nod. You understand this, but do you?"

"Yes."

"Are you sure?"

"Yes." He also nodded.

Slowly moving her hand back from the cutting board, she asks, "Then, what has changed on the table? You have said three times that you are paying full attention to everything, but I am only holding you responsible for what is on the table. So, what has changed?"

The reporter scanned the table.

She leaned back, sipping on her coffee. "Take your time. Think about everything." He continued to look at the table, the tablecloth, the cutting board with its fruit, and the large knife she had not touched. He was confused. She watched quietly, leaning against the stove and sipping her coffee. She counted the times he scanned carefully from one end of the almost empty tabletop to the other. Then, believing he had missed something, he had started again.

Finally, he admitted defeat and leaned back in his chair, taking his mug with him. "Okay, I give up. I didn't see it. What changed?"

None of the three siblings laughed. This was never a trick to them. But setting down her mug, Betsy smiled. She pointed to the fruit. "My mother was a grand magician. Her father had taught her well. These three fruits (the potato being Walt) represent us." She picked up the large knife and hefted the weight, then quickly brought it down beside the fruits, burying the tip deep into the wood. The reporter jumped. Betsy looked over and commented gently, "Don't spill your milk."

The reporter looked at the glass mug of milk in his hand, checking for a spill, and then took a sip as Betsy continued. Pulling the large knife out of the board with a slight wiggle, she laid it gently back on the board. "The knife is quiet—it just lies there. It is very much like the quiet of our being deaf. But in other people, it is as large as when I stuck it in the board. Our silent hearing is loud and gets other people's attention. There were also three of us, with no father. The story of his being killed abroad during the war is also another quiet thing. In its quiet, it is also very loud. Women doctors were scarce, and even rarer were women who were also surgeons."

She paused, took up her coffee mug, and took a sip. Pointing toward the reporter with the mug, she continued. "With all that noise, nobody was paying any attention to the curly hair, or a little darker complexion on a woman who is living where we pride ourselves about a skin tone, we jokingly call Northwest White. The intricate details were as unnoticed as your coffee."

The reporter glanced at his mug of white milk and took another sip.

"So the magic she performed was that she had no husband, but was a widow left with three children to rear, who were profoundly deaf." With each point, she chopped the fruit or potato in half. "Nobody had time to take their eyes off the children to notice she might be something she wasn't. She was like creamy coffee that wasn't really milk." Pointing with the large knife at the reporter's mug for the third time, she asked. "Would you like a refill on your coffee?"

The reporter once again glanced down at the glass mug full of milk and started to say he was fine. His head dropped back down as he stared in disbelief at what was definitely not the coffee he had watched her pour into the new mug with nothing to hide. The change had been in plain sight, and he had even taken several sips of the milk and still did not notice the difference.

Walter placed the original clear mug with coffee back on the table where he had switched them. "Now you understand how our mother could be white, and adopt all three of us—even though we were deaf. We were her cover—her distraction. And then, became every bit her family."

Leatha, leaning back against the counter, sipping her

coffee, chuckling. "Especially after you asked her if we were her children, why weren't we named after her parents?"

Betsy feigned offense. "Hey. I was always Betsy."

Walter chuckled. "Yes, Bethany, yes, you were."

"Well, it's closer than Robert and Alanna."

The reporter thought, and chuckled, as he looked from one mug to the other, and then at the siblings. "I don't think I will ever look at coffee and milk in the same way." Looking up at the three smiling faces, he added, "Or deaf and black."

Then, thinking for a moment, he nodded toward the two classically shaped gold candlesticks in the center of the dining table, softly reflecting the light from many decades of loving care and polishing.

"And I don't think I will ever judge something just because it looks like brass."

The four laughed in their own ways.

ALSO BY BAER CHARLTON

The Very Littlest Dragon: NEW Editions
(All-new full-color ebook, a paperback with
coloring pages, and a full-color Collector's Edition hardback)

Stoneheart — Pulitzer Nominee 2015
Angel Flights
What About Marsha?
Pirate's Patch
Flat Surf

I Drink Coffee and Make Shit Up
One Writer's Journey Without Signposts

Everyone Deserves a Home

JOLIE "ROCKET" ROBERTS SERIES
Dry Bridge of Vengeance – Book One
Dry Ridge of Redemption – Book Two

THORNY WALLACE SERIES
Death in the Valley – Book One
Light to Light – Book Two

SOUTHSIDE HOOKER SERIES
Death on a Dime – Book One
Night Vision – Book Two
Unbidden Garden – Book Three

Boomtown – Book Four
One Day Under the Grass – Book Five
Southside Hooker Series: Books 1–5 Box Set
(Collector's Edition hardback & ebook available)

Nash Running Bear Mysteries
A Skeleton in Bone Creek – Book One
Double-time Out of Taos – Book Two
Three Crows East of Empty – Book Three
Four-corner Spread – Book Four
Cinco D' Mojave – Book Five
Six-sided Crap Shoot – Book Six
Seven Grams of Vengence – Book Seven
Eight Ball Sand Trap – Book Eight
Nine Minutes to Midnight – Book Nine

Nash Running Bear Shorts
Shrinkage

ABOUT THE AUTHOR

Bestselling author Baer Charlton graduated from UC Irvine with a degree in Social Anthropology, monkeyed around for a while, and then proceeded onward with a life of global travel, multi-disciplinary adventure, and meeting the memorable array of characters he would come to describe in his writing. He has ridden things with gears, engines, and sails, and made things with wood, leather, and metal. He has been stitched back together more times than the average hockey team; his long-suffering wife and an assortment of cats and dogs have nursed him back to health after each surgery.

Baer knows a lot about many things in this world. History flows through his veins and pours out of him at the slightest provocation. Do not ask him what you may think is a simple question unless you have the time to hear a fascinating story.

You can find more at
www.mordantmedia.com